A SCREAM FULL OF GHOSTS

12 GHOST STORIES

JANE NIGHTSHADE

www.DarkInkBooks.com

ISBN: 9781943201891

Library of Congress Control Number: 2022941781

The Warriors of the Sand, first printed in Horror USA: California, Soteira Press, edited by Gabriel Grobler and R. C. Bowman, 2019.

The Stone Wife, first printed in Voices in the Darkness, Steem Fiction Press, 2019.

First Published by *Dark Ink Books*, Southwick, MA, 2023

www.AMInkPublishing.com

Dark Ink Books is a division of *AM Ink Publishing. Dark Ink* and *AM Ink* and its logos are trademarked by *AM Ink Publishing.*

Contents

For my sisters,
who bought me my first book of ghost stories as a child,
and my husband and children.

Foreword

Blame the Whitman Publishing Company. They were the ones who printed the first ghost stories I ever read, two anthology volumes called, respectively, *Tales to Tremble By* and *More Tales to Tremble By*.

They consisted of reprints of old classic ghost stories from the masters of the 19th and early 20th Centuries: M. R. James, Charles Dickens, F. Marion Crawford, Ambrose Bierce, Bram Stoker, and many more. I received them for Christmas one year when I was eight or nine. I read and then re-read them numerous times. I fell in love then with my favorite of all horror genres—the ghost story. Especially the old-fashioned kind, with slow-burn action, eccentric characters, and subtle, creeping chills.

I had to write my own versions of the classic ghost story someday. And so here they are. A couple of them, *The Warden's Office* and *Footdazzle*, were actually inspired directly by stories from the Whitman anthologies: *The Judge's House* by Bram Stoker and *The Suitor of Selkirk*, a traditional Scottish folk tale by an anonymous author.

My stories feature, in their turn, most of the classic elements: haunted old houses, vengeful ghosts, sinister servants, and befuddled main characters trying to make sense of it all. But they also take place in the current era, updating these tropes for the Internet, smartphones, and social media. It took some doing to preserve the magic of the classic ghost story while incorporating the hard reality of the 21st Century, but I think I did justice to the spirit of my old favorites.

I hope you enjoy my stories.

Jane Nightshade

The Beekeeper's House

"Goddamn—those are some creepy-looking boxes." Rickey whistled in a soft tone and pointed at a clump of dilapidated wooden structures in a far glade beyond the garden. "Funny how I didn't really see them that way when we first toured the house."

Adrienne shrugged. The grassy meadow slumbering in the June afternoon light seemed charming to her, not creepy at all. The real estate agent had told them that the old lady who previously owned their new house lived with a nephew who was keen on keeping bees.

"They're just old hive-boxes. We can get rid of them easily enough."

"I take nothing about bees lightly," Rickey replied. "I do not lug about this cumbersome EpiPen for fun." Rickey was deathly allergic to most types of insect venom and never went anywhere without his emergency adrenaline injector. "Do me a favor, love, and call someone to come and get them as soon as you can. Please?"

"Of course, dear heart. Anything for my love." Rickey was terrible at doing practical things and they most often fell to Adrienne to take care of, which she normally accepted with grace. Rickey looked after the intellectual side of things, as befit his position of a retired English professor from Boston College, reborn as an aspiring novelist. His students had called him "Professor Fuzzybrain," in affectionate recognition of his general absent-mindedness and complete lack of practicality.

"Thank you, Adri. I appreciate your efforts to make me more comfortable out here in the barren boondocks. As you know, it wouldn't be my preference to live so far away from the city."

"It'll be lovely once we get settled. Really, this house will be like a dream come true. An old country manor full of books, well-broken-in furniture, paintings, and jars of homemade preserves. You will have your separate writing quarters and I shall have my own art studio. No more kitchen table for me. Plus, all this land to meander about in. Heaven!"

Rickey grumbled. "Hmmm. Yes, the peace and quiet will be welcome. It's just that there are a lot more bees and wasps and black widow spiders in the countryside."

"There were bees and wasps aplenty at the park in the city where you used to walk with Pettigrew—don't deny it."

"Well, I won't belabor the point—speaking of Pettigrew, where is the spoiled little scamp?"

"Exploring the barn, I think."

At that moment, as if aware that he was being talked about, a little yellow Yorkie terrier bolted out of the barn, barking wildly. Pettigrew headed straight for Rickey and ran around him in circles, assaulting his and Adrienne's ears with continuous short, sharp barks.

"Hold on there, Pettigrew," said Rickey in a stern tone, and the dog quieted down a bit. "What's got you so excited?"

"I suspect he's uncovered a rabbit or some other large rodent in the barn," said Adrienne. "I should go and investigate, shouldn't I?"

"Yes, dear. While I find something less exciting for

Pettigrew to do in the house."

But they didn't do either of those things, as Rickey and Adrienne shortly heard the unmistakable sound of gravel being crunched by automobile tires. Then they saw a station wagon with wooden sides making its way up the long driveway that ended at their new house.

"Looks like the welcome wagon is here," said Adrienne. "And it's literally a wagon. Ancient, too."

The station wagon parked on the gravel oval next to Rickey's venerable Saab. A middle-aged couple, a few years younger than Rickey and Adrienne, alighted from the car. Adrienne noticed in a small disapproving way that the woman wore stretchy red pants slightly inappropriate for her age and weight, with a matching floral top and shiny red sandals. She carried a square casserole dish covered by a checked cloth. The man wore droopy beige cargo shorts and a striped shirt.

"Halloo," the man shouted at Ricky and Adrienne, as Pettigrew answered with a ferocious string of barks. Rickey yelled, "Stop it, Petti!" and the little dog complied, but still regarded this new pair of humans suspiciously.

"We're the Morrisons," the man continued when the couple reached conversational distance. "My wife is Florrie and I'm Vance. We live down the road. You might call us your closest neighbors, if such a moniker can be applied to someone who's five square acres away." They shook hands all around.

"Excuse us for barging in without calling, but we didn't know if you'd got your phone in yet," said Florrie, beaming with good will. "And we wanted to make sure you had everything you needed."

"We're fine for now," said Adrienne. "Thanks

awfully! And we'd invite you in, but the house is full of boxes. The movers only left two hours ago."

"Oh, that's quite all right," said Florrie hastily. "We didn't expect to be invited into…*that house*." The woman almost shuddered as she said, 'that house' and Adrienne noticed it. *What an odd choice of words*, she thought. *Why say* 'that *house'? Why not* 'the *house'? There's a story behind that* 'that'!

There was an ungainly pause.

"I've brought you the proverbial welcoming casserole," said Florrie, thrusting it forward in an awkward manner. "Southwestern scramble with bell peppers and shredded pork."

Adrienne could see that there was no getting around it; she had to make some hospitable gesture for the new neighbors, or she'd feel embarrassed about it forever. "Smells wonderful! Thank you! We could sit on the front porch," she said, with a sudden inspiration. "We've got our old wicker chairs set up and I can bring some beers."

Florrie seemed glad that a nod to conventions would relieve the awkwardness of their meeting. "That would be lovely—"

"But Florrie, are you sure? The *house*—" broke in Vance.

"The house isn't the front porch, Father," she said firmly.

Vance seemed somewhat mollified. "Well, if you say so, Mother—"

Adrienne took the casserole into the house and set it on a shelf in the refrigerator in the kitchen. It was one of the old '70s models, harvest gold with artificial wood trim, and would have to be replaced once they got settled in. She placed several bottles of craft brew, glasses, and an opener on a tray and at the last minute added some cheese and crackers, then took it out to the front part of the porch. The porch was covered by an overhang and wrapped around the house in a lovely way.

Rickey had ushered the Morrisons to their battered wicker patio set, four chairs and a side table and square tea table, and they'd all settled in comfortably. She thought for the second or third time how she loved the way the wicker set looked on the porch, as if it had always belonged there. The old, worn-in, loved furniture and the porch that likely had seen numerous generations of card games, luncheons, and tea parties on warm lazy days.

"Now, I recommend adding a rider to your home insurance that covers lost jewelry or other personal items…" Adrienne heard a male voice drone, as she arrived with her tray. Vance was regaling Rickey with information about property insurance. She gathered that he owned a small brokerage in the nearest town. Just the sort of person who would bore the pants off of Rickey. She hoped her husband would try hard to hide his boredom—he usually wasn't very good at it.

"Well, here we are," she said gaily, setting the tray on the square table. "Sam Adams, good and cold, and I've found some stoneground crackers and smoked Gouda cheese to go with it."

"Looks delish," said Florrie. Adrienne settled into the last empty wicker chair, next to Rickey, and adjusted her "company face." After some polite inquiries about the Morrisons (she taught school part-time in town; there was a daughter at Worcester State named Mandy), Adrienne worked her way around to their own house's former occupants.

"Did you know them well? The old lady and the nephew?"

There was a pause and the Morrisons looked at each other in an odd way.

"We knew Mrs. Simpson quite well. Although we saw less and less of her when Randolph moved in with her," said Florrie.

"Randolph was the nephew? What was he like? I mean aside from the fact that he was a beekeeper?"

"Randolph—"

"Now Mother," broke in Vance firmly. "I'm sure our new friends are not interested in the county gossip."

To Adrienne he turned and said, "Randolph only lived here less than a year. He kept to himself, and people talked—invented all kinds of silly things about him and his bees. He was obsessed with the creatures—the way that some introverted people do get obsessed with things. We are really quite insular in this county, unfortunately."

"Yes, I think I understand…" Adrienne trailed off, suddenly catching Rickey's eye. His face was frozen and purple with some negative emotion. She followed his gaze and noticed with a start that a small circle of bees was hovering near the tea table. Rickey put his hand beneath his shirt. Adrienne knew he was reaching for the EpiPen he kept in a little shoulder holster under his arm.

"Bees!" cried Florrie, freezing in her place. She actually looked to Adrienne to be more frightened of the bees than Rickey was. Vance stood up suddenly, also looking tremendously stressed.

"Awfully sorry, but we must leave. I—I think I left the water running in the garden. Water rates are exorbitant around here. Mother, come on, let's go." He grabbed Florrie's arm and almost pushed her upright.

"We must do this again sometime," Florrie said, looking strangely wistful and haunted, as if she'd just lost something precious. All of a sudden, the bees dived toward the Morrisons and the two of them immediately took off, as Adrienne and Rickey watched, open-mouthed.

They ran to their station wagon with the bees in pursuit. Vance opened the passenger door and pushed Adrienne roughly inside, then slammed the door and ran around to the driver's side and got in. They closed all the car windows frantically—they were old-fashioned ones with hand cranks—and then Vance pulled out of the gravel parking space with a squeal and a great crunching of tires and drove away.

Adrienne exhaled loudly. "What extraordinary behavior!" she cried. "Are you all right, Rickey? None of the little buggers have gotten to you, have they?"

"No, they've dispersed. Thankfully. It's almost as if the bees were deliberately targeting the Morrisons," said Rickey. "As if the insects were acting with sentience."

"They *were* chasing them, and what's more, the Morrisons behaved like they knew what was coming—like it had happened before."

"Let's hope they don't come back," said Rickey, lifting his bottle of Sam Adams to his lips, and Adrienne couldn't decide whether he meant the bees or the Morrisons.

* * *

Adrienne and Rickey spent the next two days cleaning their

house and unpacking furniture and belongings. Adrienne helped Rickey set up his writing room in the study on the first floor and he admitted that it was a larger and better space than his old one in their city apartment.

Mercifully, they did not have any repeats of the bee incident. On their second night in the house, they even sat on the porch and played cards and drank Sam Adams, undisturbed by any invading insects. The strange incident with the Morrisons started to fade in importance for both Adrienne and Rickey. "Maybe one of them has insect venom anaphylaxis, as I do," Rickey allowed.

Adrienne started working to set up her art studio in the spare room on the second floor. She was excited. The room seemed perfect for the purpose: the light was coming in from the right direction and in the right quantity. There was even an old built-in flat file that she could use to store her watercolors. Mrs. Simpson's long-dead husband had been an engineer.

Rummaging through the flat file, Adrienne found some ancient, not-terribly-interesting blueprints and a Styrofoam board. She turned the board over and saw that there were rows of dead bees of various sizes pinned to it, in the manner of professional insect collectors. Bumblebee, queen, drones. *So*, she thought, *this must have been the room that the mysterious Randolph used to study his bees.*

Something fell off the board, a slip of folded paper that had been pinned at the bottom. Adrienne opened the folded paper and found a message scrawled in green ballpoint ink:

Mandy & Randy
Forever My Queen

Mandy! Wasn't that the name of the Morrisons' daughter? There was also a strange drawing on the note, in the same color, of a young woman's face on the body of a bee, with an oversized stinger drawn in red ink over the green, as if the stinger had been added later.

"Creepy drawing," said Adrienne aloud. "I wonder what the story was with Randolph and Mandy."

"What drawing?" asked Rickey from the doorway. "You are talking to yourself, woman."

"Oh, Rickey! It's just this bizarre note I found in the flat file. I think it's from the Randolph kid who liked bees."

Rickey looked at it briefly. "Disturbing. Poor Mandy, whoever she is."

"I think it might be the Morrisons' daughter! They said they had a daughter with that name, who goes to Worcester State. And they were very weird about Randolph. Vance shushed Florrie when she brought him up. I wonder if I should invite them over again and wiggle out the real story?"

"Vance is a dreadful bore, and his wife isn't exactly Miss Personality either. And why on earth would you want to immerse yourself in their affairs? Likely they wouldn't welcome a busybody sticking their nose in."

"It's that look Florrie gave me when Vance was dragging her away. As though she's missing something very important to her. It haunts me."

"Nonsense," grumbled Rickey. "I doubt they'll accept an invite anyway. They clearly despise this house. Best you should just drop it."

"Then I'll just have to contrive a way to talk to Florrie in some other venue," said Adrienne serenely, ignoring the warning.

* * *

Adrienne was pushing a grocery cart through the small country store nearest her house when she came face-to-face with Florrie Morrison. Florrie was trying to decide between ice cream flavors in the frozen products aisle.

"Oh, it's you!" exclaimed the new neighbor. "So sorry about the other day. It couldn't be helped." Florrie was almost unrecognizable: she was wearing huge, oversized sunglasses, and a hat that covered her forehead. Adrienne immediately suspected that she was a victim of domestic abuse. Vance hadn't seemed the type at all, but who could really tell, especially from just one meeting?

"That's quite all right, Florrie. Forget it! My husband Rickey doesn't like bees either. He's allergic, you know."

Astonishingly, Florrie began to cry: "I know. Because of that, we can't visit your house anymore. You see, we brought them there. That's why I didn't want to go inside—because it's easier to get away from them when we're outside."

"What?" Adrienne could feel her jaw drop; she had no idea how to process this extraordinary information.

"The bees. They follow us everywhere and attack us." Florrie pushed up the brim of her hat and removed her sunglasses. All across her forehead and around her eyes were large, painful-looking red and purple welts. "This is what they did to me yesterday when I was watering my roses. My skin looks like hamburger."

Adrienne yelped in shock. "My God, that's awful! But bees don't have the intelligence to follow people around."

Florrie grabbed a carton of vanilla ice cream from

the freezer section. "Yes, they do!" She cried tearfully. "You may even find that out for yourself someday. It's that boy!"

"Randolph? Mrs. Simpson's nephew?"

Florrie nodded as a car horn screeched from outside the store. "Vance is waiting in the parking lot. I have to go!" Then she turned away and fled with her carton of ice cream.

Adrienne wheeled her cart into the store's single check-out terminal just as Florrie was exiting the store. The cashier was an older woman who looked like she'd lived in the county for a long time. Adrienne guessed that if anyone knew all the current gossip and local lore in the land, this woman would be it.

"We're the new people in the Simpson house," Adrienne said, as the cashier scanned her purchases—most of which were cans of dog food for Pettigrew. "Our name is Wagner, Adrienne and Rickey." It wasn't like Adrienne at all to be so forward, but her curiosity about the Morrisons was stronger than her habitual WASPy reticence.

The cashier, who wore a name tag that read *Dora*, exclaimed, "Oh, the Simpson house! Lovely old place. Was in the same family for generations." She seemed friendly and eager to talk, and Adrienne silently congratulated herself on her ability to read people.

"Indeed?"

"Until that nephew arrived," sighed Dora. "He was supposed to inherit everything and keep the place up, you know."

"It didn't work out?"

Dora laughed dryly. "You could say that. He

basically murdered old Mrs. Simpson."

"*Murder?* But no one told us that! The real estate agent—"

"Oh, I don't think you could officially call it murder. Mrs. Simpson died from a heart attack, after being stung multiple times by a bee swarm."

"Oh, how awful! But surely it wasn't the nephew's fault, unless he was blamed for keeping the bees in the first place."

A man with a cart pulled up behind Adrienne and cleared his throat impatiently. "Dora, my frozen peas are defrosting."

"Sorry, Bill. That's $87.59," Dora said hurriedly, ringing up Adrienne's total. She fixed Adrienne with a penetrating stare. "Folks around here believe he could communicate with bees and get them to do what he wanted. He sicced them on the Morrisons' daughter. Then his aunt."

"Mandy?"

"She was a sweet girl. I mean *is* a sweet girl. She never comes home anymore. The Morrisons go up to Worcester to visit her. Felt sorry for the nephew and befriended him, and he fell in love with her. She tried to let him down easy, but he didn't understand. Mental, or something close to it. Mandy was attacked by a whole swarm when she went over there to help Viola—Mrs. Simpson—one day. Well, after that, Viola called the moving men to come take away his hive boxes—bees and all—and the nephew was very, very upset. Viola died before the movers were scheduled to come."

Dora lowered her voice. "And the strange thing was, the attack on Viola happened right inside the house. *With the windows closed.* Or so I've heard."

Adrienne was stunned. *What a story*, she thought. Rickey would sneer at any supernatural implications, but she allowed her imagination to get a little ahead of itself and make her shiver a bit. All this drama at that charming and sleepy old house, and then there was the fact that Mrs. Simpson had died in it—the real estate agent had kept quiet about *that*.

"What happened to the nephew?"

"Well, he was sent to an institution in Springfield by the court after his aunt died. A cousin took control of the house and sold it and now, here you are!"

"Dora!" growled Bill.

"She's done," Dora called back in an irritated voice. "You've nowhere to go anyway, Bill. Been retired for fifteen years."

Adrienne drove home feeling uneasy. Not just because of the gruesome story she'd just heard, but because something was nagging at her, and she could not put her finger on it. But as she pulled up her long gravel driveway, she passed a junk hauler's van leaving in the opposite direction.

Of course! That was it. Today was the day the hive boxes were being moved. She'd made the arrangements herself, then forgotten when the haulers were planning to come. Adrienne began to feel more uneasy as she parked the Saab.

She thought of Mrs. Simpson being swarmed after the old lady tried to have the boxes removed. The real estate agent had assured her that all the bees in Randolph's hive boxes were either dead or had flown away, without anyone to feed them for months. But what if they'd had enough honey in their hive boxes to last all that time? What then? Randolph would be angry if he knew they were still alive, and their homes disrupted.

"Silly girl!" Adrienne said aloud to herself. How would the unfortunate boy even know they'd had the hive boxes removed? He was in an institution in Springfield. She got out of the car and began to remove the grocery bags. The dog food was heavy, and she wondered where Rickey was; usually he could be persuaded to help when he heard the Saab pull up.

As she struggled with the dog food cans, she heard a series of anguished high-pitched yelps coming from the back of the house. And then Rickey calling out: "Pettigrew! No, no, not Pettigrew!"

Adrienne felt the bag with the dog food slip from her arms to the ground with a loud crash. She stepped over the rolling cans and ran around the side of the house to the back.

There was Pettigrew, stretched out on the ground, yelping and barking in pain, almost obscured by a massive swarm of stinging bees.

"Help him, Adri! For god's sake help him!" shouted Ricky from the strip of lawn edging the back porch. He was crouched behind their bulbous old Weber barbecue. "I can't do anything —I'll get stung!" he croaked out. "I was too scared to even run for the house."

Adrienne stood rooted, unsure of what to do, while the bees droned their hateful collective buzz all around Pettigrew. Then she ran to the water spigot at the back of the house; there was a garden hose attached to it with a sprayer at the end. She turned the water on full force, planted her feet firmly on the ground, and sprayed the swarm away from the dog. She shot water at the angry bees for almost twenty minutes. At times they dived toward her or Rickey and she furiously sprayed them back. Finally, the swarm gave up and retreated.

She ran to Pettigrew and picked him up. He was still breathing but not moving, as if he were comatose. "I'll drive him into town and find a vet somewhere. You go into the house and stay there," she cried to Rickey, as he stood and removed himself from behind the barbecue. She saw with relief that only his dignity appeared to be injured.

When Rickey turned toward the house, Adrienne saw someone standing in the meadow where the hive-boxes had been. The figure was wearing a protective costume with helmet, visor and a full, vinyl robe, which seemed menacing and alien. She blinked and it was gone, and she realized she had no time to ponder who it was or why it was there.

She carried Pettigrew to the Saab and laid him on the back seat, then gunned her motor toward town. About halfway down the road, she heard a small, painful bark and stopped the car on the shoulder. She got out, opened the door to the back seat, and saw with an anguished heart that the dog was dead.

Poor little Petti, she thought, her heart full and leaden. *How on earth am I going to tell Rickey?*

They buried him on their grounds, as far away from the place where the bee boxes had been as they could find.

* * *

A day later, Adrienne left a morose and grieving Rickey upstairs in bed with a hot-lemon-honey-and-bourbon toddy and started calling mental health facilities in Springfield.

She found him at The Springfield Institute for the Mentally Challenged. A male receptionist confirmed that a patient named Randolph Ford had once lived at the Institute.

"He's not living there anymore?"

"No, ma'am. He was here for a year but left when his cousin got conservatorship and removed him."

"His cousin? What was the cousin's name? And do you have any idea where he lived?"

"I'm sorry, ma'am, but I can't give that information out. Privacy rules."

"It's all right. I think I know. Thank you for your time." Adrienne realized the cousin was probably Gary Ford, the man who'd signed their house's sales papers.

She looked up the documents and saw that he'd given an address in Boston as his permanent residence. But she remembered the real estate agent saying that he'd lived in their house for a couple of months, fixing it up.

She thought of the figure she'd seen in the bee meadow and was certain now it was Randolph. He'd come back somehow, maybe escaped from Gary Ford's supervision and found his way back to his beloved bees. What if it were true that he could control them? And wanted revenge against the Morrisons because of Mandy, and also against themselves, for removing his hives?

She didn't think she could talk to Rickey about it. He already wanted to sell up and leave as soon as possible. Adrienne, however, was firm in her resolve; she wanted to find Randolph and talk to him, to convince him they meant no harm. It was all just a misunderstanding—the kind of thing she was very, very good at fixing.

But where to begin? Track down Gary Ford? She needed more information first. She thought of Florrie Morrison. It was obvious that the woman knew more than she was letting on.

Possibly, Florrie even knew where Randolph could currently be found. She drove down the road to the first house she saw, set far back like their own and half-obscured by large trees. She'd passed it on the way to the store before. There was a sign on an arch in front of the driveway reading "The Morrisons." She figured it was the perfect time of day; a weekday afternoon and school was out, but also before Vance would be coming home from his insurance office.

The first things she noticed about the Morrisons' house were large, thick metal screens on every window of the house and a full-length one on the front door. It gave her a chill. She also noticed with relief that the ancient station wagon was parked out front, so Florrie was likely home. Vance must have his own car to drive into the office.

As Adrienne stood in the summer sun at the Morrisons' front door, the odd hope floated up that Florrie would perhaps offer her wine or better yet, a stiff cocktail. She punched the doorbell next to the metal screen door and at first there was no response. After several more rings, she heard Florrie call through the door, "Who is it?"

"Florrie," shouted Adrienne. "It's Adrienne Wagner, from down the road. Your new neighbor. I must speak with you. It's very important."

"It's not a good time, Adrienne. I'm sorry."

"We've been *attacked*, Florrie! I think you know what

I mean."

There was silence, and then a loud buzz, which unlocked the metal screen door. Adrienne opened it and then Florrie threw open the wooden door behind it.

She wasn't wearing the sunglasses she'd had on in the grocery store the last time Adrienne saw her, but her face was still marked with the evidence of numerous insect stings. She showed Adrienne to a living room that was packed with photos of a girl Adrienne assumed was Mandy.

"You've been attacked?" Florrie stammered through trembling lips. "How—how did it happen?"

"Pettigrew. Our Yorkie terrier. He was stung all over by a swarm and he died yesterday. While my husband watched, unable to help because he's deathly allergic to bee venom."

"Oh heavens, I'm so sorry." Florrie put her head in her hands briefly in despair. "I thought you two were safe. You haven't done anything to offend...*him*. Please sit down." She gestured toward a rust-colored velvet couch. "I suppose I should offer you something. Lemonade? I just made some, freshly squeezed. Or maybe tea?"

Adrienne shook her head. "I hate to be forward, but have you got anything stronger?"

"I can dump some vodka into the lemonade," said Florrie dryly.

"I'll take it."

She disappeared for ten minutes and came back with two tall glasses of icy lemonade on a tray. She set the tray on a side table and procured a bottle from a low cabinet set next to a side wall.

There was some buzzing suddenly, and two bees

appeared as if out of nowhere and settled on the tray. Florrie grabbed a magazine from a rack nearby, rolled it up, and smacked them away.

"That's seven in the house today," she said with a grim chuckle. "I don't know how they get in, but they always do." She added several liberal splashings from the bottle to each glass of lemonade and then handed one to Adrienne.

"Thank you," Adrienne said, after a couple of hefty gulps. "This is what I need. We *have* offended him, I'm afraid. We had his hive boxes taken away. Somehow, he found out about it— I think he's been watching us! I saw him out in that little meadow behind the house, where he kept the boxes."

Florrie plopped into a brown leather club chair as if in shock. "You *saw* him?"

"Yes. He was wearing beekeepers' gear. Standing perfectly still and looking straight toward us. Only for a moment and then he somehow just slipped away. I'm sorry to tell you this, but I think he's living around here again."

"That's impossible!" Florrie dropped her drink suddenly on the carpet. She looked as if she were about to burst into tears again, as she'd done at the store. She crawled to the floor on her knees and began scooping up the scattered ice and putting it back into her glass. "He *can't* be living here," she said, staring up at Adrienne from the floor with agonized eyes.

"I'm afraid so. That cousin of Mrs. Simpson's— Gary Ford—got him out of the institution. I'm not sure what happened, but maybe he ran away from Gary and turned up around here?"

"Gary Ford!" Florrie looked even more distressed

than she had previously, if that were possible.

"You know Gary? I was hoping to get him to tell me where Randolph was, so I could talk to the boy. Maybe convince him to stop making his bees attack. Yes, I believe he can talk to bees now, somehow. I've googled some research at Virginia Tech."

"That can't be," said Florrie firmly, standing up and pointing her glass at Adrienne as if to punctuate her statement.

"Do you think so? I have a neurodivergent brother. I know how to talk to people with mental challenges. My brother is obsessed with fish. Catching fish, eating fish, reading about fish, even wearing clothes with fish designs on them. He's not so different from Randolph."

"No. Whatever order Randolph gave to the bees, it can't be undone." Florrie was suddenly bitter about it, and Adrienne was taken aback.

"But why?" she finally asked.

"Because he's dead. He can't undo whatever he did. We thought it would stop the attacks, but instead they got worse."

Adrienne stared at her in disbelief, the implication of *we thought it would stop the attacks* slowly seeping in. Through unsteady lips she mouthed: "What? I don't understand—?"

Florrie's face took on a far-off look, as if she were willing herself to exist on a different plane, in a different dimension.

"We can't go anywhere. We kept making excuses to our friends, until they stopped calling us or inviting us places. We thought about leaving, but we've got almost everything we own sunk into this house, and it's hard to unload these old white elephants. Your house was on the market for almost a year. Oh, Adrienne, I've been so lonely, so terribly, terribly lonely. I quit my teaching job. It's just days and days of sitting alone for the most part, in this house, behind all the screens. Scared to even open a door on a hot summer's day."

Adrienne set her glass down on the coffee table in front of the couch. "Florrie, I don't understand. How do you know the boy is dead? I saw him in the meadow only yesterday—"

Florrie collapsed into the brown club chair, with a dark, defeated look on her face. "Don't you get it? Because we killed him. Me, Vance, and Gary Ford."

Adrienne gulped in shock. "You what?"

Florrie nodded. "The bees attacked Gary, too, when he tried to take down the boxes, while he was fixing up the house. And then Vance convinced him that it was the only way to escape the attacks—take Randolph out of the institution and do away with him. I played along. I lured Randolph to where they were waiting, by telling him that Mandy was home and wanted to be his girlfriend... So help me, Adrienne...I lied to that poor boy with the misshapen mind, about the one thing he cared for more than his precious damned bees. I don't know what they did with the body."

She slammed the empty lemonade glass on a lamp table next to her chair in a defiant gesture. "Go ahead, call the sheriff's! I don't care anymore. One day, the bees are going to kill me anyway. I know it."

Adrienne sat in silent horror. If Randolph was dead, who was it she'd seen wearing the beekeepers' gear and standing in the meadow? She shuddered at the memory.

Then she stood up. "I'm terribly sorry. But I've got to get going now," she said, feeling idiotic, as if she'd just had a convivial afternoon tête-à-tête with her neighbor, instead of being told the incredible things she'd actually heard.

Florrie nodded and showed her to the door. "I hope you can be my friend, and we can, sort of, help each other through it all," she said, sounding absurdly hopeful in view of the circumstances. "Believe me, if the attacks continue, you'll have it better with help from someone who understands. Don't bother with an exterminator by the way—it doesn't work."

Adrienne said nothing and walked out to her car. Her mind was racing as she drove home to Rickey. What were their options, after all? Put the house up for sale, and maybe they could leave in a year's time; they hadn't enough money to go back to Boston and rent a new place without unloading this one first. That was if they survived as long as a year. Turn in the neighbors to the sheriff? Adrienne longed to do what was right. But calling in the sheriff about a murder at the Simpson house would make it even more unsalable than it already was. Word would spread throughout the county, and into the neighboring counties as well. And what about Rickey? As much as he now disliked the house, Rickey would never want to unload it on some unsuspecting buyers without telling them everything.

As her driveway came into perspective, an abrupt memory surfaced through the brew of Adrienne's murky thoughts: Pettigrew. Poor little thing. Barking furiously as he ran from something in the barn. She'd never checked what all the fuss was about. In the *barn*...

As she parked on the gravel oval, she tried to avoid

looking at the hulking structure, because she now knew with a terrible certainty where Vance and Gary Ford had buried the beekeeper's body. Maybe, just maybe, she should dig it up and burn it—would that stop the attacks?

Rickey would never have to know about it…she was the practical one, after all, the one who took care of everything. Maybe that would work. Maybe the Morrisons and Gary Ford just hadn't gone far enough in obliterating Randolph.

There was a shovel in the trunk of the Saab, she remembered. Rickey had left it there after burying Pettigrew, meaning to take it into town sometime to have its loose handle fixed. Or rather, meaning for Adrienne to do the task for him.

She got out, slammed the car door shut, and retrieved the shovel. It was still usable; the handle wasn't really all that loose. She steeled herself for the task awaiting her. What would Randolph look like after being buried for so long? Adrienne cringed at the thought, as she started up the pathway to the barn. She bit her lip and tried not to cry out as a few bees settled nonchalantly on the spade end of the shovel.

The Devil Winds

October in Los Angeles County was a terrible time to be stripping wallpaper, but Annie needed to finish remodeling her dining room. There was a strange discoloration on the room's wallpaper that had made her feel insane. The big, light brown splotch seemed to grow every time she saw it, spreading out and assuming odd shapes that seemed vaguely familiar.

"Shit," she said aloud, putting down the stripping trowel. A rivulet of sweat dripped into her eyes from her forehead and temporarily blinded her. The old house in Pasadena she'd inherited from her great-aunt Sophronia didn't have air conditioning; she was trying to cope with just a portable floor fan. The fan wasn't doing much about the heat, but even the best central air conditioning was no sure guard against discomfort when the Santa Ana winds blew.

The Spanish called the Santa Anas the Vientos de Diablo, the "Devil Winds." They drove a man or woman loco—those hot, bone-dry winds that hurled a furnace blast from the San Gabriel Mountains down into the valley below. Assault, drug overdoses, and homicide rates for Los Angeles County spiked during the Devil Winds. They usually came in October, when Southern California was already baked yellow-gold and olive-brown by its endless summer, and brought wildfires, broken dreams, and derangement with them.

Her phone buzzed. It was Jake. Probably going to

chide her again about keeping the house instead of selling the lot for millions to a condo developer.

"You could put five or six million-dollar townhouses on that prime lot in Garfield Heights," he kept saying. "As opposed to the huge amount of money that old white elephant will cost you as long as you own it."

The memory of his words annoyed her. She was in a cross mood when she pulled out her phone and barked, "Hi, Jake."

"Whoa, Babe. What's been getting on your tits? Is it the money pit?"

"Sorry, Hon, it must be the Winds. Still working on stripping the goddam dining room. That stain, or whatever it is, keeps growing."

"There's possibly damp or mold in the wall."

"Nada. It's as dry as Methuselah's bones, like everything else in L.A. County in October. But you're right, it's something in the wall itself, not the paper. I stripped that one wall first. But the stain was still there when I got all the paper off."

"Weird."

"These old houses are full of surprises. I'm gonna have to get new plaster anyway, and then I gotta paint it. That stain for sure won't show through a new layer of plaster and paint!" Her voice rose in frustration. "That is, if I can just get that freakin' plasterer to call me back! My dinner party's in two weeks!"

"Hey, calm down, Babe. Are you sure you wanna go through with the dinner right now? Why not postpone it until everything is finished?"

Annie snorted. "You know I can't postpone it. It's the only time the Big Cheese can squeeze it in for months."

The Big Cheese was a location scout for one of the hottest production companies in Hollywood. Annie planned to make the money pit pay for itself by leasing it out as a shooting site for film and television productions. She believed that the quaint eight-bedroom Edwardian on a two-acre tree-studded plot—once fully repaired and restored—was perfect for period dramas and Gothic horror films. She hoped that wining and dining the Big Cheese would plant that suggestion firmly in his mind. Who knew, if he liked the house enough, he might even get his company to spring for some of the restoration costs.

Jake sighed. "Awright...I see you're determined to make this hare-brained scheme work. But did you have to invite my ex-girlfriend Caroline, too? That's gonna be so awkward, if not worse than awkward...worse as in a 'Miss-Caroline-in-the-dining-room-with-the-wrench-thing.'"

Annie laughed. "Oh, Caroline and I smoked the peace pipe quite a while ago, my dear. Back when you were so busy with your landscaping business and not paying attention. And I *had* to invite her, silly boy... The grapevine says that the Big Cheese has a crush on her. She's kind of the bait."

Jake whistled. "You schemer! Still, I'd watch my back if I were you. You should have seen her when I dumped her...*talk about a woman scorned*. I wish I could be there to keep an eye on her, but I gotta go to that landscaping convention in Florida."

"It's okay. Caroline's biggest enemy is herself. I gotta hang up now, Babe—I've got a whole 'nother wall to strip. Kisses."

When Annie began stripping the new wall, she

noticed for the first time that the discoloration on the opposite one seemed to be following a definite pattern.

She could make out a couple of long vertical smudges bracketing a darker, vaguely rectangular smudge. A long horizontal blob with smaller, slatted rectangles crossing it at regular vertical intervals. Something droopy that hovered a significant distance above the horizontal blob.

The arrangement looked so familiar that it was making Annie crazy trying to figure out what it was.

Eventually, she gave up and returned to concentrating on the stripping. She finished by the late afternoon and treated herself to a bottle of India Pale Ale. She took it outside to the long, covered verandah that wrapped around most of the house, and sat in an oak rocking chair, sipping directly from the bottle. She thought ruefully that Aunt Sophronia probably would have insisted on a glass.

The winds were coming up, and she sat for a while as kinetic waves of heat blasted her face. Everything beyond the verandah was blanketed in a shimmering golden haze, even the dark circle of shade that enveloped the bottom of Aunt Sophronia's large and ancient weeping willow tree. The trees, flowers, and garden ornaments all looked like they were melting.

"This is too surreal for me," she told herself, surveying the shimmering garden. "It's no wonder people go crazy in the Devil Winds."

She lost her thirst for the IPA. She placed the half-empty bottle on the floor of the verandah and went inside. Passing the dining room, she couldn't help but go in and look at the stained wall. Although it was still light outside, it was dim in the musty old dining room, which had only a small set of mullioned windows. She turned on the crystal chandelier from the quaint, push-button light switch.

"Oh!" She let out a sharp little cry when the light revealed the discoloration on the one wall. The shapes had become sharper than they were just a few hours ago. And finally, Annie recognized the familiar pattern that had been nagging her for so long.

Why, she thought, *I know what it is. It's this room! The way it looked before I moved all the furniture out to strip the walls. There's the long horizontal oblong thing—that's the table. The thing hanging above—that's the chandelier. And the two long marks—those are the wood columns on either side of the doorway to the butler's pantry.*

She couldn't think of any explanation for what she saw, but she was certain of what the stain depicted. Suddenly, there was something sinister about the dining room. The back of her neck began to tingle. She grabbed her phone and took a few quick snaps of the discolored wall, then hastily turned off the chandelier light and left the room.

* * *

Annie had never been afraid to stay alone in the old house before, not in all of the three months she'd lived there. Even though it was creaky, very large, and full of odd, dark niches where a boogeyman could hide easily.

That night, however, was different. Buffeted by the noisy, hot fury of the Santa Anas, the house seemed to wake up and become a living, breathing thing.

The antique mahogany and walnut furnishings

looked like hulking beasts in the darkening rooms. The fronds of the potted palms resembled fingers, grabbing at her as she hurried by. Even the designs on the oriental carpets became giant crawling insects and slithering snakes.

Her bedroom—once Aunt Sophronia's—seemed normal in full light, but she was afraid of what it would look like when the lights were off. She put her phone in her speaker cradle and flipped on the loudest, jazziest Spotify playlist she had. Dance tunes and theme songs from action movies.

The music blared while she took a bath and washed her hair in the adjacent bathroom. She blow-dried her blonde waves and found the roar of the dryer comforting. Shutting it off, she thought she heard noises downstairs. She debated whether to go investigate or not.

"If this were a horror movie, I'd be shouting at myself to *not* go downstairs," she said aloud, almost laughing.

But then she heard the scream.

It was fairly faint; the walls of the house were sturdy. Maybe it was the wind; a gale-whipped branch scratching against a windowpane. But she didn't think so. And she was pretty sure that whatever it was, it was coming from the dining room.

Now, she *had* to go investigate. There was no getting to sleep unless she made sure she was alone in the house.

The thought came to call Jake and talk to him while taking the stairs down to the ground floor. But that wouldn't work; he'd just say, "I told you so about that old white elephant!" and demand again that she sell it to a condo developer. Besides, she didn't want to warn any intruder of her approach. So, she crept down the stairs in the dark like a heroine in a Gothic novel, except that she was using her phone to light her way and not a candle—and wore navy sweats instead of a floaty white nightgown.

She shivered as she slid through the doorway of the dining room, feeling for the push-button light switch and exhaling deeply with relief upon finding it. She half-expected someone to jump at her when the light came on. But nobody was in the room. The adrenaline rush made her unsteady on her feet. She braced herself against the wall with the light switch and forced herself to look at the stain.

It had expanded and sharpened yet again. She wasn't surprised, but it was still horrifying. Now, there were oval blobs positioned just above the long oblong. Heads, her mind shouted. Heads of people eating at the table—that's what it was. She counted *seven* oval blobs in total.

Then she noticed that at the head of the table, an elongated blob was bending or crouching over another blob that looked like it was seated. The elongated blob seemed to be threatening or attacking the other blob.

She quickly turned off the chandelier light and fled upstairs to her bedroom. She hit the speed dial to Jake's phone with unsteady hands.

"Honey, I'm coming over to stay the night. I can't sleep here until that fucking stain is gone!"

* * *

Annie woke up to the sound of her phone buzzing on the nightstand. She was groggy and disoriented, having slept in a bed not her own and passed a fitful night dreaming about haunted smudges.

"But Jake," she cried once in the middle of the night,

after waking from a nightmare in a shivering sweat. "I think it's a recording of some kind. Someone died in that room, and the wall recorded it." And he had stroked and soothed her, and then told her it wasn't possible.

Now she was cranky from being woken up so abruptly, after finally getting back to sleep.

"Who is it, goddamn it? It's seven-thirty. It's an ungodly hour to call."

The voice at the other end was edgy and masculine.

"Lady, I'm Teodoro, here for the appointment you made yesterday. The plasterer. I can't get into the house because you are not here."

"Oh no! Teodoro, I'm so sorry! I'll be there in fifteen minutes. Thank you so much for waiting."

He grunted resentfully. "Not a minute more."

Jake groaned and turned over to find his girlfriend already up and frantically dressing.

"Going so soon?" He consulted his phone. "It's not even eight yet. Where are you running off to?"

"The house! It's the plasterer. I finally got ahold of him. If I don't get there in fifteen minutes he'll leave, and God knows when he can come again."

"But—but—last night you said you never wanted to go into the house again."

"Oh, Jake, that was different. After a couple of crappy nightmares. It's daylight now. And it's not the house—it's the stain. The plasterer is getting rid of it today! Hallelujah!"

"I guess that house is always going to come before me, isn't it?" he shot back, in an uncharacteristically nasty tone.

"I gotta leave," she answered back, hurt. "The house

is kind of my job now."

She arrived in twenty minutes to find Teodoro packing his tools in his truck. "Oh please, please don't leave," she implored, "I got here as soon as I could."

Teodoro stared at her angrily. "I should leave, but Los Vientos are telling me to stay. Loco, is what I am. I already waited for you for twenty minutes before I called, then you made me wait another twenty on top of that."

"I'm sorry, I'm sorry!" Annie wailed. "I'll pay for the lost time."

Teodoro smoldered a bit, but then started unpacking his tools. "All right then," he said grudgingly.

"It's in here," she said, leading him into the dining room. "I need all new plaster on the ceiling and walls. Especially the wall with that hideous stain. Double-plaster it if you have to. I want it gone." She spoke with such vehemence that Teodoro appeared slightly shocked.

"It's just a stain, lady. It'll be easy to fix. I do it all the time." He still sounded put out.

"I'll leave you to get to it," Annie replied. Why was everybody being so angry and mean today? First Jake and then this tradesman. Another strike for the Devil Winds.

"I'll be in the kitchen, making tea," she said. "If you need me for anything. Would you like a mug?"

"Do I look like the kinda guy who drinks tea?" He gave her an annoyed look and began setting up his tools and supplies.

"Uh, no?" she said lamely. "I'll just be in the kitchen, then," she repeated, but he wasn't listening.

"What a dick!" she said to herself, settling down at the kitchen table with her steeping tea. She couldn't afford to offend him, though, as he was a specialist in plastering historic homes and had little competition. She busied herself first with looking at blueprints, paint, and wallpaper samples, and then with finalizing plans for the dinner party. Her friend Cherie, who catered film and TV productions in Hollywood, was coming to help her prepare and cook the all-important meal for the Big Cheese.

Teodoro came into the kitchen twice for water to mix up his plaster. Both times he ignored her. When the late afternoon rolled around, he returned to the kitchen a third time to announce that he was done for the day.

Annie jumped up and hurried into the dining room. *The stain was gone!* She felt immense relief. She wanted to hug Teodoro, as hostile and grumpy as he seemed to be.

"I'll have to come back tomorrow to do the ceiling," Teodoro said gruffly. "But that coat of plaster should do the trick for your stain."

Annie wasn't listening. She was already envisioning the dining room as it would look the day of the dinner party for the Big Cheese. Freshly painted, and with all the furniture put back and Aunt Sophronia's huge silver candelabras on each end providing romantic lighting. It would be sublime.

* * *

Annie got her hair done and had an oxygen facial the morning of the party. Cherie, up to her elbows in chopped veggies, told her she looked fantastic.

"I *have* to look good," she replied. "Jake's ex is coming tonight and she's gorgeous."

"Why'd they break up?"

Annie shrugged and picked up a carrot to chop.

"Sooner or later, everybody breaks up with Caroline. There's something 'off' about her, but you can't really say what. She can be wonderful when she wants to be, but there's always something lurking under the facade that makes people uneasy."

"Sounds like Jake dodged a bullet when he dumped her."

"Possibly."

* * *

Caroline was the first to arrive when evening rolled around. Annie had told her she could come early to hear all the deets on the Big Cheese before she met him. Annie didn't know the Cheese all that well, but she knew all about him through the publicist firm she'd worked for before inheriting the house. His production company was a client.

Caroline looked dazzling. She was wearing a smoke-gray cocktail dress covered with sparkles. Eye-catching but not vulgar. Its body-conscious, sheath design displayed her perfect figure exceptionally well. Her shiny black hair was done up in a fashionable "messy bun" that probably took an hour and a half to achieve. As a bit-part actress in several series, she knew how to present herself. Annie felt uneasy. She wondered if she looked drab in her simple black tank dress next to Caroline. Thank heavens Jake wasn't there to make comparisons.

Caroline accepted a glass of Chardonnay from Annie and they both lounged with their wine in the front parlor, which was bedecked in oriental rugs, oak paneling, and elaborate plasterwork.

"So, tell me more about the Big Cheese," Caroline

began.

"He's quite a catch. He's got this cool Jake Gyllenhaal-meets-Dax-Shepard vibe. Scruffy, but hot. And he'll probably end up as VP of location services at one of the major studios. Word on the street is that he saw you in that Wheat Thins commercial and was smitten."

Caroline laughed a tinkly little laugh. "I can't tell you how many dates I've gotten from that commercial. I'm more popular dressed as a dowdy hausfrau in that ad than I am wearing a bikini in the Caribbean resort ad."

There was an awkward pause and then Caroline asked about Jake.

"He isn't here. He's at a landscaping convention in Florida."

"*Jake?* Jake at a convention? He must have *really* changed." There was the slightest edge of scorn in her voice.

"He's doing very well with his landscaping business," Annie replied defensively. "His company takes care of Bob Dylan's lawn in Malibu. He's positively raking in the dough and working from dawn to dusk." Unspoken came the thought: *Why, Caroline's still in love with Jake after all! I didn't realize it.*

Caroline flashed a smile that seemed forced. "Of course. I didn't mean to sound sarcastic. I'm glad Jake has settled down and is successful. It must be the Devil Winds getting to me. I suppose he's lost all of his famous bad boy charm, now that he's respectable?"

"Not between the sheets."

Caroline flinched—barely perceptible—but still a flinch. Her smile didn't change, though.

Why did I say such a mean thing? thought Annie. *The*

Devil Winds are getting to me too.

Aloud she said, "Would you like some more wine?"

Thankfully for the two women, the doorbell chimed soon after and the other guests arrived—the Changs, who lived across the street; Bob and James from her old workplace; and lastly, fashionably late and somewhat coked-up, the Big Cheese. With Annie, Cherie, and Caroline, that made eight for dinner—the perfect number for a dinner party.

"Does anybody want to join a tour of the house?" Annie asked after cocktails were served and consumed.

Of course, everyone wanted to see it. She took them all around, pointing out the unique features for the benefit of the Big Cheese. She was giddy with the excitement of showing off her prize.

"Here's the dumb waiter—it still works perfectly. Here's the telephone alcove—that was added in the 1920s. You can sit here and gossip on the phone in perfect privacy... The verandah has a spectacular view of the gardens and the mountains... There's the Tiffany stained-glass window, which would look so great in any scene... Of course, a lot of work needs to be done to restore and refurbish it. I could see a Merchant-Ivory-style film being shot here."

"Starring *me*, of course," broke in Caroline, giving the Big Cheese her flashiest smile. Annie was relieved that he seemed besotted with her, and she looked rapt when he spoke. Maybe she wasn't really still stuck on Jake after all.

* * *

When the dinner hour came around, Annie grandly opened

the carved double doors to the dining room. The guests made appreciative sounds as they took in the sight. Aunt Sophronia's silver candelabras stationed on each end of her mahogany table (with slow-burning candles, due to the heat); the white damask tablecloth and napkins, starched to perfection; the centerpiece of fall roses from the garden; the gleaming china, and the oak wainscoting that Annie had polished herself. And of course, the freshly painted plaster walls—no stain visible! The only discordant notes were the two large floor fans that Annie had rented and placed in the corners.

"Oh my," said Mrs. Chang. "It's smashing in here. Bravo, Annie! You've done a fantastic job."

"I hired the best historic homes plasterer in SoCal, Emily. But I did a lot of the work myself, such as stripping the wallpaper, which was incredibly grim looking before."

The Big Cheese looked around and Annie thought even he looked impressed. "I love those mullioned windows. This would make a great set for a seance, wouldn't it?"

"For sure," said Annie happily.

"Has anyone ever died in the house?" asked Bob. "It may just be my gay man's intuition, but I'm getting some weird vibes from this room."

Annie froze. For a moment she felt a creepy chill, remembering how she'd woken up in the middle of the night at Jake's, convinced that the spreading stain was a recording of someone's murder.

She forced herself to smile and answer in a light tone. "I don't think so. But I plan to investigate the history of the house once I have more time. If someone did die in this room, anyway, it would just get more publicity for any film that was made here. As we used to say at the office, all publicity is good publicity!"

James laughed. "We still say that. And *all* old houses are creepy, especially if they are Victorians."

"Edwardian," corrected Annie. "Victoria was gone by the time this house was built in 1905. Her son ruled as Edward VII—the fat one with all the mistresses."

"Ah, I stand corrected," replied James. "And here is what appears to be dinner."

Cherie made an appearance, parading into the dining room from the butler's pantry with a chilled, roasted goose on a platter, surrounded by warm baby potatoes and bright green fennel. She set the platter down on the sideboard and expertly flayed off a few slices and parts with a carving knife. Then she went back to the kitchen and returned with side dishes and bottles of dinner wine.

"Guys, this is Cherie. She's the best caterer in the business. She does cast and crew meals for *Grey's Anatomy* and other big shows."

The Big Cheese said, "Kudos, Cherie. It looks fabulous. And may I congratulate you on the creative choice of entrée? You don't see cold goose every day."

"Oh, that was Annie's idea," she replied. "It's too hot and heavy for red meat. And turkey is boring, while chicken isn't large enough for a party of seven."

"*Seven*? You're not staying? But I've got the table set for eight," said Annie.

"Alas, I've got a double shift tomorrow, so I need to make an early night of it. I hope you all enjoy the goose!" With that, Cherie took her leave.

Annie felt another little chill. *Seven at dinner?* Something was nagging at her memory, but she couldn't think what. Something about the number seven.

"Shall we all sit down?" asked Mr. Chang. "I'm famished!"

Annie dimmed the electric chandelier and lit the candles. "Yes, let's do! Everyone pick your seat—I'm sitting at the head—and then help yourself to the goose on the sideboard."

They chose seats at random, and Annie was surprised that Caroline placed her gray silk wrap on the chair next to Annie's right, with the sideboard and the formerly stained wall directly behind her. The Big Cheese chose the chair on Annie's left, directly opposite Caroline. Everyone got their roast goose and then grabbed their seats. Caroline, Annie noted, was the last to visit the sideboard. When all were sitting, Annie poured wine, and everyone passed side dishes around.

The Big Cheese lifted his glass and gave a toast: "To beauty in all its forms. From grand old houses to the graceful feminine form"—he paused to look meaningfully at Caroline—"and to the grandeur of new and old friendships."

"Here! here!" cried everyone, downing their glasses.

Annie happily drank her wine and then poured more. It was all going so well. But then she paused with her glass in mid-air, startled by a sudden glimpse of the wall behind Caroline, and she froze. Now she knew why the number seven had bothered her. The seven heads bobbing above the long oblong table, the windows, the columns framing the doorway to the butler's pantry—they all cast deep shadows on the wall by the slow-burning candles, making exactly the same pattern as the mysterious stain she'd had covered by the plasterer.

Now she knew. *Not* a stain—shadows! They were shadows all along.

"What's the matter, Annie honey? Your face looks positively petrified." It was Caroline, with a strange edge in her voice. Her hands appeared to be buried in her lap, but Annie couldn't think why that struck her as odd.

Annie put down her glass. Her first instinct was to get up and run, but she fought the urge down. It was only shadows; maybe they weren't exactly the same pattern as the stain after all. She'd check the snaps on her phone later. For now, she couldn't afford to alienate the Big Cheese. Things were all going swimmingly, and he seemed to be having a great time.

A heavy gale of wind shook the mullioned window ominously.

"The Vientos!" Annie proclaimed, with strained gaiety in her voice. "What would we do without them! How is everyone getting along with the Vientos?"

"I've invested in a collection of disposable paper shirts," joked Bob. "Saves on the laundry costs. And James is buying enough Xanax to pacify an entire coven of Beverly Hills housewives."

Annie forced a small, nervous laugh. "I don't blame him. We all go a little loony when the Devil Winds blow." Another gale rattled the windows, and Annie jumped slightly in her seat.

"Yes, we all go a little loony in the Devil Winds," Caroline echoed. "They make every little bad thing seem so much worse. Like faithless lovers *who walk out without so much as a shrug of regret…*"

Then she pulled her hands up from her lap and showed the long carving knife she'd taken from the sideboard platter when no one was looking. She fixed her gaze at Annie with frightening eyes and stood up abruptly, one arm raised with the knife, pointed straight at Annie's neck.

Annie couldn't move. She was vaguely aware for an instant of the stricken faces around the table. She saw the Big Cheese on her left stand up suddenly and spill his wine all over Aunt Sophronia's damask tablecloth, and then she saw he was reaching across the table for the knife clutched in Caroline's right hand, and then she saw blood spray all over his face and she realized it was her own, spurting out of her neck.

Oh God! The stain on the wall wasn't a record of murder after all, came Annie's last thought, ever. *It was a* prediction*!*

Hangwood

At precisely nine-forty-five a.m. on a spring morning, Tom Korner, the executive editor *slash* publisher of the *Lodesville Mountain Chronicle*, turned the key to his office door with a resolute wrench (it was an old lock), and then sauntered down Main Street toward the Lodesville City Hall. He'd given himself plenty of time to make the ten o'clock semi-monthly city council meeting, even at the most leisurely walking pace. And leisurely was how he wanted it, because he was in no hurry to witness what he knew would be a deeply unpleasant shouting match.

Arriving with three minutes to spare, Tom eased open one of the heavy double doors at the entrance to City Hall. The building dated from the 1870s and exhibited the typical grandiosity of public architecture from the era. *Still a magnificent old girl*, Tom thought, admiring the carved wooden friezes, marble floors, and mahogany paneling.

Tom nodded to the craggy security guard, well past sixty, who sat behind an incongruous folding table just inside the entrance. "Morning, Mack."

"Morning, Tom. Marge still out with the baby?"

"Yeah, that's why I'm here covering the council meeting."

The Mountain Chronicle had a permanent staff of exactly four: Tom; Marge Cahill, the senior editor; Wade Garcia, the layout man, and Cory, a part-time staff writer, who was a journalism student at a community college in nearby Sierra Pines. Tom was used to filling in for Cory,

Marge, and even Wade when the need arose, and he also sold advertising space. At forty-five, he was a local boy, the son and grandson of two beloved county sheriffs. He had long ago become that venerable small-town cliché: the "prominent citizen." Which meant he was often "comped" at the town's two main watering holes and invited to judge either the livestock competition or the beauty contest at the annual El Dorado County Fair. He didn't have a remarkable or exciting life, but on the whole, it suited him very well.

Mack waved him along, but Tom paused to sign the daybook anyway, because it was the rules, even though Mack had known Tom since he was a toddler.

"Gonna be a bit of a corker today, dontcha think? What with all the folderol about ol' Hal and all."

"I reckon so. Seems a bit ridiculous—after all these years. Arguing in a city council meeting over a department store mannequin! But I guess that's life in a small town."

Mack leaned forward and spoke in a low, off-the-record tone, "It ain't a good idea a'tall to take down that dummy, in my humble oh-pin-yun. Older folks like me can tell more'an a few tales about it...*strange* tales."

"I'm sure you can," smiled Tom. "See ya, Mack." He began whistling as he sauntered toward the stairs to the second-floor meeting chamber, as Mack sighed after him.

"It's the lady of the hour," said Tom as he greeted Susan Cain on the landing. A transplant from Marin County in the San Francisco Bay Area, Susan had moved to the mountains about five years before, seeking to start a new life after a painful divorce.

Tom had always liked Susan; she had a kind of relentless peppiness, a dash of sparkle to her personality, that he found intriguing. And she was trim and neat and compact, with well-groomed dark, shiny hair framing a pixyish face. He guessed her age at about forty, five years younger than himself. He'd taken her out for a few months when she first arrived in town. He'd enjoyed himself, but that was as far as their relationship had gone.

He knew that most of Lodesville still considered Susan an outsider. She ran a small shop on Main Street that sold herbal supplements, healing crystals, and other products considered essential for what she called "natural living," and she also kept a room in the back for yoga lessons and health seminars.

Susan flashed him a wry smile. "Good morning, Tom. Gonna give me a fair write-up?"

"I always try," he replied.

"Well, I guess it's time for the Christian to get eaten by the lions. I wish I had a gladiator helmet and maybe a sword."

Tom rather thought that Susan was the lion, and the rest of the town were the Christians. She certainly knew her way around City Hall, where she showed up often to lobby for all kinds of causes and complaints. The staff at the Hall thought she was a nuisance, but they treated her politely. Until today.

Tom shrugged. "Hangin' Hal is a pretty emotional subject, Susan. The people here have valued it for so long, and it's naive not to expect fireworks."

Susan had no reply. She set her mouth in a determined line and entered the meeting chamber with Tom trailing slightly behind her.

Tom took his seat in the small gallery section and opened the recording app on his phone. Susan sat down a couple of chairs over with her folder full of papers, instinctively marking out her own little space. Tom nodded to many of the other gallery attendants, most of whom he'd known for years. It was a packed house.

Someone tapped him on the shoulder from behind. "Good to see ya here, Tom," said Sammy Silva. Tom sympathized with Sammy. Out of anyone in the room, he had the biggest stake in the upcoming proceedings.

"So, Tom, can I count on the *Mountain Chronicle* to respect the history of Lodesville against *that…that Bay Area invader…*iffin' the vote goes her way?"

Tom gave him a bland, non-committal smile. "I can't write the story until I see how it plays out, Sammy."

Sammy's family had owned the Hangwood Inn on Main Street since the 1930s. The ramshackle tavern was the oldest building in town, put up only a few years after the beginning of the Northern California Gold Rush of 1849. In those days, Lodesville was a miners' tent city known as Hangwood—and called that for good reason. Hangwood was the hanging place for El Dorado County and most of its surroundings: the hangtree itself was a giant oak that once stood in the middle of what became Main Street. When civilization and solid buildings replaced tents and lean-tos, Hangwood formally became Lodesville, but locals still relished the old name, even a hundred and seventy years later.

"I'm not usually a superstitious man," Sammy mumbled to Tom. "Not t'all. But between you 'n me, there's something about ol' Hangin' Hal that just *wants* to stay put."

Hangin' Hal was the town's nickname for the battered department store dummy that hung by a noose from a flagpole affixed to the Hangwood Inn. Red-haired, red-bearded, and dressed in miner's clothes, Hal and his predecessors had been the Inn's macabre mascot since Sammy's Great Uncle Balthazar operated the tavern in the 1930s. The dummy was the most popular landmark in Lodesville, so much so that residents would set their lives by it. "I'll meet you for lunch under Hal," they'd say to their friends. "Take a left turn just after you see Hal to get back on the highway," they'd tell lost visitors. The graduating class of El Dorado County High School took their senior prom pictures with Hal in the background, and young men proposed to their girlfriends while Hal loomed above them.

The dummy was a beloved community landmark for more than eighty years, but in the last five years or so, the Bay Area transplants arrived in large numbers, and many began to complain that Hangin' Hal was "offensive." Susan Cain was their leader, and she was determined to get Hal taken down. Her lobbying was so effective that it led eventually to this packed, contentious meeting at the Lodesville City Hall, on what should have been a glorious and happy spring day in the mountains.

The five city council members took their places around the meeting table. Everyone knew their names: old Eb Turner, the mayor; Andy Sakamoto, a small-time rancher who farmed a place his family settled in the 1890s; Dot Bailey, who ran a diner on Main Street and always had her finger in every town pie imaginable; Carol Sanders, the English teacher at the high school; and Chuck Hawkfeather, who worked at the small tribal museum just outside of town.

Eb Turner welcomed everyone to the proceedings,

and then banged the meeting open with his gavel.

"Ummm, well, let's not pussyfoot around, folks—let's just get to it. There are two town ordinances under the proposed council vote, Ordinance 74 and Ordinance 75. The first ordinance establishes regulations for signage and symbols displayed by businesses outside of their establishment…" here a chorus of "boos" went up from the gallery and Eb held up a hand for silence. "And Ordinance 75 establishes an official committee to draft the regulations should Ordinance 74 pass."

The first to address the council was Sammy. He lumbered up to a podium facing the table, looking nervous and uncomfortable. Sammy didn't have much formal education and he seemed well-aware that he was over-matched by Susan's smooth diction and advanced vocabulary.

"That dummy is a big hit with the tourists," he began. "Always wantin' to get their picture taken with it. Take it down and it'll cut into trade—everyone's trade. Here in the Gold Country, whatta we got? Not much. Tourism and a little ranchin'. They closed down the mines 'n destroyed the loggin' camps. Tourists come here to see a real Wild West Town—if we start gettin' rid of our history, no one will come."

The majority in the gallery clapped loudly as Sammy finished his statement. Those were the established townspeople. Susan Cain and the smaller contingent of Bay Area transplants sat silent and stony-faced.

After Sammy returned to the gallery, it was Susan's turn to address the council members.

"Lodesville is a wonderful, special place—one that has welcomed me and made me feel so at home," she began, and Tom looked up from his phone and pondered the sudden thought that Susan always found a way to bring herself and how she felt into nearly every issue that anyone wanted to discuss.

"And it's because I love Lodesville so very much, that I want to see us all move into the future of a modern, progressive and...*inclusive*...community that we can all be proud of. And of course, I feel we can't really do that if one of the first things our visitors see is a brutal reminder of an instrument of execution. And one that comes with an unfortunate association with racism of the worst kind."

Someone heckled from the gallery. "Hey Susan, I don't know if you ever noticed it, but Hal is a white dude!"

Eb banged on his gavel. Susan ignored the comments and continued: "We already saw last summer how an African American tourist was deeply upset by the sight of that...*thing*...and wrote to the *Mountain Chronicle* about it! This is how we're perceived by people outside of our community."

"We don't give a crap about how them Bay Area trendy-oids see us," yelled another heckler from the gallery.

Susan looked taken aback for a split second, but she quickly regained her composure and finished up.

"History is good, but not when it's harmful or cruel. Hangin' Hal doesn't project a modern, progressive image of Lodesville. This is our chance to put our town's checkered past to rest and move onto a brighter future."

The Bay Area contingent clapped quietly, and Susan returned to her seat.

Tom was recording everything on his phone. He switched over to his notes section and typed, "CONTRADICTORY" in all-caps.

She keeps talking about how much she loves it here, but then says we all need to change, he told himself. *If you love something, do you really need to demand that it changes? Contradictory.* He thought Susan was exasperating; maybe it was a good thing their relationship had never gone anywhere.

Sammy was determined to have the last word. "But our past is why people come here in the first place," he shouted out of turn. "If we hadn't been Hangwood once ago, we'd be just another old dyin' mountain town."

* * *

In the end, it was old Eb Turner who cast the deciding vote, after the rest of the town council vote deadlocked at 2-2, with Carol Sanders and Andy Sakamoto voting "yea" and Dot Bailey and Chuck Hawkfeather voting "nay."

"You voting with the racists, Chuck?" called out one of the Bay Area transplants.

"You can't just go around taking away someone's way of life, just because a bunch of new folks don't like it, Phil," Chuck replied. Tom lowered his head and stifled a snicker.

Eb hemmed and hawed and squirmed in his seat, but eventually he sided with the "yeas." He was known throughout El Dorado County as being the type of man who just wanted everyone to get along. Tom typed, "SPINELESS" into his notes section.

Ordinance 74 was thus duly passed, and Hangin' Hal's fate was sealed. Afterward the council passed Ordinance 75, which made Susan the chairwoman of the committee that would design the new regulations for business signs and symbols. It would take a while for the committee to draft the regulations, but everyone knew the vote was the end of the road for Hangin' Hal.

"Why we gotta take it down after more than eighty-five years just because that little bit o' Bay Area fluff don't like it?" Sammy burst out. "Eighty-five years!"

"Now Sammy," began Eb, looking distressed. He hated confrontation and spent much of his time as mayor trying to make sure no one ever got their nose out of joint. "Miss Cain wasn't the only one—"

"You won't like it one bit when Hal comes down, Eb Turner!" Sammy barked, his face almost purple. "Just ask Rose MacGreevey's granddaughter!" Then he stomped out of the room with a final glare at Susan.

Susan arose and addressed the room with a gracious smile. "It will be an adjustment for many of us to observe the new sign and advertising rules, but in the end, it will make for a kinder, more cohesive community that rejects racism and embraces openness!"

Some of the folks in the gallery smiled and nodded along. But most—those who had deep roots in Lodesville—glowered at Susan with set faces.

Sammy stuck his head back in the room. "She don't care nothin' about that black lady tourist," he roared. "She tried to get me to take Hal down *before* that lady even showed up. She just wants to shove her Bay Area nonsense down all of our throats."

"That simply isn't true, Sammy," Susan said evenly, facing him with squared shoulders. He glared at her and pulled back out of the room, slamming the door shut again.

Tom was already typing a rough draft of tomorrow's editorial into his notes section:

Nobody wanted this anger and divisiveness. But now that the anti-dummy crowd has had its way, then what? Where will it stop? Will they next come for the big brass plaque on Main Street that marks where the hangtree used to be? How about the annual one-hundred-year-old Christmas Parade? Will there be lobbying and hectoring until the name is changed to be more 'inclusive'? Yes, it's trivial and childish to hang the First Amendment upon the chipped plaster shoulders of Hangin' Hal, but that's what we've come to as a community.

Tom closed his phone and left the council chambers, heavy of heart. He sensed that something very important had been lost by Lodesville, but he wasn't sure if he could articulate it well enough in his editorial.

He was stopped in the City Hall lobby on his way out by Susan, the last person in the world he wanted to talk to at that precise moment.

"Tom, it worries me that Sammy Silva was so angry," she frowned. "And more than just mad—almost as if he were afraid of something! What do you suppose he meant when he said we wouldn't like it when the dummy came down?"

"I'm sure he was just talking about the divisions it would cause in the community. It's a local landmark and people get attached to those. Sammy talks a lot of shit, but he's harmless."

"But I'm doing this to *improve* the community."

"Improve it according to *your* views, but not other people's. Look, the locals already dislike the Bay Area transplants for pushing up the price of real estate so our young folks can't afford housing, and for acting like we're a bunch of ignorant hicks."

Susan opened her mouth to say something, then abruptly closed it. "It'll be fine, you'll see," she said, pushing up her chin.

"Yes, we'll all see."

"What was that stuff about Rose Something? What did it mean?"

"Oh Lord, it's nothing. An old woman who drank at the Hangwood Inn died a long time ago, and it was a strange kind of death. She stumbled into an iron fence and her neck scarf caught on a post and she somehow strangled herself. Some folks assumed foul play, but there was no evidence. It was decades ago—poor old Rose MacGreevey."

"He made it sound like it had something to do with the dummy."

"Before my time. Some old rumor about a curse—campfire story stuff. Look, I gotta go, Susan."

He left her in the lobby, frowning, as if her victory suddenly wasn't satisfying anymore. He bought a takeout sandwich at Dot's diner for lunch, and intended to retrace his steps back to the *Mountain Chronicle* offices. Then he changed his mind on a whim, and took a detour past the Hangwood Inn. He thought for the thousandth time how pretty and unique Main Street was, how preciously preserved. There were still double-decker sidewalks in some stretches, in front of mid-19th Century buildings with their high false fronts to make them appear taller, after the fashion of the times. At that very moment, Clint Eastwood could have ridden into Lodesville looking for his fistful of dollars, and not seemed out of place. How he loved the Gold Country--the foothills and mountains of the Sierra Nevada range—and its people and unique culture. He felt sorry for people like Susan, who didn't have a place they felt rooted to, a place they belonged.

As he approached the Hangwood Inn, he was surprised to see a small crowd gathered around it, clumped together around Hangin' Hal.

Sammy had set up a very tall ladder on the sidewalk near Hal and was just about to climb it. He carried a pair of wicked-looking garden clippers, which Tom assumed would be used for cutting Hal's rope.

"News travels fast," Tom muttered to himself. "Damn."

"Don't do it, Sammy!" someone yelled from the crowd. "Show them Bay Area folks that we don't back down!"

"I heard one of 'em as much as called Dot Bailey a racist," shouted another onlooker. "Damn fool don't even know that Dot's been keepin' company with Chuck Hawkfeather since *forever*!"

"You fixin' to take it down already, Sammy?" asked Tom. "They probably won't have the new rules finished for a month, or maybe longer."

"It's best to get it over with, Tom. No use prolongin' the agony. Now move aside, so Kit can get into position to catch ol' Hal when he goes down."

Kit Shorelong had worked at the tavern ever since Tom could remember. Now he was standing on the fringes of the little crowd with a hangdog expression on his face, carrying a big folded quilt. "It's for catching Hal. We can't let him smash on the sidewalk," Kit explained. "Not after all what he's meant to us."

"I'll help hold it, Kit," said a man from the crowd. "My pleasure to do anything for Hal," said another volunteer.

"Everybody that's not catchin' needs to stand clear

back," yelled Sammy, ascending the ladder. Kit and the volunteers from the crowd spread out the quilt and held it up under the dummy.

When Sammy reached the horizontal flagpole, he grabbed the rope that hung around Hal's neck and chopped angrily at it. "Watch out everyone!" he shouted, as the last brutal cuts sent Hal crashing toward the ground. It landed with a loud thud on Kit's outstretched quilt.

"There—it's done!" Sammy cried out, his voice shaded in dark, angry tones. He and Kit carried the dummy inside the Inn, and nobody knew what happened to it after that. Some people said that Sammy put Hal in the basement of the tavern, next to the ancient stump of the dead Lodesville hangtree that Sammy kept in trust for the town—a fitting grave companion for poor ol' Hangin' Hal.

* * *

At four o'clock that afternoon, Eb Turner left his office at City Hall and made his way to Susan's shop. He found her dusting shelves in the storage room behind the front shop floor.

"Cleaning and straightening always make me feel better when I'm antsy," she explained to Eb. "It's not easy to be on the right side of history, but I'm glad I made the effort. Thank you for voting our way."

Eb didn't know quite how to answer her. It was as if she only saw fancy words on a paper, not flesh-and-blood people.

"Well…you heard that Hal's already been taken down?"

"Yes, I did. Thankfully."

"Well, it's like this—Sammy Silva and his gang and a lot of other folks are real angry about it. I was thinkin'…maybe you could…you know…make some sort of gesture to get everyone reconciled."

"What did you have in mind?"

"I dunno." Eb looked around the stacks of inventory. "Maybe you could give Sammy and his employees a gift certificate or something…"

She almost laughed. "I don't think Sammy's the healing crystal or yoga type. And besides, that would be like admitting I was wrong…and I'm *not* wrong! *I'm on the right side of history!* I can't believe what people around here get away with. They say and do stuff that would *never* be tolerated in Marin County."

Eb was alarmed at the shrillness in her voice. "Now, now settle down, Susan. Just try to think of something for Sammy. As a favor to me."

"All right, I'll try to think of something. And you can do something for me, now that you're here."

"Glad to oblige." Eb was relieved to drop the subject of Sammy and Hangin' Hal. "What can I do you for?"

She pointed upwards toward a high shelf: "It's that pile of macramé belts that I can't reach, even with a step stool. Would you mind?"

Eb was a tall man, well over six feet, and Susan was very petite.

"Of course!"

He looked around more closely at the storage room and thought it a dismal place. There were too many dark shadows and corners and niches, and the single window to the street hadn't been washed in months.

And then—Eb gave a little cry.

He saw someone looking into the window. He flinched at what he saw. A head covered with a light blue hood...no eye holes...with a thick noose tightened around the neck. He strained to look closer, and then the hooded head was just—*gone*.

"Eb? Is there something wrong   ?"

"Nothing. Letting my imagination run away with me. I thought I saw some kinda creepy scarecrow or something looking in the window. Probably just a high school kid in those hoodie things they wear."

Eb was embarrassed. He thought his little lapse of sanity was because of some nonsense about the dummy rattling around in his head. He suddenly resented this uppity girl, this outsider from the Bay Area, for dumping such a touchy problem in his lap. Life was so much easier in Lodesville before the Bay Area people came. Who would have thought, even ten years ago, that Hangin' Hal would be such a divisive issue, tearing the whole community apart? No one had a problem with Hal until the Bay Area people came. That was the trouble with them; they ranted and raved about things that didn't matter, but when it came time to do something useful and important, like sandbagging the town when the spring snowmelt was threatening to flood, they were nowhere to be found. Still, the Bay Area people brought sorely-needed new money and jobs into the county—that couldn't be denied. Susan herself had donated a generous sum to replace the dilapidated playground at the Lodesville Elementary School.

"Eb?" Susan broke into his thoughts. "Anyone home in there? The pile of macramé belts is up there on that shelf—"

"W-w-what? Oh yes, hand me the step stool, I'll get them right down."

The shelf was right above the window where Eb imagined he saw the hooded man with the noose around his neck. He had a strange aversion to approaching the window, but he'd already promised to help and couldn't back out. The girl was just so much trouble, he was beginning to regret his tie-breaking vote that morning.

I should have left her twisting in the wind like ol' Hal, he told himself.

He made a point not to look at the window as he stepped on the stool and reached for the pile of the belts. He thought there were an awful lot of them; who would buy so many of these things anyway? People in Lodesville wore proper belts, made out of leather. Dot Bailey had a side business where she tooled leather belts and wallets in old cowboy patterns, not this flimsy crap that probably came from some purple-haired hippie in San Francisco.

For the first time, Eb noticed that the heavy wooden floating beams across the ceiling looked very old and not that steady. The building, he knew, was almost as old as the Hangwood Inn.

He handed down the first few belts to Susan's waiting arms.

"You should have those beams fixed, Susan. Some of them look to be rotten or loose."

Susan sighed. "Yes, there's so much to do, and so little time."

Eb grunted skeptically. He figured she'd have had plenty of time to do the repairs if she hadn't spent so much effort gallivanting around town lecturing everybody about a harmless dummy.

He handed down the last of the belts and then stepped down. "Well, I've got to be gettin' on...just think about what I said about making nice with Sammy."

"Thank you so much, Eb. Hey, did you...did you hear from Tom Korner about what he thought of the vote?" Her face was a little flushed and Eb realized that she was carrying a torch for Tom.

"Tom's a fair man," he began cautiously. "But he's gotta fierce devotion to the people of Lodesville, to the whole Gold Country. That's the way them Korners are—his dad and his grandpa took care of the place for decades, and while he's not in law enforcement, he kinda feels the same way."

Susan looked rueful. "Yes, I know. He once asked me why I wanted to change Lodesville into the same thing I ran away from in the Bay Area."

"To be honest, it's what a lot of people around here are thinking these days."

Susan didn't have an answer for that. "Well, I guess I better not keep you from going about your business. Thank you for your help."

"Good evening, Susan," nodded Eb, "I'll see myself out." He edged out onto the front shop floor and was nearly at the front door, when he heard a tremendous crash coming from the storage room. The crash was accompanied by a terrified scream from Susan.

He ran back into the inventory room and saw a pile of clothes and some limp limbs sticking out from them. Then he saw a heavy floating beam lying horizontally across the body of Susan Cain.

Eb rushed toward the pile. Susan lay face up, staring at the ceiling, and he noticed that the beam lay straight across her throat, crushing it and the upper part of her chest. Eb was over sixty; he struggled for far too long to lift the beam, but finally pushed and dragged it off the still form.

Susan Cain died fifteen minutes before the EMTs managed to rush in from nearby Bourbon Flats.

* * *

In the morning, Eb didn't know what to do after suffering a hellish night with EMTs and police. He decided to go to his usual refuge: his feed store off Main Street, where he hoped his routine of setting up for the day's business would take his mind off the awful death of Susan Cain. He was just opening up the store when Andy Sakamoto came barreling down the sidewalk, looking like a wild man.

"I heard about Susan," he said, out of breath. "It's…it's terrible, *awful*. Eb, I want to rescind my vote from yesterday. There's something you need to know!"

Eb stared at Andy, surprised and disturbed. It was unlike him to look or act so distressed. He was known around town as "Easy Andy."

"Why, come on in, Andy. Yes, it's a horrible thing. I got some coffee brewing in the back room."

Eb locked up again, and turned the sign in his front window to "closed." He and Andy sat together in the back room where Eb kept a coffee maker, a sink and a hotplate.

"Don't need coffee, Eb."

"Okay. So, what do you want to talk about? The vote? It's not on anyone's mind now with this awful accident and what's happened to the Cain woman. I didn't know you were especially close to her."

"I wasn't really. It's not that. It's... look... Eb... you're a level-headed guy. Do you ever think there might be such a thing as...*ghosts?*" Andy looked embarrassed at his own words, as if he were hoping that Eb wouldn't laugh at him too much.

"Well, Andy, I dunno. I never gave it much thought. Why?" Eb shuddered, thinking about the hooded head he'd seen (or *thought* he'd seen) in the window at Susan's shop.

"It was about four o'clock yesterday, around the time the accident happened. I was in the barn stacking hay when...I saw...something. A figure of a man. Just standing there. He had a light blue hood over his head, with no eye holes. There was a noose around his neck, tightened over the cloth of the hood. He...took a few steps toward me. I swear this is all true. I don't mind admitting it, I almost wet my pants."

"Well...what happened then? Did he stop comin'?"

"He...it...disappeared. *But that's not the end of it.*" Andy paused for a minute, collecting himself, and then started talking again: "I went outside, and you know that big ol' willow tree that I got near my barn? I was standing under it, trying to figure out what the hell I'd just seen, when some of the branches trailing down swayed across my throat and...it was like they had a mind of their own...like they were trying to strangle me, and then I felt like they *were* strangling me. I couldn't breathe. *Don't look at me like that, Eb. I'm not making this up!*"

"Now, calm down, Andy. You're gettin' all your morning exercise by jumpin' to conclusions." Eb was on the verge of telling Andy about his own sighting of a strange figure in a light blue hood, but then thought better of it. He had next year's elections to think of, and then there was the feed store. His customers might start thinking he was going off the deep end—undependable-like. Aloud, he said simply, "How'd you get away?"

"I grabbed the branches and pulled at them until they loosened and then I sort of wrenched away from them. When I got loose I ran like hell, got in my truck and drove to town to see you. Eb, I remember all those old stories about Rose MacGreevey and even remember some people saying it had something to do with Hal. Don't tell anyone, but that's why I want to change my vote."

Eb sat back in his chair and lost himself in grim reflections. Even in death, the Cain woman was a troublemaker. Now, Easy Andy was a nervous wreck and Eb felt responsible. He didn't know what was going on, but he realized that he should never have voted to remove the dummy.

"Look Andy, you just go home to Naomi and the kids and rest a spell. And stay away from that damn willow tree! I'm not gonna enforce that ordinance. In fact, I'm goin' over to Sammy's place right now and have a li'l talk with him about it."

* * *

Eb sat at the bar in the Hangwood Inn, enjoying his "comped" Diet Coke. "All right, Sammy, out with it. What's the story behind the dummy? I mean, I usually don't even believe in this kind of crap, but I gotta know, one way or the other."

"I tried to warn you, Eb." Sammy wiped down his bar with a wet cloth, working in vigorous, exaggerated circles. He was still mad. "You wouldn't listen."

"Well, I'm listening now. 'Cause that girl's dead. And this mornin', Andy Sakamoto says he got near strangled by his own willow tree. You *know* somethin'. You said all that stuff about Rose MacGreevey at the council."

"I never told no one. I'm not sure I'm a-*supposed* to tell. And besides I can't afford to lose trade 'coz folks are scared o' my place."

"I'm the mayor," Eb said. "A mayor's gotta right to know what's goin' on in his town, don't he? And I won't tell no one either, if it's *that* important to you."

Sammy put down his cloth and crossed his arms over his barrel chest.

"It's like this," he finally said, leaning in close. "This town's gotta hankerin' for hangin'. And if it can't get a hangin' it'll settle for the next best thing—a chokin' or a garottin'."

"What the ever-lovin' eff? The town does effin' *what?*"

"It's Simpy Jim, come to get his revenge, like he always does."

"Simpy Jim?"

"He was this retard—sorry—this *mentally challenged* fellow who worked at the stamp plant in the '30s. He put a curse on this bar."

"Simpy Jim? *Simpy Jim*...that fella who supposedly haunts the old pioneer cemetery?"

Sammy nodded. "Well, that's just a kid's campfire story. The real story is right here in this bar, handed down to me by my Great Uncle Balt. And I'll hand it down to my nephew Timbo when the time comes."

"Sammy, I never did have patience for riddles. I

think I feel a complaint to the health department comin' on...when's the last time you cleaned the tavern's fridge?"

Sammy shot a hard look at Eb. "So that's how you wanna play it, Eb?"

"I gotta right to know what's happenin' in my own town, Sammy."

Sammy snorted, shook his head, and then disappeared into his back kitchen. He came out carrying a leather-bound chest, which he unlocked with an ancient key. He took out a ledger pad, the pages of which were yellowed and fragile.

"Uncle Balt wrote down everything about the bar in his journals. Lists of supplies, debts, customers. This one's from the '30s, when he was a young man just startin' out. Now, you're gonna listen Eb, unlike yesterday."

He flipped the ledger pad to a back page and started reading aloud:

> *On this date, I, Balthazar Silva, am puttin' down the history of the man called Simpy Jim for the benefit of the posterity of Lodesville.*
>
> *He came to work in the stamp plant in the second year of the Great Depression. He wasn't an operator but a water boy and a general dogsbody, on account of bein' "simple." His odd ways were put down to his bein' all mental, but he had his cunnin' side, too.*
>
> *Simpy always come into the Hangwood on a Friday night after pay day, with a group of stamp men. Would have a plate of ham, fried eggs, and a beer, usually. He could do tricks—that's where the cunnin' part came in. He would do them for the workers and usually money changed hands, and Simpy would make some dough on the side to keep body and soul together.*

He could make quarters move across the bar with nobody helpin' them go. If you asked him how he did it, he would just smile and say, "it's a secret." He could do other strange stuff too, like tell dogs to stop barkin' and they'd do it.

One night at the tavern, Simpy made a lot of money off a guy named Skell with the quarter trick. I wished later I'da stopped it, because Skell wasn't the kind to be trifled with. Soon he got madder 'n madder, and then he got his boys to tie Simpy's hands together, and it didn't make no difference because the quarters moved down the bar, same as always. Then Skell wanted to put a hood over Simpy's face, and someone produced an old blue pillowcase and put it over Simpy's head and covered his face all up, and still the quarters moved same as always, and Skell kept losin'.

Skell was drunk and mad. Then someone suggested that they take Simpy outside, into the cold night, and "pretend" to give him some "frontier justice," like the old days in Hangwood. I yelled at them to stop tormentin' the poor simple creature, but no one paid no mind. At that hour, it was just me and the dumb silly girl in the kitchen against all those drunk, rough-cut plant men. They said they were only jokin'.

We didn't have no telephone in those days, but I sent the girl down the street to find one of the Sheriff's men and bring him back.

I could tell from the befuddled sounds comin' out from under that hood that Simpy had no idea what was happenin'. It was only after someone found another, longer rope and made a noose and looped it around Simpy's neck that it finally dawned on him that somethin' awful was afoot. And then such a sound of terror came out of that poor *simple creature's mouth—oh my! I shudder to even write it down. I yelled at them to stop one more time and someone pushed me on the floor and then they rushed passed me while pushin' Simpy out the front door.*

I got up and followed them outside and tried to get them to leave poor Simpy alone, but they wouldn't listen. They kept joshin' in a mean, drunk way about hanging Simpy from the flagpole in front. And Simpy started to cry from under the hood. "I ain't a cheat!" He bleated like a scared sheep. "I'll give the money back!"

Skell just laughed and made the noose tighter. "Well if this mental case wants to give my money back, don't that mean he's guilty?"

"Hangin's too good for him!" one man yelled. I was startin' to get pretty scared myself, truth be told.

And then, Lord be praised, along came the deputy, young Billy Korner, and the girl.

"That's enough," Billy shouted. "Leave that man be!"

There was an embarrassed silence, and the other men started to leave, except for Skell, who looked Billy up and down and then jutted out his chin.

"He cheated me out of three dollars!" Skell shouted. "Three whole dollars! You should arrest him!"

"Is that true?" Billy said to the lump under the pillowcase.

Simpy sputtered through his sobs. "No, Billy, no! I just always been able to move them quarters and other things…"

"Oh, the quarter trick," said Billy. "By gum, it's Simpy under that pillowcase! You should know better than to do the quarter trick for a varmint like Skell." He pushed

his way passed Skell and took the noose from around Simpy's neck, then removed the pillow case and untied Simpy's hands.

"I demand my money back!" said Skell. "And you arrest him for...for conductin' an illegal wagering operation."

Billy laughed. "For a bar bet? Go on, Skell! Simpy, you wanna give him his money back? Give him two dollars. You can keep the other dollar in fair payment for the scare."

It took Simpy a long time to figure out that he no longer had anything to fear from Skell. With trembling fingers he finally reached into his overalls and pulled out two dollars and gave them to Billy, who handed them over to Skell.

"It's done, then," Billy said. "Go home and sleep it off, Skell."

Skell saw he was defeated and took his leave, but he wasn't done with Simpy.

"You mind your ways, cheater," he yelled. "I'll be lookin' to get even some day."

Simpy's face turned dead white with terror, and then he got a horrible look in his eyes. It was kind of like a trance, where he acted like he'd gone into some other place and couldn't hear or see anything normally. When that look came into Simpy's eyes, I was more scared of him than Skell.

"You mind yourself," Simpy said, in a strange voice. "This town's got a hankerin' for hangin' and best you not tempt the Hangin' Tree to claim its own."

Skell shoved Simpy's shoulder hard and then he left.

Simpy Jim died the next day. No one knew why and the county eventually said it was "cause unknown." His heart gave out sometime durin' the night, and everyone said *it was because he was scared to death by Skell. Billy Korner blamed himself. He seemed to think that Simpy would've lived if he'd kept an eye on him. But Simpy wanted to go home to his own little apartment over the drug store and there was nothing Billy could do about it.*

And then Skell died too. There was an accident at the stamp plant where they sifted the gold. Somehow, Skell had been caught in a rope someone was using to lift a crate. He was chokin', but they cut him out, too late. His last words were: "This town's gotta hankerin' for a hangin'."

After that, a few days later, the dummy appeared. Hangin' from the yardarm in front of the Hangwood. Some folks thought it was the ghost of Simpy that done it, to remind Skell's buddies of what they tried to do him for. Others thought it was Skell's boys, mockin' poor Simpy's memory. I took it down of course, but then accidents kept happenin', people almost gettin' kilt for no reason, most by hangin' or stranglin'. All accidents, so they said.

I put the dummy back up, and it all stopped. And I never took it down no more except that time when the rope broke, and it fell. And poor old Rose MacGreevey paid the price—Simpy made sure he choked her with her own scarf. As God is my witness, this is the truth.

—Balthazar Silva. (date unknown)

Sammy finished reading and gave Eb a hard look that said: "I dare you to challenge what I just read."

"That's...that's some story, Sammy."

Sammy pushed his lip out a little bit. "And if you don't believe Uncle Balt about Rose MacGreevey, I got my own story too. When I took over the bar, he gave me the journal, but I didn't *believe* in those days. I had ol' Hal hauled down and given a change of clothes and a fresh coat of face paint. Well, while he was down, a customer choked on a ham sandwich, and he almost died, right here where you're settin' now. Kit saved his life with that there Heimlich Maneuver."

Eb was solemn. "I believe you, Sammy."

"What? You *believe* me?" Sammy was dumfounded.

"I saw Simpy *myself*. Simpy was looking into the window of the Cain woman's shop just before the accident. But if you ever, ever tell anyone I said that, I'm a-gonna sic the county inspector on that ancient industrial fridge you got in the back that grows moldy science projects."

"I ain't tellin' nobody, Eb. You think I'm crazy enough to yak about something like that around town? Now can I put the dummy back?"

"Yes. I ain't enforcin' that ordinance. Andy told me he wanted to rescind his vote anyway."

* * *

Heavy-hearted and slightly numb, Tom Korner drove with Eb down to Marin County a few days later. They went to pay their respects to Susan's parents and attend her memorial service. The service was held in a spring meadow near a place called Lucas Valley. It was officiated by a very tall woman, who wore bright goldenrod robes and a dyed, cobalt-blue coif. The statuesque yellow-and-blue woman reminded Tom of the tropical flower that Dot Bailey once planted in her garden, against all advice of those who said it would never survive the first frost. But Dot had a plan to drape it with lightbulbs and wrap it in plastic when the weather dipped. The plant limped along for a while in the early chill, but eventually died. It didn't belong in the mountains.

The Stone Wife

Billy Stone had never minded that his favorite jogging trail went past the old Heartwood Pioneer Cemetery. In fact, he sometimes would stop and explore the place on the way back to his car, after finishing his run. He liked it. The crooked, lichen-covered tombstones leaned every which way; the variegated ivy climbed peacefully on the brick or stone mausoleums; the mock strawberries nudged the flat gray markers in the spring. In his view, it was a charming place, not at all gloomy or foreboding.

It was very early on a weekday morning in the first week of November. The air stung like a needle-prick in its chilliness, which was typical at this time of year for his mid-sized city in Southern Oregon. He chugged along the gravel trail that ran beside the north border of the cemetery, his warm breath pluming out in front of him like a soft white feather.

He thought about his break-up with Candace as he ran, *pound-pound-pound,* with his running shoes hitting the gravel trail harder and harder in grim time with his thoughts. He was thirty-three and wanted to settle down. He'd thought that Candace was The One, until she had started "working late" at night with the new, handsome executive at her firm…Austin Peek. Fucking *Austin Peek.*

He stopped short at the thought of that hateful name, and he found that he was breathing hard and gasping for air. He decided to take a small detour to view his favorite nook in the cemetery. He wended his way to it through an ivy-covered arbor that desperately needed cutting back. Some of the graves were more than a hundred and fifty years old, with markers that were so worn they weren't readable.

For the two years he'd been using the jogging trail, Stone enjoyed making up brief, whimsical bios for the stones and markers that were still legible. An infant girl named Oregonia Elizabeth had a small, mottled stone bearing a birth and death date in November of 1849. Oregonia Elizabeth, he wondered often why her people gave her such a name? Hopefulness for a new life in a new land after the long trip on the Oregon Trail, from unknown points East? A hopefulness that was cruelly dashed when little Oregonia Elizabeth died just two weeks after she was born.

And then there was the praying woman statue that kept guard over a flat granite marker a few twisty aisles from Oregonia Elizabeth. The figure in granite was exceptionally well-crafted, and Stone was fascinated with its face. It was a standing woman with her two hands pressed together in a steeple peak, her chin resting slightly above the apex. He had visited the praying woman many times over the past two years. A discreet legend on the front of the statue read *Devoted Wife*, presumably the spouse of the man who rested under the marker, but no name was given for the woman on the legend. Yet it appeared that Devoted Wife had never joined her husband in the Heartwood Cemetery, as there was only a single gravestone under the figure's shadow.

He had taken to calling the statue The Stone Wife. A play on his own name and his fascination with the statue's face. Today, he stopped to pay his respects to

Oregonia Elizabeth and then rambled off in search of The Stone Wife. Which, to his surprise, he could not find.

She wasn't where he expected her to be, and he spread out further into the nook and turned down more rows of stones and statues, but *she* could not be found. He had never bothered, he suddenly realized, to look at the name on the marker beneath the statue—the name of The Stone Wife's dear departed spouse. That would have made it easier to find her.

"I could have sworn it was over *there...*" he mumbled to himself, pointing to an aisle near a mini-square planted with rose bushes. However, he couldn't be sure. Perhaps it was near a different plot of rose bushes, in a different aisle.

Or perhaps he'd got the location right, but someone had taken the statue down for cleaning or repair; perhaps vandals had stolen it. The last thought made him slightly angry, as if he imagined the figure could feel its own violation and mistreatment.

Or perhaps he was simply wrong, and the statue was further on from Oregonia Elizabeth than he remembered. He shrugged and trotted back to the gravel jogging trail.

Somewhere, while he shivered in the frosty November air, Candace was showering in Austin Peek's lavishly appointed bachelor pad. She would be using the Neutrogena shampoo with the distinctive smell, and her beloved Aveeno soap. Always the Aveeno soap, or else her seasonal eczema would start to flare up—or so she always claimed. Maybe Austin Peek had a double-sized shower stall; maybe he would be joining her and soaping up with the Aveeno soap and washing his hair in the Neutrogena... *Stop! Stop these punishing thoughts!* he sternly reminded himself.

He had to suppress his thinking about Candace, somehow. She was the past, she was *over*. Time to concentrate on the future. Returning to his jogging, Stone picked up his pace and followed the gravel trail to the bus shelter that was stationed near it. It was plastered with a faded poster advertising a Mariah Carey concert that took place more than two years ago. No one had bothered to take it down or replace it with another, more current poster. Stone took a cursory glance at the shelter and almost turned away, but strangely, he felt pulled toward it. He heard a slight sound, like a quiet sob, and he stopped running and peeked around the side of the shelter to see where the sound was coming from.

There was a figure huddled in the bus shelter. Probably a domestic worker, who worked long hours and wouldn't be taking the bus back home until it was long past dark. The domestic worker, if that's what she really was, seemed to be quietly crying.

Stone normally had a strict "don't get involved" ethos when it came to odd encounters with strangers in public. He'd been a lawyer for eight years, and he knew what happened to Good Samaritans all too often, when they were just "only trying to help."

But this girl appeared to be young, and there was something fleetingly familiar about the way she held herself, in a pose that was almost supplicating… Stone sighed. He knew he was going to talk to her, against his better judgment. And he knew he was going to regret playing Good Samaritan.

He cleared his throat. "Umm, excuse me, Miss, but is there a problem? It's pretty early for you to be out here…alone," he said. "Aren't you cold?

He checked his watch. It was just past 6:45 in the morning. She raised her head and Stone got a good look at her face for the first time. He gasped slightly; she was heartbreakingly beautiful, with bones carved in Donatello-like delicacy; glowing pale skin; and a haunted, smudged-shadow look about her eyes. Her fair hair had a silvery cast, as if it had been spun from the softest spider silk.

She was as different in appearance from Candace as chalk was from cheese. Fair where Candace was dark-haired; lanky where Candace was petite; silvery pale and deliberate in her mannerisms, where Candace was olive-skinned, vivid, and quick in everything she did.

The girl had an oddly familiar face, but Stone couldn't place it. He didn't think she was a domestic worker after all; nobody that beautiful would be scrubbing floors. Maybe she was one of the girls who toiled downstairs in the deli in the ground floor of his office building. They came and went; it wasn't a great place to work.

"No, I'm not cold. I…I don't have anywhere else to go," she stuttered through small, occasional sobs.

"You're homeless?"

"What—what is homeless?"

"You don't have a place to live?" He said, incredulous that she didn't seem to understand the meaning of the word "homeless." Maybe she was hard of hearing.

"Oh, yes, homeless—now I see what you mean. No, I don't have a place to live."

"You have no family?"

She shook her head.

"No one to take you in?" She shook her head again.

"Look here—what's your name?"

"Why—I don't know. I've never really thought about it." An amnesiac then—or a druggie. But she didn't look under the influence of anything. She was just vague and strange.

"You've had a shock; you may have amnesia."

"If you say so."

He was frustrated with her enigmatic answers and beautiful—but slightly blank—expressions.

He made up his mind that he would take her in to the police station downtown when he got the chance. But for now, he had a court date at 8:00 a.m. which couldn't be postponed.

"I can take you to my apartment. Don't worry, you will be safe. You can wait outside in the car for me while I shower and change into my work clothes, if you want to. Then you can come with me to a place where people can help you."

She hesitated.

"I'm safe. My name is Billy—er, William—Stone. I'm an attorney who works downtown near the courthouse. I'm one hundred percent trustworthy." He smiled what he hoped was a charming and confident smile.

Oddly, she jumped on his name. "Stone? It's a good name. A good man with a good name."

"Well, I like it," he said, lamely. Inwardly, he thought: *What a weird chick. I really know how to pick 'em. First Candace turned out to be a gold-digging slut and now I seem to have adopted this peculiar street woman.*

Aloud he said, "I'll walk you to my car. I'll stay a safe distance from you while we walk." She nodded, and he helped her up from her seat and guided her to the place along the gravel trail where he'd parked his car.

Along the way, they passed the old quarry below the jogging trail, and she stopped for a moment and stared across the surrounding fence and into the pit, with a pensive, undefinable look on her face.

"What place is this?"

"It's just a quarry. They used to dig stone out of it. For walls and things. It hasn't been used for many years."

"Oh."

"Did you live near a quarry before?" he asked, with a sudden inspiration.

"I-I can't say," she said. "It just looks like something I *know*."

He drove her to his apartment building, and she waited for him in the car in the parking lot. After showering and putting his court suit on, he brought her a sweater jacket that Candace had left behind. He should have realized sooner that her long, flowing dress was too flimsy for the chilly morning weather, but she didn't seem to be cold. The jacket was a bit short for her, but it mostly fit, after a fashion.

Stone's courthouse appearance was at the City Hall complex, where the main police station was also located. He'd planned to drop the girl off at the station before court and hoped there would be no time-consuming hassles from the authorities.

As they parked and approached the complex, however, he noticed the girl becoming more agitated.

Why, she's shaking with terror, thought Stone. *It's rare to see someone so frightened for no reason.*

She stared straight ahead at the plaza in front of the

complex and halted stubbornly on the sidewalk.

Holy crap, he thought, *she's staring at old Mayor Dougherty! It's Old Dough-Dough that is giving her the heebie-jeebies.*

"Old Dough-Dough" was a granite statue of a mayor from another age, which had been erected in front of the courthouse many years before.

"Please," she pleaded, "I don't want to go. I can't go."

"It's just a *statue*," cried Billy, bewildered. "It isn't real. Why don't you like it?

"I don't know. It just looks...*lonely*. It reminds me of something I don't like, but I can't remember what it is."

He tried to sound soothing, but he was plainly disturbed by the odd reaction. "I'll take you to the police. They can help you! They can find your people and get you a doctor who will help you with your memory," he implored. "Really! Come along, and I'll come back and see you when I'm done at the court. I promise."

She clutched his arm in an iron vise grip. "No! Take me back then! Take me back to where you found me!"

"I can't take you back to that dismal bus shelter. And besides, it's started to rain."

Eventually they decided that she would wait for him at a coffee shop near the courthouse called The Docket. Stone ate lunch or breakfast there at least once a week. He found her a good table and gave her money for coffee and breakfast.

"I'll be back around noon," he said. "Promise me you won't go anywhere?"

"Where would I go?" she asked. Again, there was the blank, far-off look on her face that he found so disconcerting.

II.

It was still raining when Stone hurried into The Docket. He felt a sense of great relief that he was finally able to get away for his lunch hour after his court business was completed and his morning office work was under control.

The girl was still sitting where he left her. There was a plate of waffles on the table before her, and a half-filled glass of orange juice. The waffles were swimming in maple syrup that had started to congeal, and were only half-touched.

"Food not good?" he asked, jerking his thumb toward the waffles.

She brightened up when she saw him. He was annoyed with himself for being glad to see that happy look.

"I just didn't know how to...you know...use the things to eat with. I had to watch the others until I learned, and I was slow."

"What an extraordinary thing to say."

The words were out of his mouth before he knew what he was saying.

"Look," she said, with a shy smile. "I can use this cutting thing now." She sawed a piece of waffle with her knife and fork and plopped it in her mouth, chewing slowly and carefully.

"It's a knife," Stone said, perplexed. "Not a cutting thing."

"Yes, then."

"Look, what is it that you wanted me to do? You

can't stay here forever, and you don't want to go to the police, who can help you. Don't you want to know who you are? They can help you get to someone who'll assist you in getting your memory back."

"*No!* I don't want to go near...*there*! Can't I come with you?"

Stone was doubtful. But where else would she go, if not home with him? The county hospital? They wouldn't look after her properly without insurance and she wouldn't know how to deal with them anyway.

"Can't I stay with you? At least until the memory comes back."

"Do you think it will ever come back?"

"Well, I remembered something important while you were away."

"What was that?"

"I remembered my name."

"Really?"

"Selma. My name is Selma."

"Oh, that's a beautiful name," he said, letting out a soft whistle of admiration. "That's great that you remembered. Do you know your last name too?"

"I don't know if I have another name. I'll try."

Stone sighed. Without a surname to go on, he'd make little progress in tracking down her identity. He made a quick decision. He figured he still had time on his lunch hour to drive her back to the apartment before his next appointment. Maybe she would remember her surname by dinnertime.

As they parked in his building's lot, he ran into Mrs. Ronan, the neighbor. Stone cringed. He had been feuding in a cold but cordial way with the old lady for several weeks over the spare parking space that Candace used when she lived with him. It had been a bitter fight, and the old lady obviously still held a grudge.

Now, she looked Selma up and down in a critical way, a habit that had always made Stone furious when she did it to him or Candace.

"If you have a new *friend* staying over, I expect you'll try to be quiet? The last girl was so loud."

The nasty emphasis on the word "friend" infuriated Stone even more. Selma didn't have anything to say. She had her typical blank, uncomprehending look on her face.

"This is Selma, an old friend," Stone snapped back, in a frigid voice. "She's staying with me while she's recovering from a long, painful illness, so I'd appreciate it if you kept the drama to a minimum while she's here."

Mrs. Ronan was momentarily taken aback, then her eyes narrowed, and she reached out as if to grab Stone's lapels, but her claw-like hand halted in mid-air.

"Very well, Mr. Stone. Does she have her own car?"

"No!"

Mrs. Ronan's face creased into a goblinesque smile, displaying yellowed teeth and tarnished silver fillings. "Good," she said, smugly. "My son can use the parking space when he visits."

"Whatever!" Stone replied, with disgust. He watched while she waddled out of the parking lot and down a covered cement passageway to her own apartment.

Stone let out a deep breath and shook his head, before he led Selma to his own place, and then fumbled for his apartment key.

"This is it," he said, pulling her in through the door. "Home sweet home."

"It's a very different place from what I'm used to," she said.

"Really? What do you mean? Do you have any more memories coming back?"

She shook her head. "No. I just remember that it was cold a lot. Not warm like here."

He shrugged. The apartment was actually rather chilly this evening. But instead of turning up the heat, he put on a sweater. She seemed to like things on the colder side.

"Well, I'll show you where you can sleep."

Stone lived in a two-bedroom, two-bath apartment. He used the second bedroom for an office. It contained a desk with a very large monitor that plugged into his laptop, his spare desktop computer, and a printer. There was also a futon that could be expanded and made into a bed, and a closet with some old clothes that Candace had left behind.

Stone told her she could have any of the clothes she wanted, although he could see Selma was significantly taller than Candace. He showed her where the attached bathroom was, and demonstrated how to turn on the shower.

"You probably want to clean up sometime soon," he said. "Plenty of hot water, but it comes out a little fast sometimes—be careful!"

Then he made up the futon into a bed. "You can take a nap here, if you're tired."

He showed her how to boot up the spare computer and access the Internet.

"You can search on here for anything that might jog your memory. Or you can watch movies from my Netflix account or on YouTube." He gave her the password and showed her how to find YouTube and Netflix's streaming site. She seemed especially fascinated with YouTube.

He returned in the evening with ingredients to make dinner. He normally had bachelor tastes and habits; his usual evening meal was take-out or frozen pizza. But he could make pasta, garlic bread, and salad, and he unpacked these simple provisions and laid them on the kitchen counter to prepare for the meal.

However, when he tapped on Selma's door, there was no answer. He peeked in and discovered that she was fast asleep, under the blankets he'd placed on the futon.

How still she is, he thought. *Almost like she's not even breathing. Almost like she's petrified.*

But that was impossible, and Stone closed the door softly and sat down to have dinner with himself. Having dinner alone had been a common occurrence since Candace moved out. Selma wasn't much for conversation, but at least she was company, a warm living body. He still had no clue what he was going to do with her. Maybe it would become clear the next morning after a decent night's sleep.

III.

Stone was having a dream about the Heartwood Pioneer Cemetery. It was not a pleasant dream. He was jogging by the big, rambling graveyard on the gravel trail, as usual. But then a woman drifted past and beckoned him to follow her into the cemetery. She was headed toward his favorite nook, the leafy one that contained the burial plot of

Oregonia Elizabeth and the statue of The Stone Wife.

He followed, feeling as if his legs were somehow disconnected from his mind. He moved as if walking on some soft, doughy substance, like marshmallows or a sea of foam pillows.

The woman kept pulling away from him just when he thought he was catching up to her…in the dream it seemed so very important to catch up to her…at his heels something grabbed his ankle, up from one of the graves, a bony hand with an iron grip.

He heard a hostile, metallic voice bark at him: "You're not wanted here…you're too warm for us."

And then he felt another bony hand…gripping his throat, while he gasped for air.

Suddenly, he awoke to find that something was on his throat for real…in the dark, he could feel ragged breath on his face. It was Selma.

She was draped, naked, over his prone body. Her hands were around his neck, pushing his head up close to her face, kissing his face and lips in a ferocious, animalistic way. Almost as if she wanted to eat him.

But—but! he tried to sputter, *this is not what I expected…* He tried to speak again, but now her hands were moving down his body, touching and massaging… "You're almost too warm for me," she whispered in a heady, lusty voice.

He felt a small thrill of revulsion at the words, and briefly thought of pushing her off, but then the thought was buried in the swirling darkness surrounding them. And in the end, he gave in to her insistent passion—first reluctantly, and then hungrily, almost as lustful and frantic as the woman.

IV.

In the morning, Selma was gone. He searched the whole apartment, and she was gone.

"Was that a dream?" he wondered. "Or am I just losing it?"

It was a Saturday. Normally he would have slept in a bit, then gone out for lunch. He dressed and went out into the common grounds around his building, searching for Selma.

There was a little boy playing with a red ball near the barbecue area. Stone realized it was Mrs. Ronan's grandson, who frequently stayed with his grandmother. The kid was a brat, known for causing trouble for the other tenants

Stone approached and asked him if he'd seen a woman who looked like Selma.

"It's Philip, isn't it?" he inquired.

"It's Phil, really. I'm called Little Phil, after my dad."

"Okay, Little Phil, have you seen any lady walking around out here? A tall lady, dressed in a white, floaty kind of dress?"

Little Phil shook his head. "I only saw the stone lady."

Stone didn't understand what the boy meant.

"A stone lady? What's that?"

"She—*it*—was over there." The boy pointed to a grassy spot in front of a large sycamore tree growing in the common area. "I thought it was a new thing for the garden. Like, for decoration. My grandma has these little, glass elves she puts on the patio, you know—"

"There's nothing there," Stone interrupted impatiently, annoyed. "You're making all this up, aren't you?"

The kid was apparently as crazy as his grandmother. Stone turned to leave, but Little Phil was insistent.

"Somebody *moved* it," Little Phil cried. "I went to find my ball in the bushes, and the stone lady was gone when I got back. Maybe the gardening man moved it to a better place."

Little Phil was useless, Stone thought. Clearly, he was trying to put one over on Stone, and Stone wasn't amused.

A shameless liar like dear old Granny, he thought. He noticed that the boy had the same beady, rodent-like eyes that Mrs. Ronan possessed, and those eyes moved around a lot, like the little brat was hiding something.

He went back to the apartment and was surprised to see Selma, standing at the front door, with a gray towel wrapped tightly around her right hand and lower arm. He recognized it as one of the towels the apartment managers provided for the complex's gymnasium.

"Selma!" he cried. "Where have you been? I've been out looking for you."

She looked at him with her typical, slightly blank stare. "I was just out for a walk. It seemed like a nice morning. You locked me out."

"It's a shit morning," said Stone, red and flustered. "It's colder than an ice cream cone in an igloo. Next time leave a note."

"Oh, I'm sorry. Billy, I'm so sorry. I guess I thought I'd be back from my walk before you woke up. I'll leave a note next time."

"Did you hurt your arm?"

"My arm?"

"The towel—"

"Oh that. Yes, I just had an accident, with the water, in the shower. The place you showed me for washing. It came out too hot at first. It burned."

"Oh my god, you got scalded! I warned you about that. May I see it?"

He reached for her injured arm, but she pulled it away quickly, holding it protectively against her middle section.

"*No!* I mean, it would hurt to unwrap it now. It will be better in a couple of days."

She wouldn't unwrap her arm for the next couple of days, and Stone was a bit worried. She repeatedly rebuffed his entreaties to let him look at the arm or visit a doctor.

A couple of times, he bumped the arm accidentally, and through the towel, it felt strangely hard and cold. But she continued to claim vigorously that the arm was fine and would be all right soon.

She stayed in the second bedroom at night for several days, and there were no more passionate midnight visits to his bed. Beyond that, she was sweet, helpful, and pleasant.

She walked to the corner market each day and bought food for dinner, and had the evening meal ready for him when he came home from the office. She loved to watch the cooking videos on YouTube, especially the baking ones.

One evening he came home from work and the homemade bandage was gone from Selma's arm. Selma was beaming over the dining table, which contained a plate of Chicken Parmesan and steamed Brussels sprouts. She'd also made sourdough bread from scratch. The fresh-baked smell filled the apartment.

She held up her right arm with a beaming smile when she saw him. The arm was pink and healthy and perfectly fine.

Stone lifted it for a moment, and gently kissed her hand; it was not hard or cold or scarred.

Over dinner, she told him proudly: "I remembered something again. My other name. It's Stansfield. S-T-A-N-S-F-I-E-L-D."

"That's wonderful," said Stone. "Now we can search on the computer to see if there are any records or other posts with that name."

She frowned. "What if you don't like the person I used to be? What if I was something *bad?*"

"That wouldn't be possible," said Stone gently.

After dinner, he did an Internet search on the name "Selma Stansfield." He came up with only one record, which was for a seventy-five-year-old woman in Columbus, Ohio.

"Well, that can't be you," said Stone. "You're not an old crone. But maybe she's a relative. Does Columbus, Ohio, mean anything to you?"

She thought for a long moment. "No," she said. "It's not familiar at all."

"Hmmm—nothing seems to be all that familiar to you."

"*You* do," she said with a small, mysterious smile. "You seem *very* familiar to me."

In the middle of the night, she came to him again, finally, after so long away. Passionate, insistent, fierce and devouring. He kissed her and touched her with equal ferocity, losing himself in the lustful strangeness of the night.

"You're almost too warm for me," she whispered.

V.

They stayed together many nights afterward, and Stone dropped all pretense of trying to find out who she was. He just accepted what was happening, fatalistically.

If it happens that she remembers, he thought, *that's okay. If not, it doesn't matter.*

On the next clear weekend, he took her to the upscale shopping mall downtown to buy some new clothes. Candace's cast-offs weren't sufficient for her size and what she needed. Stone hated seeing her in them anyway. He no longer cared about Candace and didn't want to have any reminders of her around. He would toss her clothes out or drive them to Goodwill when Selma got her new wardrobe.

And first Selma was delighted by the mall; she acted as if she had never seen one before. She was fascinated by the display windows for the garden supply store and the cookware store, full of so many bright and lovely things.

"I want to make a strawberry soufflé!" she exclaimed, looking longingly at a ceramic soufflé pan in the cookware store's front window. "I watched a lady make one on YouTube yesterday."

Stone promised he would get her the pan on the way back. He steered her toward the big department store where Candace used to buy most of her clothes. He had accompanied her there on many, many shopping trips in past days.

Selma, however, became visibly agitated when she saw the display windows of the big store, full of Christmas decorations and holiday clothing.

"I don't like this place," she whispered. "They look so lonely."

"They?"

"In the window. The people in the window."

"But those are only mannequins," he reproached. "They aren't real."

"But they look *lonely*. It makes me sad. Isn't there another place to buy clothes, where the window doesn't have lonely people inside?"

She was already pulling him along by the arm. He chuckled slightly. There was no point in trying to figure out what she meant; he loved her anyways. Unlike Candace, she made few demands and was never unreasonable—just mysterious. He could put up with her strange quirks and occasional odd remarks, as otherwise, he was happy. Happier than Candace had ever made him, that was for sure.

They found a mid-size boutique where clothes were displayed on tree-like racks, very modern and trendy, and Selma was suddenly serene again. They bought shirts, pants and dresses; underwear, socks and shoes; two coats, and a bathrobe. Amused, Stone had to convince Selma that it was all right for her to wear jeans; she favored long, flowing dresses and skirts.

"Almost like you're from another century," he teased.

Stone didn't mind the substantial total at checkout;

he made good money and had no debts. They stopped off at the cookware store on the way back to the parking lot and bought the soufflé pan, to Selma's delight.

"I'm going to make you the most delicious soufflé—it will be the most strawberry-ish of strawberry-ness," she cried happily.

"I think you were a chef in your old life—or a baker," he said, giving her slim waist a squeeze. "Chef Selma, Queen of the Kitchen Domain."

She stopped walking suddenly and looked straight into his eyes. "You may be right. I do so love to cook and bake things. It's like I've always been around wonderful kitchen smells and tastes. I almost feel like I have a memory now, thanks to you."

And she impulsively kissed him. "I'm going to look for a job next week. A job in a bakery."

"It's not necessary that you work," he protested. "I can support us."

"Oh, but I *want* to. I want to be Chef Selma, Queen of the Kitchen Domain."

Stone laughed. It was the happiest he had been in a long time; before Candace, before even law school. Maybe it was the happiest he had ever been in his whole long, boring life.

VI.

The next weekday morning, Selma was just coming out of the bathroom after finishing her shower.

Stone, already dressed for work, approached her to get his goodbye kiss. When she leaned forward awkwardly for the kiss, the right sleeve of her robe fell open and he could see that her arm and hand were wrapped in the gray towel once again.

"Did you hurt yourself again?" he cried, alarmed. "What's going on?"

"It's just a little thing," she said, defensively, while he looked at her skeptically.

"Okay," she sighed, "I'll come clean. The truth is, I have an embarrassing skin condition on my arm that flares up every once in a while. I said before that it was a burn because I was too shy to tell you about it. I've had it for a long time and it's nothing—just a nuisance—really. It usually goes away in a few days."

"Oh," said Stone, relieved. "Maybe you should see a doctor about it?"

"Yes, maybe so. But for now, it's just a bother, nothing more. No worries, sweetheart," she added.   "I will still be able to make you your strawberry soufflé for dessert tonight."

"You'd better! I'm counting on it," he said, with mock severity.

VII.

Candace still had a key to Stone's apartment. She thought she'd drop by when she knew he was at work and get that embarrassing object she'd left behind.

So much easier not to have to ask him about it. She was sure he'd stuffed it somewhere in a drawer to the desk in the second bedroom. Of course, he could have tossed it out in anger, but it was worth trying to find it.

She was looking for a thumb drive containing photos of her in various poses of undress, suggestively posed. When they were still together, she'd made him delete the photos from his phone and computer files. Unfortunately, he'd kept the thumb drive of them.

Just in case she changed her mind and wanted them someday, he'd said. Well, *she wanted them now.* She wanted them very, very badly.

She had to make sure that the thumb drive would never fall into the hands of Austin Peek. She was pretty sure that Austin was on the verge of popping the question, and she wasn't going to have that thing hanging over her head on her wedding day. Billy had been so upset when she'd broken it off with him and moved out, he was capable of doing anything in revenge.

With her key in the front door, she looked down the concrete walkway, feeling watched. She saw the crazy lady, Mrs. Ronan, who had made her life so miserable when she lived with Billy, standing at the other end of the walkway. Mrs. Ronan was staring at her blatantly, watching her every move.

For heaven's sake, what an awful snoop! I hated that old hag so much when I lived here, she thought. *Thank God I'll probably never see her again, after today.*

She got the door open and quickly slipped inside Stone's apartment. She stopped in the hallway and took in the kitchen and eating area, which were on either side from the front door, shocked. The place was spotlessly clean. It was no longer the old, rumpled Billy Stone bachelor digs she knew (and deplored) when she lived with him. There was a vase of Gerbera daisies on the dining table, and a hard-backed cookbook atop the kitchen counter, spread open to a recipe for strawberry soufflé.

Billy couldn't boil an egg, she thought. *He's got someone new!*

She felt a pang of disappointment, seasoned with a small side of outrage. She had been picturing him as pining away desperately for her in solitary misery—and all along, he'd had someone new! Someone who cared about more than careers, status, and clothes, from the tidy looks of the apartment. It was insulting!

Candace marched into the living room and was shocked to see "the other woman" standing next to the sofa there, as still as a tombstone. The pale and fair-haired woman seemed almost rooted to the floor, somehow.

Candace saw with a pang of jealousy that she was very beautiful. More beautiful than herself, if she was honest about it. She didn't want Billy back, but she hated the idea of him being with a new woman who seemed like an upgrade. It *was* insulting.

She noticed suddenly that the other woman had a sort of bandage, gray in color, that was wrapped tightly around one of her arms.

"Oh! I'm sorry!" said Candace. "I didn't know anyone was here."

"Who are you?" the still woman asked.

"I'm…uh…the *ex*-girlfriend. I still have a key. I was meaning to mail it back to Billy, but I didn't get around to it. And I'm just here to get something that belongs to me. It's kind of important."

The pale, still woman said: "I packed up your old clothes. They're in a bag in the second bedroom."

She had a blank, tranquil expression on her face, and spoke in a soft monotone.

What a weird chick he's hooked up with, thought Candace, feeling her previous outrage somewhat mollified. *Maybe she's not as much of an upgrade as I assumed.* She felt a small dart of happiness at the thought.

Aloud Candace said: "Oh, you can keep those. I just need to look for something in the computer desk."

"That's Billy's desk," the other woman stated. "I don't think he would like it."

"Well, we just won't tell him, then," Candace said quickly. "He'll never know."

Candace started to push her way aggressively past the strange, pale woman, but the stubborn girl lumbered forward, almost as if she were dragging something heavy along with her right leg, and blocked Candace's path.

"That's Billy's desk," she stated in the soft monotone. "You can't go in there. I love him, and we are going to be together forever."

"Good for you," said Candace, sarcastically. "You don't need to invite me to the wedding though. Now get out of my way, you—!" She pushed the other woman's shoulder roughly

But then she gasped out loud, shocked.

The other woman's robe had parted when she'd moved and Candace, looking downward, suddenly got a good look at the girl's right leg.

"Your leg!" She shrieked. "What is wrong with...your...*leg*? It doesn't look *human*—"

Candace screamed and screamed.

"Be *quiet!* You'll bring that old gossip over here. And I can't let you tell Billy. Billy *mustn't* know about me...ever."

Candace screamed again, and then, there was a dark

explosion in her head, and then more darkness. She went tumbling down, down, down…into a black void of nothingness.

"I *told* you Billy wouldn't like it," Candace heard a soft voice say above her, before she stopped hearing anything at all.

VIII.

Stone had left work early, as he'd promised Selma.

He whistled a happy tune as he unlocked the front door to his apartment. Coming home to Selma was now the high point of his weekday. How he looked forward to her lovely dinners and quiet conversation—her comments were always sweet and kind, if sometimes incomprehensible or teasingly mysterious.

Tonight, however, he sensed something wrong the minute he stepped into the entryway of the apartment. There was a strange, coppery smell in the air.

"That smell seems familiar—what is it? It smells almost like the fresh meat station at the supermarket."

There was an open cookbook spread out on the kitchen counter, but no strawberry soufflé baking in the oven. And, most alarmingly, no Selma puttering around happily in the kitchen.

Well, she may have gone out for one of her strange walks, he told himself. *Maybe she changed her mind about having dinner at home. Maybe she wants to eat out. Or maybe she needed some last-minute ingredients and walked to the market to get them.*

But even as he was turning these thoughts around in his mind, he didn't believe them. He could feel a prickling at the back of his neck that warned him of danger. Something was *wrong*.

"Selma?" he called out, uncertainly, throwing his overcoat on the dining table.

He hurried into the living room.

Something bloody was heaped in front of the sofa.

"Selma!" he called out again, this time desperately. "Selma!"

Stone rushed to the crumpled heap, knelt down near it, and lifted up its head.

It wasn't Selma as he had feared; he could now see black hair swamped in all of the congealing blood surrounding the heap. He recognized the flowing top and jeans suddenly, and he realized sickly, that the scrunched-up, bloody thing was…Candace.

What. The. Fuck? he thought, bewildered. *What is Candace doing here? And where's Selma?*

The crumpled thing that had once been Candace stirred, groaned and briefly opened its eyes when Stone lay the head back down on the carpet.

"She…*hit*…me," croaked out Candace's familiar voice, in between sharp gasps of breath. "With her *arm*… Her horrible *hard* arm…"

She tried to say more, but her whole body shuddered, and her lungs emitted a horrible rattling sound. The fresh meat smell got stronger, as a trickle of fresh blood spewed from her mouth.

Candace was dead, staring at him accusingly, with open eyes. Stone tried frantically to revive her, but it was no good. She was gone.

Candace was dead! He couldn't believe what was happening. *Who* hit her? She couldn't possibly have been talking about sweet, quiet *Selma.*

"Her *hard* arm…" Candace had said.

Hard arm. Selma with the towel bandage wrapped around her arm this morning.

An unwelcome thought was trying to work its way into his upper, conscious mind, and he tried desperately to push it back down to where it belonged.

"Selma, are you here? Selma?" he cried out again, standing up.

He entered the short hallway that led to the two bedrooms. The door to the second bedroom was slightly ajar, and Stone noticed a wrinkled, red-stained cloth lying in the entry.

He picked it up; it was the same gray towel from the gym that Selma had used to wrap her bad arm with that morning. Stained all over with what could only be Candace's blood.

"What? What is going on?" he mumbled to himself.

Her *hard* arm. He himself had felt its coldness and hardness accidentally, the first time she'd covered it with the towel. That strange morning that seemed so long ago…

He pushed open the spare bedroom door and forced himself into the room, all the while feeling the same sense of dread and neck-prickling he'd felt since first entering his apartment.

There was deadly silence all around the room for a quick couple of minutes, and then suddenly, Stone began to cry out in horrified anguish, *"My God! The Stone Wife! The Stone Wife!"*

Then he started to scream inconsolably, until he, too, fell into darkness and tumbled onto the carpet.

IX.

A pair of policemen, DeMare and Rodriguez, broke into Billy Stone's apartment two days afterward, acting on a tip from Mrs. Ronan. They were accompanied by a detective, Fancher.

Fancher had been contacted by Austin Peek, who was frantic about the strange disappearance of his girlfriend, a petite, dark-haired girl named Candace Hilligoss.

Stone's apartment smelled strongly of death, a smell that Fancher unfortunately knew quite well.

They found Candace's crumpled, bloody body on the floor near the sofa. The detective knelt down to get a better look, while the other two searched the rest of the apartment, guns drawn.

"The old lady on the phone said there was another woman living here, a fair-haired girl who kept to herself," said Rodriguez, coming out of Stone's bedroom, after finding nothing out of place.

"Poor girl," Fancher muttered, straightening up with a sigh. "Peek said the ex-boyfriend was pretty broken up when she left him. She must have come back for some reason, they had a row, and he smashed her up with an unknown weapon, something heavy. At least that's what it looks like."

"Do you think he killed the other girl too?" Rodriguez asked.

"It's possible," replied Fancher. "He's an upstanding guy from all I've heard. No record, member in good standing of the Oregon State Bar. Of course, that doesn't mean anything, if he suddenly just snapped."

"You'd better come in here, Detective," interrupted DeMare, ducking out of the second bedroom. "It beats anything I've seen in years."

Fancher followed the cop into the second bedroom to find Stone lying on the carpeted floor in a fetal position, still breathing but totally unresponsive.

"Catatonic," said Fancher. "I've seen them before. Guy's had an enormous shock. Call an ambulance," he ordered Rodriguez, who was standing behind him. "Actually, make that two ambulances. One for the emergency room, and one for the coroner's. And get the crime scene investigation unit here with a photographer for the...girl...in the living room."

A bloody towel, gray in color, was lying next to Stone's curled-up form. "Must have been wrapped around the murder weapon, whatever it was," said Fancher, squatting down for a closer look.

Then he cried out as he stood up and took in the other strange form in the room.

"What the—?"

It was a large, gray statue of a woman in what he assumed was granite, its hands steepled together in prayer, standing in the middle of the room, as if it had been rooted there forever.

"Beats all, don't it?" said DeMare, grimly. "This guy is a real nutjob. It even says 'Devoted Wife' on the front. Like it's a memorial to the ex-girlfriend he bashed to death."

"Actually, I think I know what it is," replied Fancher. "Believe it or not. There was a statue stolen from the Heartwood Pioneer Cemetery a few weeks ago. A praying woman in granite. The cemetery's manager lodged a complaint, but we haven't had time to do much on it. This may be it."

"He stole a statue from a *graveyard?* Jeez, what a sicko!" said DeMare, shaking his head.

Fancher stepped around the catatonic Stone to examine the statue. He paused at the back of the base, then he crouched down to examine it.

"Yes, this *is* it, the stolen statue from Heartwood. It was donated to the cemetery in the early 1900s, by a family who ran a successful chain of bakeries, to commemorate their father. The mother couldn't be buried here because she committed suicide, so they substituted the statue. If you look closely, there's a pattern of wheat carved around the bottom of the figure's dress. All according to what the cemetery managers included in their complaint."

"Are you *sure* it's the same statue?" asked DeMare. "Why would he steal someone else's memorial statue?"

"Yes, I'm sure. There is an inscription on the base of the statue in the back. It was described in the cemetery complaint."

Fancher retrieved a notebook from his overcoat pocket and flipped back a few pages. He read out to DeMare:

STANSFIELD MONUMENT COMPANY
Selma, Alabama. 1905.

The detective could hear twin ambulance sirens shrieking from some distance away. He wondered what his wife was making for dinner.

She was a very good cook.

The Brotherhood of the Traveling…Thing

Ash McCartney, dealer in items of the strange and macabre, was excited about his newest acquisition. The ancient shipping crate for his latest collector's item was a plain wooden coffin; the coffin had travelled a long way throughout an apparently colorful hundred years-plus of history. The coffin-crate showed travel stamps and stickers for Providence, Rhode Island; Bangor, Maine; Tulsa, Oklahoma; New Orleans and Milwaukee, among others that were unreadable. The oldest stamp, in faded red ink, was from Carson City, Nevada. Since Ash had purchased it online three weeks before, the crate could now add Sacramento, California, to its travel itinerary.

He pried it open and gave a delighted little gasp at the figure inside. *Why, it's even better than it looked in the online pictures, except for those weird green spots on the face*, he told himself. It was a wax figure from the late 19th Century, the beginning of the golden age of the wax museum in America. It had graced wax palaces, both celebrated and obscure, since at least 1880—that was the date of the earliest stamp on the crate. The figure had no name, but "Wild West Outlaw" was inscribed on a small brass plate inside the wax creation's final resting place.

He wasn't quite sure he could sell it, but he thought it would make a magnificent publicity prop for the shop. On good weather days—there were hardly any bad ones in sunny Sacramento —he planned to display it outside the front of his shop. Of course, he would have to be careful on the hottest afternoons, for temperatures of 105 °F—or more—were not uncommon in the city in the summer. He didn't want the thing to start melting, right there on the sidewalk.

The figure was of a full-bearded, pale-skinned man with dark brown hair and brown eyes. It was dressed in the style of a Hollywood saloon gambler, with a green brocade weskit over a formerly white linen shirt, closed at the neck with a black ribbon tie. It also wore black twill trousers and a belt with a large, tarnished buckle, and scuffed and slightly rotted black leather cowboy boots. On the figure's face, there were a few visible repairs to the wax surface that looked amateurish, especially the ones that tried to cover the green spots.

Ash sniffed. His well-traveled Wild West Outlaw smelled of aged cloth, old wax, and chemicals. There was also an underlying odor he couldn't identify, which was faintly unpleasant.

Well, I don't have to smell it, I just have to display it, he reasoned. *Our Outlaw needs some repair in places, and he needs a name.*

He knew the exact person to call: Bodie Hawkfeather, who lived up in the Sierra foothills near the old Gold Rush town of Lodesville. Bodie was a very fit and active seventy-year-old Miwok, whose brother Chuck ran a small tribal museum just outside of town. Bodie could repair anything that was man-made and many other things that were created by God or nature. Ash had hired Bodie so many times for various projects he was thinking of putting him on retainer. The hitch was Bodie himself; he didn't like the thought of being tied down by regular hours and accountability for his time.

Ash planned to motor up to Lodesville in his SUV the next day, a seventy-minute drive when traffic was good. He closed the coffin and pounded its lid in place, and then dragged it out to the small parking lot behind his store. He got a few strange looks from a couple of teenagers using the alley that bordered the lot as he shoved the coffin in the back of his SUV, and slammed the hatch shut. He always looked forward to seeing Bodie, although he dreaded seeing Bodie's bill for each project.

He went back to the shop. It was a slow day, and most customers were looky-loos anyway. He made his real money online, answering inquiries from movie production departments and rich but weird collectors who lived all over the world. He kept the shop because it made him feel human and connected to the world. He liked seeing physical customers, exchanging pleasantries with them and shooting the shit with them about the history of the Gold Country and all kinds of other things.

He sat down at the front desk of his shop and started playing with his accounts on his computer. He made a good living from his business, but he always had to be scrappy to break even, and there were times when he didn't want to scrap. But that was life for a small business-owner.

"No rest for the wicked, Ash old boy," he said aloud to the empty shop. He was somewhat worried about his dwindling movie business. With Hollywood's CGI software getting so good, prop managers were skipping the real things and just ordering up facsimiles from the graphics department. He had to work to convince even longtime movie customers to stay with him.

His head came up as he heard someone enter the shop. It was a girl of university age—a blonde with a pair of sunglasses pushed up on top of a messy head of hair. She was dressed in a lime skort with a matching lime-and-white patterned blouse. She took a swig out of her camelback water bottle as he rose to greet her.

"Hot as hell out there and it's early *October*. How do you people live in it!"

"It's Indian Summer, not that unusual here. And it's all I've ever known," said Ash, smiling broadly. "I'm a local boy. You're not from around here?"

"I'm from Seattle! I don't 'do' heat like this!! It rains in October in Seattle! Whole lot of us down here from UDub on a special exchange month-long program at Davis. Go Huskies!"

Ah! A sorority girl, thought Ash, with a mental chuckle. Too young for him, alas. "Is there something I can help you with?"

"I'm looking for a prop to use at a Halloween party. Like maybe, a coffin? One of those old-fashioned ones that are shaped like…you know…a coffin. Not one of those modern casket thingies."

"What do you want to use it for?"

"A table. For nom-noms and drinks, you know. Just clean fun!"

"I'm sorry, I haven't anything like that. Most of my stock is for collectors and very expensive. They're not for use as a throwaway prop."

"Oh…" she looked disappointed. "I wanted something special!"

"Well," said Ash. "I can't offer you a coffin, but I've got a little novelty display over there"—he pointed to a glass case near the front desk—"where you might find some unusual trinkets or candy for your party."

The girl looked crushed but walked over to the display case and picked out several bags of painted sugar skulls that Ash got from a special distributor in Mexico.

"These will be cool for the party," she said, as Ash rang them up. "But if you find a coffin before Halloween, let me know." She grabbed a scratchpad from the front desk and scribbled her name and contact information on it.

The pen scratched the paper at the same time as a loud crash came from outside, behind the store. It sounded like a car crash.

"The SUV!" cried Ash. He closed the register and dashed out the back, to find that his car had somehow slipped its gears and crashed part of its back bumper into a Dumpster in the parking lot. The crash had caused the hatchback door on his SUV to pop open.

Ash swore loudly and ran up to his car. "I'm dead sure I set the parking brake!" he yelled. "I always set the parking brake!"

"Hey, there's my coffin," squealed an excited voice nearby, pointing at the back of the SUV. It was the UDub sorority girl; she'd followed him outside. "With a creepy old fake dude inside."

Ash looked into the back of the SUV. The crash had somehow dislodged the lid of the coffin-crate and the container of ice he'd put on top of it to keep the wax dummy from melting in the heat. The outlaw wax figure was now on display. From the scowling expression on the dummy's face, it almost looked like it was angry at him.

"Hi, Scowler," he said to it. "Did you cause this?"

"Hey, can I buy that coffin?" broke in the sorority girl. "Is it for sale without the creepy fake dude?"

"No!" said Ash.

* * *

Ash's bumper was ignominiously marked with a deep gash on one side, but the SUV was still perfectly drivable. He drove up to the foothills a few days later with the wax figure he'd christened Ol' Scowler and found Bodie Hawkfeather puttering around in his workshop in the pines. Bodie once again declined Ash's idea of a retainer covering set hours devoted to restoration projects for the shop.

"I'm an Indian and a country boy, used to being my own master. I might wanna get out the canoe and go fishin' in the middle of the day."

"I thought we were supposed to call you guys Native Americans now?" Ash asked.

"Oh, that's *so* ten years ago, Ash. Now you're supposed to call us 'indigenous.' The great and the good keep changing our name every few years, just like they do to our African American brothers. At my age, I've lived through Indian, American Indian, Amerind, Native American, and now this new word pushed by college professors. Me, I'll stick with what I've been called the longest. Indian. Or N-D-N if you're into the whole brevity thing."

"I'll probably just keeping calling you Bodie."

"Works for me. So, whatcha bringing me this time?"

"A wax figure of an Old West Outlaw that's traveled all over and traded hands many times. From around 1880. Not in terrible shape but needs a few improvements. It's kinda got these green splotches on the face that look gangrenous."

"Let's take a look."

The two men dragged the coffin-crate from Ash's SUV into Bodie's workshop. Ash pried the lid open.

"It's gotta weird smell. Other than that, I can fix it up to look a bit more presentable."

"How much?" Ash dreaded hearing the total.

Bodie sketched some figures on a scratchpad.

Ash gulped. "*Really*…Bodie?"

Bodie laughed. "It's the Custer tax, paleface."

"Aahhhhh…I guess I don't have a choice. You're the best in the business. How long do you think it will take to spruce up Ol' Scowler?"

"Scowler?"

"That's what I call the thing. On account of how it seems to scowl at you in anger."

"I don't see it. He looks like a rather solemn fellow to me."

Ash leaned forward and peered into the dummy's face. "Hmmmph. You're right. The other day in the car after it crashed, I could have sworn I saw him scowling."

"Trick of the light maybe. Or just your imagination."

"Yeah, I guess. I'll give you a week, Bodie. How about that?"

"It'll be done."

But he heard from Bodie far earlier than in a week's time. Bodie called two days later with an ominous tone in his voice.

Ash sat down, expecting Bodie to give him some grim update on how it would cost many more times than estimated to restore Ol' Scowler.

"Ash…you better sit down. I'm not sure you want

me to keep working on this thing."

"I'm sitting down. Go ahead."

"Your Scowler isn't a wax figure. It's a corpse."

"What?"

"A dead guy. A stiff. A horizontal. It's been preserved via 1880s embalming techniques, probably with arsenic. Somewhere along the line, someone got the bright idea to turn this stiff into a wax museum exhibit."

Ash whistled softly into his phone. "Holy crap! Are you sure?"

"Yup. I scraped a bit of the wax down to skin and bone—what's left of it."

"Jeezus. That's so messed up. I don't know what to say. I'm sorry, Bodie. Don't work on it. I don't think I can legally sell a human corpse. Looks like this is a sunk cost unless I can get my money back from the seller. I'll come get it."

"Well, do. And hurry. I don't like having it around. Between you and me, I think sometimes that it moves."

"What?"

"Things drop from the shelves in the workshop. And it fell over one day. I think it changes expressions too but that may just be the suggestion from you. Ol' Scowler is bad medicine, Ash—very bad medicine indeed."

* * *

"I swear to you, Ash—I didn't know that thing was no corpse!" moaned Minnie "Mama" Mann over her cheap, fading-in-and-out cell phone service. "I can give you back your money, but that means now I'm out of what I paid for it. And you know how hard my life's been lately —what with my rheumy knee and payin' for Jimmy-Tim's bail, I'm just barely survivin' these days."

Ash rolled his eyes. He knew that Mama—one of his best wholesalers—probably had at least a million salted away, but she always loved crying poor mouth.

"Calm down Mama, you're going to get your rheumatism all fired up. I'm looking for the person who sold you that—that *thing*. Do you have a contact number for me?"

"I couldn't possibly betray the privacy of my sources," she replied piously.

Ash rolled his eyes again. "Mama, how would it look if word got around that you sold me a stiff? Even if you didn't mean to…?"

"Oklahoma Prairie Wax Museum," she barked. "They're on the net—you can look up the number yourself. You didn't hear any of this from me."

Ash googled the Oklahoma Prairie Wax Museum and found a page on the Web that looked like it hadn't been updated since Myspace was a thing. The "museum" was a rinky-dink roadside attraction in the middle of nowhere.

He punched in the phone contact number and left a message when voicemail picked up. As he finished his message, he heard a crash coming from his back storage room —the same place he'd stowed Ol' Scowler since bringing it home from Bodie's workshop in Lodesville.

Ash jumped up from his computer desk and ran into the back. The figure was still in its coffin, propped upright against a wall. But the lid was off and Ol' Scowler was…scowling.

Ash gulped. Ol' Scowler's expression had definitely

changed since he'd last closed the lid.

There were also numerous bits of small inventory items lying on the floor near Scowler, arranged in some sort of a pattern.

No. Not a pattern. *A word!* One that began with the letter "S" and then an "E" and a "T" Then—a little ragged—but after the "T was an "L" and then another "E."

SETLE. What did that mean? Was it someone's name? He remembered the nameplate inside the coffin, WILD WEST OUTLAW. Was Ol' Scowler a famous gunfighter back in the day?

He ran back to his desk and googled on his computer: "Is Setle the name of a Wild West outlaw?" Nothing came up. There were plenty of hits for 19th Century men named Settle or Settles, but not "Setle."

His phone buzzed and he picked up. "McCartney's Curios here."

"Hello?" said a man's voice. He sounded young, younger than Ash, and he had a polite and twangy Oklahoma accent. "I'm Robbie Shaw, calling from the Prairie Wax Museum in Oklahoma. Are you the person who left the message regarding a Wild West wax figure?"

"Yep, that's me. What can you tell me about that figure? Why did you sell it? Did you know it's actually someone's body encased in wax?"

"*Oh my God.* No, I had no idea. But…I'm not really all that…surprised. There was always something wrong with it."

"Really? In what way?"

"It always seemed to be changing expressions. Often, it looked angry. Sometimes it would sort of…grimace…at you. My girlfriend told me it was all in my head. But she wasn't the one spending all day in the museum with it. I finally got rid of it for my own peace of mind."

"Where'd you get it in the first place?"

"Inherited this place and all its stock from my dad. Not many of us left in the country today. I sorta feel like I'm keeping up a tradition. Don't know how long I can last, though. I'm dead broke."

"Did your father ever say he had problems with that figure?"

"Well, no. The thing wasn't displayed in the museum in his day. It was in a locked shed with a bunch of other odds and ends. When Dad passed, I found it, spiffed it up as best I could, and put it out on the museum floor with the others. I guess he had a reason for locking it up, right? Yikes, I just realized—I worked on a corpse! And dusted it every day for almost two years! That's kind of yucky."

"*Very* yucky. Do you know where your dad got it from?"

"No, but I can look through his old records and see if I find something. Say, what are you planning to do with it?"

"I couldn't say. I can't sell it in good conscience, now that I know what it is. You'll let me know if you find anything else about it?"

"Sure, will do."

As Ash hung up, he heard more crashes and bumps from the back room. He rushed to the back and looked around. Everything looked the same, except there were more small inventory items on the floor.

"What the hell?" Ash said to himself. There was a new word after "SETLE." The floor now read "SETLE

ME."

"SETLE ME? What does that mean? Look, weirdo," Ash addressed Ol' Scowler, "I already figured your name was Setle. Not my fault I can't find you on the Internet."

Ol' Scowler just continued scowling.

Ash's phone buzzed again from the front desk. It was Bodie.

"Hey, Ash. I was just a-wonderin'. Did you ever figure out who that stiff was?"

"No. I'm workin' on it. I think the stiff's name was Setle." Ash quickly outlined all that had happened since he brought Ol' Scowler back home from Lodesville.

"SETLE ME, eh? What makes you so sure that he's trying to tell you his name?"

"Why, what else could it be? He meant SETLE, comma, ME. SETLE with one 'T'. Say, Bodie, isn't there some kinda tribal ritual that'll help still a restless soul?"

Bodie essayed a pained silence, then replied: "Tribal ritual? *Really*, Ash? ...Even if I knew of one, what makes you think it would work on the soul of your paleface outlaw, assuming he was born Christian? What you need is a priest, not a shaman."

"Okay, sorry, Bodie."

"Maybe it's not his name? Maybe he's trying to tell you to do something instead?"

"But what? SETLE ME—what does that mean?"

"Beats me. Unless he was a lousy speller."

"Lousy speller? Wait a minute, that gives me an idea! I'll call you back, Bodie."

Ash put his phone away and ran into the back storage room where he'd parked Ol' Scowler. Scowler was not scowling anymore, he noticed. Instead, the figure had an expression of what Ash could only describe as hopefulness. Ash looked again at the words spelled out on his storage floor.

"Hey Scowler, is it possible that you meant to write SETTLE ME and you just suck at spelling? If that's the case, what is it that you want settled about you?"

His phone buzzed again. This time it was an email from Robbie Shaw at the Oklahoma wax museum.

"Dear Mr. McCartney," it read, *"I found the records for Dad's purchase of that…er…figure. It seems he bought it from an estate sale of an elderly gent in Tulsa in 1978—way before I was born! And get this—the estate belonged to a retired funeral director! He was in business since 1921. I've attached a scan of a human-interest story that appeared in the* Tulsa Times *years ago about his practice, a clipping of which my dad attached to his receipt. It seems the seller displayed the dummy and its coffin in the window of his store for years."*

Ash opened the scanned file of the article about the Tulsa funeral director, Albert Swain. The story quoted Swain as saying that he acquired Scowler in 1948 from a traveling dealer, who claimed the figure was modeled after a baby-faced gunfighter named Joseph "Winsome" Carpenter.

Ash googled again. This time he searched on the name "Winsome Carpenter." After a few minutes, he found what he was looking for: a post on a blog about the history of Carson City, Nevada.

Bingo.

The money paragraph read: *"Winsome Carpenter was killed in a gunfight in 1880 in Carson City. His common-law wife, Rosita Morales, paid for his body to be embalmed according to the most successful preservative techniques available at the time. Which was using arsenic as an embalming fluid. Rosita kept the preserved body for a while, but eventually she went broke and disappeared. She may have sold Winsome's body along the way, because his remains turned up in a traveling Wild West Show in the East, where they were displayed as an example of a 'real-life Wild West outlaw.' Nobody knows what happened to the remains after the Wild West Show was disbanded."*

Ash yelled at his computer. "Well, *I* know what happened to those remains. Somebody turned them into a wax museum exhibit, and Scowler...I mean *Winsome*...just kept travelling around the country, for more than a century. And now I know what he wants and why he sometimes looks angry. He wants to stop traveling. He wants to be *settled*."

If Winsome wanted to be buried, though, where would make sense? And how? Ash, thinking of what Bodie said earlier about needing a priest, had a sudden inspiration. *Of course! Father Dillon at St. Bonifacio.* He was just the person to help.

"I'm closing shop early today, and I'm going out to talk to someone, Winsome," Ash yelled into the open door of his back room. "Someone who might help get you *settled*. I'd appreciate it if you didn't wreck my inventory any more than you've already done while I'm gone."

* * *

Ash had known Father Dillon since he was a toddler. He was aware that the padre was known around town as a "character." The priest travelled often and took comfort in the company of strange and offbeat people. He was famous for telling enthralling stories about his adventures and travels. He also had a PhD in psychology and a volunteer practice at a local mental health clinic for the indigent. If anyone could be trusted with the Winsome Carpenter affair, it was Father Dillon.

The good father received Ash at his crowded little office in the rectory. It was full of mementos from the priest's travels and photos of his many friends, most of whom were odd-looking. The dark, wire-framed Father Dillon sat behind his desk and fingered his sparse gray goatee, and then said: "What's ailin' you, boy?"

Ash cleared his throat and began the saga of Winsome Carpenter. Even Father Dillon, with all that he'd seen and done, got bulgy-eyed as Ash related the story. Ash finished up with: "It's almost like that book, *The Sisterhood of the Traveling Pants*, except it's mostly people moving around a traveling corpse, not a pair of pants."

Father Dillon lay his palms flat on his desk and spread out his fingers—a gesture Ash knew was an indicator of deep thought from the eccentric priest.

"Well, that's it, I guess. You have to bury him."

"But how, where?"

"Possibly there's a descendant somewhere who's willing to claim him?"

"He didn't have any kids."

"You could release the story to the media—some great-great nephew or distant cousin might turn up. It would be good publicity for your business. Or maybe the Carson City Historical Society would want him?"

"I thought of that, Father. But what if no one comes forward? What if it isn't really Winsome? I'd have to pay for DNA testing and all that. And I'd be known far and wide as the guy who unwittingly bought a corpse. For the rest of my life. I'm not sure I want that to happen."

"Well then, what *would* you like to see happen?"

"My gut feeling is that I should just quietly have Winsome buried on the QT, no one else the wiser. Can you arrange that?"

Father Dillon smiled a crooked, eccentric smile. "It wouldn't be exactly kosher with the Vatican, but I could probably slip him into an old, run-down Catholic cemetery I know, with few questions asked."

"You could? Oh man, that would be so great…um, I'd like to keep the coffin, though. I think I can sell it and at least recoup some of my sunk costs. There's this sorority girl from Seattle."

"I can probably get one of those cheap cardboard things the county buries the unknown dead in."

"Oh, I'd be happy to pay for that!"

"It may take me a week or two to get things arranged. Think you can hang on that long with Winsome in your storage room?"

"I think I can. As long as he knows he's gonna get *settled* soon, I think Winsome will be quiet."

* * *

A week and two days later, Ash and Father Dillon presided over the burial of the suspected corpse of Joseph "Winsome" Carpenter, at five-thirty in the morning, in the Queen of Heaven Catholic cemetery in West Sacramento. No one else attended except the cemetery's grave coordinator—a fancy way of saying gravedigger—and the grounds attendant, who kept giving Ash strange looks.

Father Dillon said a few prayers after Winsome's

cheap county coffin was lowered into the grave by the cemetery attendant's machine. "I can't say the full service because I'm not sure if he was Catholic or not. But the Vatican won't begrudge a few random prayers. *Requiescat in Pace*, Joseph Carpenter—or whomever you really are."

The grave coordinator gave Ash a long, somewhat unfriendly look after the priest finished his prayers and the two men prepared to leave.

"Why'd that gravedigger fellow keep giving me peculiar looks? I was definitely getting some strange vibes from the man," Ash asked Father Dillon, as the priest unlocked his ancient brown Saab. It was a car that looked as eccentric as its owner.

Father Dillon chuckled. "Should I tell you or not, that is the question?"

"Tell me about what?"

He fidgeted with his goatee and sighed.

"Okay. You see, I had to tell the cemetery attendant *something*. So, I told him you were a loon who believed that he was being haunted by a wax dummy and that this was the only way to cure you of your delusion. He knows me from a relative who attends my clinic, and he was willing to go along as a favor to me. He's been sworn to secrecy— even the cemetery manager won't know."

"You told him I was nuts?"

"Well, I didn't use that exact term…"

Ash began to laugh, a laugh that bordered on the demented. "So that's what I get out of this long, sorry episode. A big hole in my pocket and a guy I don't know who thinks I'm crazy."

Father Dillon gave him a quizzical look. "Are you okay, Ash? You wanna hang out at the rectory for a while today and knock back a few shots of bourbon? Four Roses, from a grateful and well-heeled parishioner."

Ash shook his head. "I gotta get back to the shop. I got a date this afternoon to hand over Winsome's original coffin to a blonde sorority girl. A hundred bucks salvaged from a bad deal is better than nothing."

Father Dillon dropped Ash off at the rectory parking lot. Wisome's battered antique coffin, recently emptied of its former contents, lay in the back compartment of Ash's wounded SUV.

They shook hands in the parking lot. "Thanks, Padre."

"Any time. By the way, the Four Roses offer stands indefinitely."

"I'll take a rain check, Padre. Next time I buy a wax dummy that's really a corpse, I'll definitely cash in that offer."

Ash drove back to his shop feeling chastened and foolish. Entering the store through the back storage room's door, he checked the section of the floor where Winsome had spelled out his messages.

Instead of SETLE ME, it now read "SETTLED."

"Hey Winsome, you finally learned how to spell," cried Ash. "Good for you." He speculated whether or not the wandering spirit of Winsome Carpenter would stay put after all. He certainly hoped so.

Footdazzle

When I lived in Hollywood, I used to know Stu Sanchez, the so-called Shoemaker to the Stars. I, in fact, did a little "creative" bookkeeping work for him back in the day.

Stu was a legend in Hollywood for forty years. He made custom shoes for celebrities— sequined platform boots for Elton John, mink-trimmed slippers for Barbra Streisand, hand-painted basketball shoes for most of the Lakers professional basketball team. The costume departments of every film and television studio in Los Angeles kept him on speed dial, and his word-of-mouth reputation was so strong that he didn't have to advertise. The movie and sports biz's great and good sought him out, searching for that special, *gen-u-wine* Stu Sanchez original that they could brag about to their friends, enemies, and frenemies.

The first thing you need to know about Stu was that he was cheap as fuck. That's why he hired me to perform my magic on his books so that his tax bite from the State of Cal didn't hurt so much. Everyone in the business knew how cheap he was. He hoarded money like Bill Shatner hoards toupées. That's why he worked out of a grungy, nondescript strip mall in Glendale. His shop was called Footdazzle (corny name, I know) and it was pretty close to Glendale's only tourist attraction, Verdant Lawns Memorial Park, the place where a shitload of Hollywood celebrities have gone to their final rest for more than a century.

Stu used to walk over to the park and "visit" Humphrey Bogart or Elizabeth Taylor during his lunch hour. It's a nice place for a walk, but he went there mostly because Verdant Lawns was free entertainment. Stu loved free stuff. He also loved watching tourists act like idiots in front of Marilyn Monroe's vault or Michael Jackson's mausoleum.

Except for his lunch-hour strolls through Verdant Lawns, Stu rarely moved his substantial tush from his shop. He made his celebrity clients (the living kind) schlep in from Bel-Air or Beverly Hills to have their pampered little tootsies measured for their fancy footwear. Business was so good that Stu discouraged walk-ins with a window sign reading "By Appointment Only." But occasionally someone wandered in, and then left when they saw that the most basic hand-painted running shoe sold for fifteen hundred smackeroos.

It all went slam-bang terrific for Stu until the night when a surprise customer came to the shop while he was working late. It was that week in December a few years ago, when a freak cold snap infrigidated LA and everybody was walking around in ski parkas and balaclavas. It was only 35 °F on the coldest night, but they acted like it was a blizzard at the North Pole.

Stu's two assistants had already gone home for the day. That would be a tiny Korean babe named Sooey and a tall, husky black dude who called himself Dave the Butt. Sooey was a whiz at hand-painting sneakers and Dave could cut leather like nobody's business. After they left, Stu hunkered down in the back of his shop and started sewing gladiator sandals for a TV miniseries about the Roman Empire. He must have forgotten to lock the front door, because the next thing he knew, the bells on the door jangled and someone walked inside. Stu cursed to himself and stomped out onto his shop's front floor, ready to flame the idiot who'd distracted him.

A tall stranger stood just inside the door. The man (Stu assumed it was a man, because of the height) was wearing a dark hood pulled down over half his face, attached to some kind of weird robe that looked like it belonged on a monk. The hood and robe had holes in them and smelled strongly of must and mildew. Oddly, the potential customer also had on a pair of bright-red knitted gloves that looked new, in contrast to his mildewy clothes.

"We're closed, dude. And we don't take walk-ins anyway. Scram!"

The stranger didn't say a word. He just pointed with a long, gloved finger to a pair of fleece-lined, glow-in-the dark sneakers that Stu had on display. Stu stared in disgust as a worm wriggled its way out of the top of one glove when the figure stretched out his hand to point.

Dude needs a fumigator, wherever he lives, he told himself. *Worms in his clothes— probably homeless, come to think of it!*

The stranger didn't seem to notice the worm. He took an ancient coin purse out of his robe and poured out something shiny, gold, and clinky into the palm of one of his gloved hands. A beetle jumped out of the purse and hopped onto the floor, and Stu was disgusted all over again.

He was about to throw the man out, but then Stu's eyes bugged out of his head as he realized the nature of the shiny stuff from the stranger's purse. It was a handful of gold coins and they looked weighty and authentic. Like a lot of skinflints, he distrusted paper money and consequently, kept a stash of Krugerrands in a safe in his crappy studio apartment a block away from his shop.

He reconsidered throwing the man out. "You wanna buy the sneakers? That's what you want?"

The hooded figure nodded and held out his palm. Balanced on it were no less than five gold coins, each of which weighed an ounce at least. At today's prices that was ten grand! Plus, it was tax-free loot—Stu told himself he could keep it off the books, and then tell Sooey and Dave he gave the shoes away as a gift to a big-spending client. Not that they'd believe it, but they wouldn't call him on it either.

Stu picked up one of the coins and held it up to the light. It was a 1927 Golden Eagle twenty-dollar gold piece. The others, he saw, were also Golden Eagles from the 1920s. He gave the coin back and noticed that the stranger had a very skinny wrist showing in the gap between his sleeve and his glove.

Dude needs a couple of Big Macs now and then, Stu thought to himself. *Skinny as a crackhead. He may be a crackhead too, come to think of it, but there ain't nothin' wrong with them gold coins!*

Aloud he said, "Sure, take the sneaks. Do you want a receipt?"

The hooded head shook slowly from side to side.

"Not a big talker, eh? Well just gimme them coins and I'll wrap 'em up for you."

The dark-hooded customer handed the gold pieces to Stu, who shoved them into his personal lockbox under the counter.

Then the stranger held up a gloved hand in a "stop" position, took the shoes right off the display shelf, and sat down in one of Stu's try-on chairs that were usually reserved for the rarified tushies of Brad Pitt or Meryl Streep. As the customer lifted the hem of his robe to put his new sneaks on, Stu noticed that he was only wearing tattered socks, no shoes. He had bony ankles, too, same as his wrists. Stu couldn't wait to get him out of his shop, but he figured the guy deserved at least to have some time to put on his new shoes.

What a weirdo, thought Stu. *Walking around in his stocking feet in this weather. Be glad when he's gone—he gives me the creeps.*

Feet securely shod, the tall stranger stood up and left the shop without saying a word. That's when Stu noticed that he didn't walk like a normal person. Stu rubbed his eyes in disbelief, for the customer appeared to be floating just slightly above ground. The glow-in-the dark shoes made the whole illusion or whatever it was seem even creepier.

"For fuck's sake," he said aloud. "Did I really see what I thought I just saw?"

Stu was so flabbergasted that he decided to follow his peculiar patron to find out what the man was getting up to with his new shoes. As he followed discreetly, guided in the dark by the glowing shoes, Stu realized that his subject was headed in the direction of Verdant Lawns. He trod along, thinking there must be an apartment building's driveway that those shoes would eventually venture into, but it never happened.

Instead, the shoes walked—or perhaps glided—right up to the front gates of Verdant Lawns Memorial Park. It was long past closing time, but the dark figure somehow squeezed in through a space in the iron fence—he was that skinny.

Stu stared open-mouthed at what he'd just seen. He could just make out the glowing shoes receding in the huge, dark maze of Verdant Lawns, and he made up his mind quickly. He decided to climb the fence, even though he was pretty old and out of shape. Plus, it was a really tall fence. He managed to get over after a couple of tries and landed with a thud on the other side.

He craned his neck and looked around as much as he could, but the glowing shoes were long gone. Now he was stuck in a huge cemetery full of winding lanes, creepy Gothic churches, and weird statues in hidden cul-de-sacs. It was hard enough to find a body's way around Verdant Lawns in the daytime, but at night it seemed even more daunting. Stu knew he was on Cathedral Avenue, just past the humongous fountain that was usually the first thing a visitor saw at the famous cemetery. On the right, he dimly perceived the park's administrative offices, which were disguised as rose-covered Tudor cottages.

He was trying to figure out the rest of his immediate environment when he caught sight of two small glowing blobs floating just above the ground some yards away from him. He turned on the flashlight on his phone and quickened his pace. When he caught up nearly to the stranger, the hooded figure didn't seem to hear or notice him, which relieved Stu greatly.

The glowing shoes (with Stu following) took a soft right off of Cathedral Avenue and started walking across a wide lawn. Stu flashed his phone light around and found the nearby grave of Tom Mix, whom he knew was a big cowboy star from the silent screen era. He realized they were in the Whispering Pines section, a very old lot where stars from the 1920s were buried. He followed the glowing shoes at a discreet distance, until they stopped suddenly. He turned off his phone's light and crept closer. Then he watched while the figure lay down on the ground and seemed to melt right into it. The last that Stu saw of his customer that night were the glowing shoes resting on the ground, toes pointed upward, and then they, too, disappeared into the indigo air.

He waited a bit until he was sure that he was alone, and then he walked over to the plot where the figure had lain down and shined his phone light on it. There was a stone marker incised with the name and vitals of one Charles "Binx" Balderwood. An inscription identified him as an actor from the silents.

Stu ran away then, as fast as he could, until he was quite far away from Whispering Pines. Then he slowed down and shambled back to his shop, where he fell asleep in a recliner in his back workroom after a couple of hours of tossing and turning.

* * *

Stu woke up to the sound of Sooey's key in the front door of the shop. She always arrived before Dave, who usually wandered in fifteen minutes after he was supposed to be at work. She came to the back workroom to start coffee and was startled to see Stu in the recliner.

"Rough night, eh boss? You look like shit!"

Stu sat up and rubbed his eyes. "I feel like shit too… I had something bizarre happen last night. Not even sure if it was real."

"Maybe lay off the booze, boss?"

"I didn't drink last night. At least, not that I can

remember."

"Okay, boss, if you say so!" Sooey chirped, and returned to making the coffee.

Then Dave came in and told Stu he looked sick. "Like you've seen a ghost or somethin'." Stu didn't think that was funny.

Stu thought about his nocturnal visitor all day long. At first, he was consumed with trying to decide whether or not the remarkable events of the previous evening were real. It seemed incontrovertible that at least some of it was real—the shoes were gone from the display shelf and the five Golden Eagles were still in his personal lockbox, awaiting transfer to the Krugerrand safe in his apartment. (He'd checked several times.) It was possible the visitor had not melted into the grave in Verdant Lawns, but somehow slipped away while Stu's eyes were deceiving him. At least, that's what he told me later when he recounted the whole story.

Yes, maybe it was true that he hadn't seen the hooded figure skulk away and there was nothing supernatural about the whole occurrence, Stu thought. There were, for instance, the new red gloves the visitor had been wearing—maybe he'd just bought them from some store downtown. Surely a ghost wouldn't need brand new gloves, even in the current unusually cold weather?

As the day wore on, the question of the ten-thousand-dollar shoes began to nag him. What if those prime walkers really were buried in Verdant Lawns? They were his best handiwork, and Sooey's painted detail was a masterpiece. It was a shame to think of them rotting away in a grave without anyone being able to appreciate them.

He googled Binx Balderwood and found his picture

and a bio on a site dedicated to silent screen stars. Dude looked like a weasel, with a pencil-slim mustache, slicked-back hair, and ferrety eyes. His most famous role was as Rasputin the Mad Monk in a long-lost film produced by Jesse Lasky. He was so proud of this film that he was, in fact, buried in his Rasputin costume. According to Stu, he was also a shitbag who ran out on his wife and baby so he could bang a new starlet every night. It bugged Stu to think of his shoes gracing the long-rotted bones of a guy who was such a dick.

Then there was the question of money. Here Stu's miserly nature got the best of him. He saw a chance to grab the shoes and resell them—making twice the moolah on the same product. What use did a dead man have for shoes? The thought nagged and nagged, and late in the afternoon, Stu made his decision.

That's where I show up, in this whole sorry saga. He called me for the name of the closest place where he could find a rope, a pick, and a shovel, and I told him to go to the Home Depot on San Fernando. Since he didn't have a car—he was too cheap to pay for the insurance—I had to pick him up and drive him over there.

"Sooey," he said, as we left, "you and Dave cover me for the rest of the day. Something I gotta do. Really, all you have to do is work on the gladiator sandals for the Roman thing. Oh, and Ryan Gosling might be calling for the cowboy boots with the blinking Christmas lights on the toes."

Satisfied that the day's remaining business was in good hands, Stu and I drove over to Home Depot. That's when he told me the whole story. At Home Depot, he bought a shovel, this pick-axe kind of thing, and some rope. Then he had me drop him off at Verdant Lawns when it was closed and quite dark.

"Are you sure you wanna do this?" I asked him. "What if you get caught? I hear those Verdant Lawns security people aren't pussies. Folks say the sappy vibes from all those kitschy churches, angel statues, and rose-covered cottages go out the window when somebody threatens their precious meat motel."

"I won't get caught," he retorted. "I know Verdant Lawns as well as anyone. I know some good hiding places, too." I wasn't quite sure, at that point, what he was gonna get up to with the rope and other stuff, but I figured it had something to do with the silent screen star he'd been ranting about to me all afternoon. I held my tongue, just as I'd learned previously not to question Stu's bookkeeping habits. After all, he paid me in cash.

I watched while Stu found a spot where the fence was easier to climb and hopped it, throwing the tools and rope over first. From what I could piece together later, he approached Binx Balderwood's grave in Whispering Pines and looked around to make sure that no bony specter was nearby. Then he started digging.

I had a bad, bad feeling about it.

* * *

A groundskeeper discovered the scandalous scene in the Whispering Pines section the next morning. I heard it from an anonymous source at Verdant Lawns. A grave was gaping open, and it had apparently been robbed. The plot belonged to one Charles "Binx" Balderwood, who had passed away in 1929. It was a serious matter indeed for The

Cemetery of the Stars, which prided itself on its reputation for never having had a plot vandalized or robbed in all of its 110-year history. Until now, of course.

It got even worse for Verdant Lawns and its august PR reputation when the groundskeeper found the body of the suspected grave robber lying some yards away. The dead man appeared to have been strangled. There were ten shallow, bruised depressions in the neck, where something sharp had pressed into the skin. The face wore an expression of abject terror and the hand clutched something tightly: a bright red, knitted glove. The dead man was Stu, of course.

The PR department at Verdant Lawns worked their asses off to keep what they found out of the media, and the authorities went along with it, not wanting to jinx Glendale's main tourist attraction. The official story was that Stu died of a heart attack after being trapped in the cemetery while on one of his visits, after it had closed for the evening.

Hollywood mourned him as much as it was capable of mourning anyone—that is, for a grand total of about five minutes. After his funeral, he was buried in Verdant Lawns. Funny thing about it, his burial plot was the one thing he hadn't scrimped on in his whole life. He paid for a prime location not far from Michael Jackson's mausoleum. Everybody said it was a tragedy that he died the way he did. I kept it to myself, but I figured that if he hadn't been such a cheap-ass miser, he'd still be alive today, sewing Roman gladiator sandals for Bradley Cooper.

One more thing: Verdant Lawns officials opened the casket of Binx Balderwood before reburying it, to see if everything was in order. They kept this out of the press, too. The remains of the silent star were lying peacefully at rest, wearing a red glove on one skeletal hand, and a pair of brand new, custom-painted sneakers on his long, bony feet.

They glowed in the dark.

The Warden's Office

Deep in the woods, Paul and Posey snaked their way through thick scrub and underbrush on the twisty trail. The tree pollen was in season, and Posey's nose trickled. She complained about it, along with all the other miseries the hike had inflicted on her equilibrium.

"It's just a little bit farther," Paul coaxed. He'd been wrong before about the distance, and Posey hadn't let him forget it.

To his relief, they soon found a pile of rusty pipes and ancient bricks sitting by the trail, which most likely came from the abandoned prison that they were searching for.

"See, Posey—there's a sign of human habitation. Or really, what *used* to be human habitation."

"Okay, Paul." Posey sighed. "Let's keep going—as long as we go back before it gets dark. I have to finish my paper for my film studies class. We're discussing Hitchcock this term."

She was a good sport, thought Paul, for all her complaining and nagging. Other girls would have bailed long before now. And you could talk to Pose about things that other girls didn't care about, like teen slasher films from the 80s and Japanese Yakuza movies. One day, when they both finished college, he planned to start a film production company with Posey. In the meantime, he made do with a successful YouTube channel that showcased ruined or "haunted" places.

"Straight ahead!" he pointed out. They trod along until the path turned to a wider road that led to a clearing. Nature had reclaimed much of it, but the prison could still be seen through the trees, resplendent in dark red brick and Victorian tracery carved from limestone. A crumbling stone wall topped with barbed wire surrounded the foreboding structure, but there was no front gate and anyone with enough gumption to finish the hike was free to walk in and explore.

Posey shivered and zipped up her hoodie. "*Jinkies, Scooby*—it's creepy. I feel like somebody's watching." She sniffled and wiped her nose again.

Paul thought that her little nose was adorable, even in mid-sniffle. He smiled at the idea of it, then laughed and said, "C'mon, I don't feel anything. That's something an actor would say in a cheesy horror movie."

"People died here, Paul. And it's been sitting in ruins for almost a hundred years. Everyone says it's haunted."

"People die everywhere, Pose. If it looks as creepy inside as it does outside, this is gonna be a bangin' YouTube video. Guaranteed to go viral!"

He took off across the clearing, his camera equipment covering his back, and Posey sighed and followed him.

They couldn't get in through the giant, Gothic-style double-doors that opened the entrance to the prison building. The doors appeared to be welded or rusted shut. Instead, the pair found a side window that was missing its iron bars and glass panes and climbed through it into a darkened corridor. Inside, the main light came from patches in the ceiling where the roof had crumbled away. The walls were covered with graffiti from almost ten decades of random vandals.

"P-e-e-w-w-w!" Posey wrinkled her adorable nose. "I smell dead people!"

"It's just the decay," Paul answered. "Every abandoned place I've vlogged smells exactly the same way. Rotting wood, ancient brick dust, often dead birds or small animals caught in the walls. And rat poop."

"Charming. This is the *best* date we've ever had."

"C'mon, let's go exploring. Look, there's a sign reading 'Administration Offices' with an arrow pointing that way. Let's shoot what we see as we follow the arrow." He removed his videocam from his backpack and fiddled with the settings until he was happy with them, then aimed the camera at Posey.

"Smile, Miss All-American."

"No! Paul!" She facepalmed with both hands. "I look awful!"

"Okay, okay." He turned the camera away with a chuckle. The echoes of their voices sounded down the corridor. "Let's keep moving."

They found a block of rooms in a caged enclosure, with a faded sign that could still be read in old-fashioned gold script: ADMINISTRATION. The front door to the block, made of metal grillwork, was sagging off its hinges.

"The administrators locked themselves behind cages? Wow, they must have been really scared of the prisoners!" exclaimed Posey.

"Ironic, isn't it?" Paul shot footage of the caged office block from several different angles. "Let's go find the big guy's office. It must be in here somewhere. The high mucky-muck, the warden."

They passed through the grillwork doorway. Posey

illuminated a short hallway with her camping flashlight. Paul filmed a row of photos hanging on the walls. She shined her light on several portraits. They were stiff photos behind cracked glass, featuring stern men in mutton chops and Victorian or Edwardian dress.

"The wardens of the past." Posey whispered. "That one looks especially vicious."

"Why are you whispering? No one can hear us… I agree that this one is remarkably nasty-looking. There's a brass name tag on the frame." He set the camera down and dusted the tag with his shirt cuff. "*O.O. Abelard, Warden, 1920-28.* He must have been the last warden, because this place closed in 1928."

"I read up on him before we came," said Posey. "He *was* vicious. At least eleven prisoners died under his watch in suspicious circumstances. The cruel punishments he meted out —dunking in water until prisoners almost drowned, flogging, food deprivation. And he insisted on attending every execution so he could watch."

"Evil bastard. Well, I've got enough here. Let's go find his office."

The warden's office was at the end of the hallway, behind a door with a cracked window made of wire-embedded glass. They walked in and saw daylight; a large window, missing panes in several spots, admitted the light. The window looked out to a courtyard surrounded by prison walls. Nature had taken the courtyard over and there were trees growing out of a baseball diamond paved in crumbling asphalt.

"The daylight almost makes it bearable," said Posey. "Except I can feel the spiritual presence of the evil bastard. Definitely."

Paul rolled his eyes and surveyed the room, planning how to shoot it. The office walls were covered in crumbling plaster and graffiti, the same as the other walls. Someone had painted "KILLER" in red drippy letters on the wall behind the warden's battered desk. The drawers of a wooden file cabinet were open, their ancient contents spilled on the floor.

Paul summoned his dramatic narrator's voice and spoke as his camera panned the room: "Nobody bothered to remove the files when this prison was shut down— imagine the history contained within them. Records of murderers and executions in the prison's electric chair, nicknamed 'Old Sparky.' This was the office of the notorious O.O. Abelard, the last warden, known for his cruelty and disregard for human rights."

"*Aaaccckkk!*"

He turned around to look at Posey, who, caught in the middle of a strangled cry, was pointing at the window. A crow perched on its sill. It cawed and screeched as if in response to Posey's cry.

"God, Pose, it's just a crow. It flew in through one of the broken panes!"

"They're harbingers of death, just like vultures. They eat carrion!"

Another crow flew in and settled on the warden's desk. And another.

"Well, go and stand outside the door then and have a smoke. These crows are gonna make some cool footage."

Posey set her backpack on the scarred wooden floor and fished her package of Kools and Bic lighter out of it.

"Okay, I'll be right outside the door. Don't spend too long with your nasty old crows. Hope you're done by the time I smoke one down." She threw him an air kiss and closed the office door behind her with a resounding thunk.

When he was done shooting the crows, Paul shut off his camera and knelt on the floor next to the pile of discarded files. The three crows watched him in unnerving silence.

He gathered a few loose, yellowed pages up from the floor, and began to read.

Wow, he thought, *here's something interesting. Abelard conducted numerous interviews with a prisoner named Carl Sachs, who seems to have been an occultist. Sachs was convicted of killing a young girl—by draining her blood!*

Another sheet was covered in occult signs and incantations. It was a treatise on the connections of the dead to their personal objects, notations about blood rituals, and an anecdote about using animals as familiars.

There was also a report about Sachs's execution in the Old Sparky chamber. It noted that Sachs refused a clergyman and left his few possessions to Warden Abelard, including "sundry books of a curious nature."

"I wonder if Ol' Abbie took up where Sachs left off with the occult stuff?" Paul wondered aloud. He stuffed the Sachs papers into his backpack, certain that no one would care if he took the file. He thought the story was much more than his usual "ruined places" videos now. It would make a gripping documentary about O.O. Abelard, one that he might even be able to sell to a distributor.

He heard one of the crows caw again, and he looked up from the floor, startled. The room was now full of crows perched everywhere—on the desk, on top of the file cabinet, on the windowsill. They all seemed to be staring at him with judgmental onyx eyes. He counted eleven of them.

Then a crow flew into the office, much larger than the others, followed by a smaller one that seemed to have an injured wing. They settled on the wooden swivel chair behind the warden's desk. The larger bird looked directly at him, with an intense gaze.

Paul stood up quickly. "Yikes! Ugly creature." He'd never seen a crow that size. He grabbed a book and tossed it, narrowly missing the big crow. The bird did not stir but continued to stare in what Paul fancied a hateful and malignant stare.

"Well, I've got enough," he told himself, after shooting more footage of the room. He turned his back to the warden's desk to pack away his equipment. Then he finally stood up and looked at the desk again.

He froze. The huge ugly crow on the warden's chair was gone. In its place sat a man—a man dressed in the clothing of the 1920s. He was staring straight at Paul with a menacing look, his features harsh and cruel, his eyes dark and pebble-like. He seemed to be made out of faded colors and some sort of grayish substance.

Paul realized, after a few tense moments, that the grayish man looked like Warden Abelard. The man in the portrait from the hall, renowned for his harsh treatment of prisoners. He sneered at Paul in a mocking way. Paul yelped in fear.

"Paul—what is going on in here?"

Paul turned to see that Posey was standing in the office doorway, trailing a cigarette in her right hand. "You crazy guy, you're white as a ghost!"

"L-L-L-o-o-ok! The desk chair!"

"There's just a big old ugly crow sitting on it! You

rolled your eyes at me when *I* was afraid of those disgusting birds."

Paul whipped around. It was true. The gray man was gone now. Sitting in the chair was the oversized crow staring at him again, with its judgmental eyes.

"You didn't see a man sitting in the chair where that crow is now? A man who looked like Warden Abelard from the picture?"

"Are you joking? It's not funny. Not funny at *all*," Posey fumed.

"I'm not joking, Pose."

"Well, then—you imagined it! Too much thinking about Abelard!"

"I guess," Paul answered in a shaky tone.

Suddenly, the crow with the injured wing half-flew, half-hopped at Posey and began pecking at her Timberland boots. She sent it away with a furious kick and it fluttered to the top of the warden's desk.

"Damn, let's get away from these nasty birds. You've got what you want, right?"

Paul gulped. "Yeah. For sure. I've got enough on Ol' Warden Abbie to make more than just a YouTube video. Maybe a whole documentary."

"Okay, so let's go. I don't want to get lost in this place when it's dark."

Paul felt a renewed surge of purpose.

"I wish we could go—I almost agree with you. But we haven't seen nearly enough. We haven't even got footage of Old Sparky. And it's only two o'clock on a spring afternoon. Don't worry—darkness won't come for hours."

"Not gonna lie. I'd rather leave."

"C'mon. Stay with me, at least until we find Old Sparky."

"Okay, but if you sell your documentary, you owe me a producer's screen credit. In a huge font above the title. A POSEY FIELDS PRODUCTION."

"I'll make your credit twice as large as mine, Darlin'," Paul promised her, followed by a quick kiss.

They grabbed their backpacks and equipment and left the warden's office. Paul stopped briefly in the hallway in front of the photo of Warden Abelard and grabbed it off the wall.

"What are you doing?" squawked Posey.

"I'm taking it. I want to shoot it in a better light for my documentary. No one will care— the state owns the land, but they don't technically keep up the prison. It's abandoned, not just closed."

Paul handed the antique photo and frame to Posey. "Here, you keep it in your pack— mine's full."

Posey stuffed it in her pack. "Creeps me out to have the old dirtbag's photo in my pack. What if I start seeing things, like you did?"

"You won't!"

Paul's map of the prison—printed off the Internet— guided them out of the administrative block and into a corridor that led to another corridor, which eventually led to a small windowless chamber. It had a heavy steel door, left somewhat ajar.

"This is it—this is where Carl Sachs and numerous other inmates bought the farm!" Paul cried.

"Carl Sachs?"

"Oh, I forgot you didn't know. I found some papers about a prisoner named Sachs. He killed a child and was into occult stuff. Described as a small, ugly guy with a deformed arm. Before he was executed, he had some kind of friendship with Abelard."

They pushed the heavy door aside as much as they could, and squeezed into a dim, dank-smelling room. It was a stark space, with walls covered in peeling, olive-green paint.

On a raised platform stood a wooden structure, a cross between a bench and a chair, made of thick heavy oak, with an over-tall back. Rotted leather straps with tarnished metal buckles were attached to the chair's arms, front legs, and back. A metal helmet, resembling an overturned mixing bowl, protruded from a gooseneck cable attached to the top slat of the chair's back. Wires and rubber tubes sprouting from the helmet led to a battered bucket. Above the platform hung a sign with words painted in crumbling white paint:

OLD SPARKY

Posey gulped. "Uh, that's quite a sight," she finally croaked. "To think that people actually died in that thing."

"It's very grim," agreed Paul, aiming his camera at Old Sparky. "This footage is gonna be lit as heck— *Aaaack!*"

They both stared, open-mouthed, as a small flock of crows flew into the room through the open wedge of the doorway. They were led by the oversized crow that Paul had first seen in the warden's office, followed by the one with the injured wing. The duo landed on the floor near the metal bucket next to Old Sparky, and the other crows landed on the floor behind them.

"How did they get in here?" shrieked Posey.

"I swear I closed the office's door," said Paul.

"Well, obviously you didn't." Posey spoke with a sharp edge in her voice. "This is starting to be a *really* terrible date, Paul."

"Well, they're not hurting anybody. They're just creepy. Maybe I did forget to close it."

He pointed to a door that led to another chamber. "I'll bet that's where the switch is. C'mon, let's explore."

Posey hesitated, clearly annoyed.

"We'll be escaping the crows," he reminded her. "Maybe they'll be gone by the time we come back."

They went through the door and found the control panel full of toggle switches and tarnished dials, with tube and knob wiring. Opposite was a galvanized sink with a rusty faucet.

Off to the side of the panel was a large, double-handled knife switch.

"Oooh!" exclaimed Posey. "There's the Frankenstein switch! It looks totally nasty."

"The Frankenstein switch?"

"You know—the switch that turns on the electric current in a Frankenstein movie! I'm sure that's the one that activates Old Sparky!"

Paul set his camera down and walked over to the switch. With grim delight, he pulled it down. There was no reaction, of course. There hadn't been electricity in the abandoned prison since 1928.

"Look, Paul—there's the telephone on the other wall! The one that leads to the governor's office, just like in the movies." It was a 1920s wall phone, with a dangling bell-shaped receiver hanging straight down from a cord, its cradle broken.

"I wonder if Abelard even answered when the governor called with a stay of execution," Posey said. "Wouldn't have wanted to miss the fun."

She put the receiver to her ear and intoned with exaggerated gravity: "Yes, Governor... We're standing by for your order...here at Nasty-Ass Stinky Corrections Institute."

Paul laughed, but then quickly sobered up when he saw Posey's face turn pale and frozen.

He lunged to her side. "What's wrong, Pose?"

"There's someone on the l-l-l-ine," she stammered.

"*What?* It's not even connected. Look, you can see where the wires are dangling loose from the box."

"The voice s-s-s-said '*Stay of execution denied.*' Here, listen for yourself." She held out the receiver and Paul took it and put it to his ear.

He heard a crackle on the line, as if there were turbulence on the other end. Then, came a definite sound of someone breathing on the line, followed by a disconnecting click.

His heart thumped as he dropped the receiver. "I-I-I... This is *unreal.* Posey, you won't believe this—there was a click on the line *as if someone had disconnected.*"

"Let's get out of here. Now!" Posey answered. "I don't want to stay here another min—"

She didn't finish her sentence. They both heard the sound of a loud buzzing hum, and an overhead light flickered on and off.

"The current's on—Paul *the current's on!* Turn it off, turn it off!" she screamed.

Paul grabbed the "Frankenstein switch" and pushed it back up into the "Off" position. Impossibly, the buzzing sound and lights both switched off.

"That's it, let's go! C'mon Paul!"

He grabbed her with this free hand, his camera in the other hand, and they exited the switch room as fast as they could, Paul leading and Posey close behind.

In the main room, they quickly froze in their places. Standing near the chair was the grayish figure of Warden Abelard. Next to him was another grayish man, small, with a weasel-like face and one arm clutched to his side as if injured. They were both looking straight at Paul and Posey with stern, malicious faces. At their feet were gathered the crows that had earlier flown into the chamber, minus two: the oversized leader crow, and the one with the gimpy wing were missing.

Paul dropped his camera with a heavy thud. Posey gripped his arm tightly.

"Is that—is t-t-that the figure of Abelard you saw?" she whispered hoarsely.

"Y-e-s. And look, the door to the chamber is shut tight now. We left it ajar!"

"Who's…the other one…the gray man?" Posey's body was rigid and seemed rooted to the floor like a tree.

"I'm guessing it's…Carl Sachs, the child-killer," he stammered.

The other gray man seemed to recognize his—*its*—name. Paul's spine seized up with fear as the figure made a "come here" gesture toward him.

Paul felt his legs and feet move, as if independent of his own will. Trancelike, he moved toward the Old Sparky platform and the two figures beside the chair. Dimly, he could hear the crows caw all around him with an obscene kind of excitement.

Left behind, Posey stood, statue-like in place, unable to speak or move.

Why am I doing this? Paul thought. *Why can't I stop myself?*

He climbed two steps to the platform and slowly sat in the chair. Warden Abelard wore a tight-lipped smile as Sachs began to buckle Paul into the chair with the rotted leather straps: first the arms, then the legs, then the midsection. As a final touch, the warden adjusted the bowl-like metal helmet onto Paul's head.

Paul was lost in a heavy mental fog. He was vaguely aware that he was in danger, but he didn't know how to fix it. And he couldn't move. He wondered who the young woman standing yards away was, her body tight with fear. Then he realized who she was and managed to croak out: "P-P-Pose."

There was no reaction from the woman. He tried to speak again but couldn't.

He turned his head to the side—an inch was all he could manage. Warden Abelard was now peering at an old-fashioned pocket watch, as if checking the time. He nodded to Carl Sachs, who took the bucket from the chair's side and made for the switch room. He walked right by Posey as if he could not see her and disappeared into the other room after opening the door. Paul could hear water spattering into the metal bucket.

"P-Pose." Paul grunted the words out as best he could.

This time there was a slight movement of Posey's head and hands. Meanwhile, Sachs came out of the switch room carrying the bucket, now filled with water. As he passed Posey—again, without seeming to see her—water splashed on her arm. Then she woke up.

"Paul. Paul!" she cried. "What can I do?"

Paul struggled to answer but could not. He could hear Sachs and the warden behind the chair, busying themselves with settling the proper hoses in the bucket. There was something he wanted to remember, but it wouldn't come into his mind. It seemed important and he tried again. And again.

While Paul was trying to remember, Sachs finished with the bucket and hoses. He walked toward the switch room again, while the warden stood guard over Paul. He tightened a random buckle, his face sporting a look of malicious anticipation. A girl's distant voice echoed in Paul's head: *"He insisted on attending every execution so he could watch…"*

As he felt the buckle squeeze his arm, Paul suddenly remembered the papers that he'd taken from the warden's office—especially the part he'd read about connections between the dead and their personal objects. And what happened when those objects were destroyed...*the dead could lose their hold on the material world.*

"The picture of Abelard...Pose! Bur… *burn*… it… with…your Bic! No time…to explain." Paul slumped to one side, exhausted from crying out while struggling against the control of inhuman forces. The grayish specter of the warden shoved his body back into position.

Then, as if for the first time, the figure of Warden Abelard seemed to realize that Posey existed and took a step in her direction. Posey looked briefly his way, trembling at the sight.

"What picture? Oh, you mean the warden's picture!"

Quick as she could, Posey grabbed her backpack and

unzipped it. Her fingers were frantic, trembling so much she could hardly move the zipper. "Please let me find the Bic right now…" she mumbled aloud in desperation. Luckily, she'd shoved it right on top of Warden Abelard's antique portrait.

She smashed the portrait's glass cover against the floor and flicked the lighter. No flame!

Paul watched, helpless to intervene. He could hear the faint noises of Sachs busying himself in the switch room. His mind pictured the grayish man adjusting dials and toggle switches. Very soon, he knew with certainty, *Sachs would approach the Frankenstein switch.*

Posey flicked her Bic Lighter a second time, and a third, as the warden moved close enough to touch her.

The grayish figure was just about to grab her arm when she got the Bic to light and applied it to the portrait. "Burn, burn!" she cried, as flames crept over the fragile cardboard.

A blood-chilling screech came from the warden as his portrait began to disappear into the flames. Out of the switch room flew the crow with the injured wing, moving straight toward the warden, whose grayish form slowly faded into the air. Soon, there were two crows sitting at Posey's feet, the big one and the smaller, injured one. The other crows in the room began to screech and flap on their perches.

Paul—released from his trance—loosened his straps and pushed the helmet away. The leather was no longer taut but rotted and barely able to restrain anything. The steel main door creaked open to a half-ajar position.

He leapt off the chair's platform and toward Posey, grabbing her arm. "Get your pack and let's go!" He found his camera and his pack, and the file of papers on Sachs fell to the floor from a compartment he'd left unzipped. Posey shouldered her pack quickly and they made for the half-opened door.

All at once the big crow screeched again and the crows lunged at them en masse, pecking and tearing at their clothes, hair, and skin. They squeezed through the door while the birds continued to attack, and ran down the hall with the creatures flying after them. The two escaped out of a paneless window and stopped just outside the prison building to catch their breaths.

"Is it over?" cried Posey, through frightened tears and gasps for air. Her hair was torn out in places and there were bloody peck marks on her face and hands. Paul thought, relieved, that she was more scared than hurt.

Paul leaned against the prison's crumbling brick exterior, panting. "Yeah, I think so. You destroyed the portrait, and I dropped the file papers about Sachs on the floor."

He himself had a nasty little wound on one hand that was trickling blood and a scratch on his neck that was painful.

"C'mon let's go," he said a few moments later, his breath recovered. They walked across the overgrown front lawn toward the prison's open entry gate, feeling the sweet release of tension.

Suddenly, Paul heard flapping and fluttering and turned to see a huge flock of crows flying out of the same paneless window they'd used to escape.

"Run, Posey! Run for the gate!"

They both took off again and sprinted toward the open gate, with the crows in angry pursuit.

The furious birds pecked and scratched at the two interlopers as they caught up with them. At one point, Posey screamed as a cloud of black feathers surrounded her head.

Thwaaaack! S-c-reee-ch… Thwaaaack! …S-c-reee-ch… S-c-reee-ch…

Paul smacked the crows away with his backpack as they vocalized with fury. He grabbed Posey with his free hand and half-ran, half-dragged her with him out of the gate.

"Keep running," she screamed, as Paul abruptly pulled up and looked back toward the prison.

"It's okay," he panted. "They're not following us, Pose. They turned back soon as we got through the front gate. And now they're flying back into the prison."

The cloud of black feathers and beaks had indeed turned around with a mass cry of disappointment.

"They're going back through that open window," Posey said. "I wonder why? Why didn't they follow us through the gate?"

"They're not normal birds. They're attached to that building somehow, and they can't leave." Paul sounded grim.

Posey was silent for a minute. Then she said: "You gonna use that footage?"

"No. I'm erasing it when we get back to the car."

Posey sighed. "If we talked about the stuff we saw in the video, it would have gotten ten million views or more. With YouTube monetization, that would have earned us a nice stake for our production company."

"I don't wanna tell anybody about what we saw. First, it'd bring more people to explore this place and who knows what would happen to 'em? And second, nobody important would believe us. We'd be a joke, like the ghost hunters on cable TV."

"I guess you're right."

"C'mon, let's go. It's more than an hour's hike back to the car and it's about five now." He wiped a trickle of blood off his face. "I've got a first-aid kit in my trunk I've never used. I'm pretty sure it's got alcohol wipes and antibiotic cream."

Posey held herself together admirably until they made it back to Paul's car and finished tending their wounds as best they could. As Paul put his car into gear and headed back to the highway, however, she began to laugh in a near-hysterical tone.

"What's so funny, Pose?" Paul cried, alarmed.

She laughed until tears started to form. Finally, she stopped enough to answer.

"My Hitchcock paper," she giggled. "I just remembered what film I'm supposed to write about."

"Not... *No!* ...Really?"

"Yes. It's *The Birds*."

They both laughed like lunatics, until Paul found the highway on-ramp, and gunned his battered RAV-4 toward home.

Red Onion

Downtown San Francisco always smelled like human piss when the weather was warm; it was some defect in the sewers, but no one at City Hall seemed capable of fixing the problem. On a malodorous mid-morning in late September, the acrid stink was a fitting punctuation for Kristy's mood. She stood on the corner of Market and New Montgomery, holding her pathetic little cardboard box of personal effects, the shameful Scarlet Letter of the laid-off.

Further down on Market, she knew that even worse smells and sights awaited pedestrians, on certain side streets used by street people as outdoor toilets.

"San Francisco at the end of the 2010s: streets covered in human poo and legions of feral vagrants who look and act like Orcs," she told herself, disgusted.

At least, losing her job meant she wouldn't have to ride the commuter train from her apartment in the East Bay to the city for a while. It would be a break from confronting the demoralizing filth that awaited at trip's end. She certainly wouldn't miss the sewer odor, or the zombie-like street people, or the druggies shooting up on random corners and dropping disposable needles for pedestrians to step on.

"It used to be different, before the tech industry came," Lorraine from Product Management had said, in the elevator just a few minutes before. Lorraine was clutching her own Scarlet Letter, her own generic box of office odds and ends. "Tech destroyed San Francisco—destroyed all of the Bay Area, as a matter of fact. I'm old enough to remember when San Jose was surrounded by cherry orchards and Burlingame was where you once got a good deal on a budget car. And nobody crapped on the street."

"Oh, Lorraine," Kristy had said, "I'm so sorry you got the ax too." Kristy felt bad about Lorraine; at her age, in her late fifties, prospects for finding another decent job in the Bay Area were slim. Tech was notoriously ageist and there was huge competition for the few legacy industry jobs that were still left in the area.

"Don't you worry about me," said Lorraine, as if reading her mind. "Not gonna waste any time trying to compete. No one's gonna hire a fifty-eight-year-old instead of a cheap, young newbie. Nope, I got some decent equity in my condo in Daly City and I'm selling up and moving to Oregon. Damn, Oregon is beautiful, girl. Looks like what Northern California used to, forty years ago. Before tech and nutty politics destroyed it."

"Will you be okay?"

"Sure, Oregon's cheap, if you stay away from Portland. I got a cousin in Medford; it's a great place. And my equity will last until I can draw Social Security." Lorraine shrugged. "You concentrate on that little Andy of yours. And at your age, I'm sure you won't be out of work for long."

"I dunno, Lorraine. I suck at finding a job. I hate hitting old friends up for work on the Linked-In site. It just seems so tacky."

"Yeah, I know, but you gotta do it. That little angel is depending on you, and you're all he's got."

"I know."

The two women had said their goodbyes and parted on Market, each swearing to stay in touch through Linked-In. Kirsty watched as Lorraine disappeared downward into the bowels of the closest BART Station, to wait for the next train to Daly City.

She would be headed the other way on BART shortly, across the Bay, all the way to Antioch in Contra Costa County. It was a miserable commute, but Antioch was all she could afford. But first, she needed a drink. No, she *deserved* a drink. There was an old bar named Pied Piper's at the Palace Hotel, which probably had free Wi-Fi. She needed to sit down, plan, and think.

She settled at the empty bar below a famous mural painted by Maxfield Parrish, leaving the shameful cardboard box on the counter, draped by her discarded jacket. She ordered a glass of cabernet from the bored server, and then abruptly changed her mind.

"Screw it. I'm having a margarita. With Patron. At ten o'clock in the morning." She didn't have to pick up Andy from daycare until six p.m., and the margarita would have worn off long before then.

"The first thing that needs to go is Red Onion," she told herself, typing a list of actions into her phone's note app. Unnecessary expenses had to be dumped ASAP, like cargo on a sinking ship.

A little pang of regret hit her as she closed out her Red Onion account. It was her lone little luxury, the box of fresh dinner ingredients delivered to her doorstep three evenings a week. And there was Wictor, the Red Onion delivery boy—er, delivery *man*—who clearly had a huge crush on her. A nineteen or twenty-year-old immigrant from some war-ravaged Balkan mini-state; his name was actually Viktor, but he pronounced it Wictor. Shy, sweet-natured, Wictor had courtly Old-World manners that seemed almost heart-wrenching among the cruel, everyday hustles of the Bay Area.

Wictor's unabashed adoration had always been Kristy's sorely needed ego boost. But Red Onion was an expensive meal service, and she couldn't justify the cost anymore—not when she, freshly unemployed, would have all day free to shop for herself. Oh well.

She thought of Lorraine's remark about Oregon: "What Northern California used to be before tech destroyed it." Then again, maybe the Bay Area had always been a cruel, stone-hearted place; at twenty-seven, she wasn't old enough to remember a different time. If only she had the means—like Lorraine—to escape to Oregon or some other place that California refugees favored for their exile.

She typed "Southern Oregon real estate" into the search bar on her phone and scrolled through dozens of listings in Medford. Damn, she could afford to rent a three-bedroom house in Medford for less than what she paid for her one-bedroom, one-bath-with-den apartment in Antioch. Most listings had a proper yard for Andy to play in, and a ton of trees. Every street she looked at seemed impossibly green, like it was a slice-of-life snapshot from the Emerald City in *The Wizard of Oz.*

Antioch had very few trees and wasn't at all green; it was a dry, faded orange, boiling-hot outback of a place, for every month of the year except for a few weeks around December and January.

Medford, Oregon. Oh, how lovely it all looked, in its

overwhelming, almost supernatural greenness. And without question, much nicer than piss-smelling downtown Market Street in San Francisco. Or *San Franshitsco*, as certain people had taken to calling it.

She and Lorraine had written a sarcastic song with that title a few weeks ago, replacing the lyrics of *I Left My Heart in San Francisco*. She'd taped it to her refrigerator door:

> *I left my poop in San Franshitsco*
> *High on a hill, shit calls to me...*

* * *

Two days later, Kristy sat in front of her laptop on the dining room table in her apartment. Outside, Antioch was as hot and gold and drab-olive as ever. She checked off each item of her task list with satisfaction.

Apply for unemployment benefits, *check*.

Cancel all unnecessary services, *check*.

Apply for COBRA medical insurance coverage, *check*.

Send direct messages to every friend or acquaintance on Linked-In, *check*.

When it came to Linked-In, hardly anyone responded; those that did mostly treated her with guarded, non-committal courtesy, as if she were leprous. Those few friends and acquaintances—the *very few*—who offered genuine help, were noted and filed away for future reference.

Then she scrolled through her email to see if Andy's dad had responded to her pleas for the child support check. The money was late by three months. Of course, there was no reply. The deadbeat.

Interruption came in the form of a familiar knock on the door: knock, *knock-knock,* knock. Wictor?

But she'd *canceled* Red Onion. Maybe he didn't get the message?

She opened the front door to Wictor, standing on the steps, holding the usual Red Onion box of dinnertime goodies.

He smiled his same shy smile. "Dinner for zhe fair lady!" He pronounced the last word *laddy.*

"I can't take it, Wictor. I cancelled my account. I can't afford you guys anymore."

Wictor looked wounded. "No, it's okay, someone else pay for it, promise."

"It's gotta be a mistake."

"No mistake. Call and ask."

"I'll send them an email. I know you've got other deliveries." She stared doubtfully at the Red Onion package, thinking how nice it would be if someone else really was paying. Free food would certainly come in handy. Half of her unemployment check would go to COBRA and most of her rent and other expenses would come out of her meager savings. She only had enough savings to last through Christmas and that was it, unless she found a job before then.

"Okay, miss. But you take this now." Wictor smiled broadly. "You need it, you don't got no job."

"How did you know that?" Kristy asked in a sharp tone. She was fond of Wictor, but the stuff he knew about her sometimes sounded almost stalkerish. She felt a little creepy chill of autumn waft through the door, even though it was warm as toast outside, and the orange, grassy hills surrounding Antioch were troubling the wildfire experts.

Wictor's green eyes, normally like a pool of shoal water floating a few brown leaves, suddenly turned opaque and dark. "Oh, I just figured. You're wearing those sweatpants, not work clothes, like if you just got home. You gonna take this package?"

There seemed to be no harm in accepting it, Kristy told herself. It was clearly a mistake, but she wasn't legally liable for merchandise she hadn't ordered.

"I guess dinner's on Red Onion tonight. Thanks, Wictor." She took the box and wished him goodnight.

"See ya next time," he said, smiling broadly.

"I doubt if this will happen again—" Kristy started to say, but Wictor had already turned and left.

Kristy went back to her laptop and sent an email to Red Onion. Then she opened the box that Wictor had brought.

Inside, everything looked normal. The box contained all of the ingredients for lamb curry, with a side of basmati rice and caramelized carrots. Two pounds of lamb shanks, spices, rice, and fresh carrots. She'd made that particular meal numerous times before.

And it turned out deliciously. Andy asked for a second helping, and shoveled forkfuls into his mouth in between verbal bursts about the new school year, his new teacher, and what he planned to be for Halloween. And, of course, what he wanted for Christmas.

Oh no, here it comes, thought Kristy. Christmas—a word that was dreaded everywhere by those who were both cash-strapped and child-laden.

"Andy, you know that I just lost my job—"

He wasn't listening. "Mom, Austin's getting a Wii

Red Bundle set for Christmas! With Nun chucks and Bluetooth!"

"Really?" She had no idea what that meant, but it sounded expensive.

"Well at least that's what he *says*. He brags an awful lot. It has all the latest games, the top console and joysticks—"

"You're only seven," Kristy said with a frown. "That sounds like a set for a big person."

"*Mom—*"

"Maybe I'll have a new job by then. Christmas is still a long way," she broke in, trying to sound soothing. After the dinner dishes were cleared away, she grabbed her phone and looked up the Red Bundle set on Amazon.

Almost seven hundred dollars! Holy crap. She wouldn't have considered it even if she was still employed, but it was out of the question now. Well, she didn't have to think about it for another couple of months. Screw spoiled Austin and his overindulgent parents.

* * *

Two days later, Kristy got an email from Red Onion customer service in response to her query about the mysterious package. It was a form message letting her know that it was against company policy to reveal the names or other details of any other accounts, even those who may be sending her regular packages.

Well, damn, she thought. *It's like they don't even* want *to know if they're giving me free meals or not.*

She startled, almost out of her chair, at the familiar Wictor knock on her front door. Knock, *knock-knock,*

knock.

"It's Wictor night!" Andy shouted happily from the floor, where he was playing a video game. "Yum, yum!"

It *was* Wictor again, with the usual Red Onion dinner package, showing up at six-thirty p.m. sharp. Always so punctual—almost like a machine.

"Wictor! I told you I don't have an account anymore."

"Somebody else pays. I swear it. You take the package now."

What.The.Fuck? she thought. *I can't keep getting these free packages.* But then she told herself: *Screw it. I tried! And Red Onion didn't seem interested in investigating the issue further. If it's a mistake, they'll find out sooner or later.*

Aloud she said, "Okay Wictor, thank you for the package."

He beamed all over. "Your hair...so...pretty tonight," he said, blushing.

"My *hair*?" She blushed back, confused. "Oh! I just put it up. Usually I wear it down."

"You look like...queen. With that object in your hair."

"Thank you! It's called a decorative comb. It's an old-fashioned thing...this came from my great aunt."

"There was lady who had one like it...in refugee camp."

His face flashed a dark, sad expression.

"Oh," said Kristy, feeling awkward. "I'm sorry about that, Wictor, I really am. But you're safe here now!"

She suddenly felt like a spoiled brat for hating the Bay Area so much. Downtown San Francisco was a toilet, but at least no one was fighting a brutal guerilla war in the middle of Market Street.

"Yes…I'm safe. No soldiers. I was just a very little child. Sometimes here, though, big roads, so many cars, they scare me. People drive crazy, no one cares if they push you off road's lane. I get scared for accidents, but it's my job so what can you do? I have my special customers I always like to see, like you."

She pinked up again. "That's nice of you to say. But hadn't you better be getting on now? You have other packages to deliver."

He seemed confused, as if he hadn't considered his other customers at all. But then his expression cleared.

Then he said, "Oh, ya, other customers," in an embarrassed manner. "Sure."

"Okay, I gotta go now Wictor."

"Okay, see ya next time."

She closed the door and opened the package. It was all the ingredients for chicken cacciatore, with a side of grilled sweet potatoes in lemon butter. Dessert was blueberry cobbler. Curiously, the portions seemed much larger than usual. There was enough chicken and other things for tomorrow's lunch as well as the evening's dinner.

She wondered if it was Andy's deadbeat dad who was sending the food. It seemed unlikely, but maybe he was turning over a new leaf.

Nah, couldn't be. Why keep it a secret? He probably would have taunted her about it. And the deadbeat wouldn't have known Red Onion from a rutabaga. He barely knew how to access Wi-Fi.

Maybe it was her former coworkers? They knew she struggled as a single mom with an unreliable ex, trying to survive in the most expensive metropolitan area in the country.

Maybe they wanted to remain anonymous because they didn't want to embarrass her. She wasn't particularly close to any of them, though, except for Lorraine.

Or maybe it was just a system error. She made a note not to count on getting the food every week. She regarded it as an ephemeral windfall that could disappear at any moment. "Like tears in rain" from the movie *Blade Runner*.

* * *

Halloween season arrived on the same smokey, velvety winds it always arrived on in Northern California. The weather was fairly warm in the daytime, but not blistering. The nights and mornings were chilly, the leaves continued to fall. Kristy turned off the heat at night to save on utilities and piled extra blankets on her bed and Andy's to make up for it.

She was waiting to hear back from a few interviews, but nothing had materialized so far. Her bank account was dwindling, and the year-end holidays were right around the corner. Nobody hired anyone during the holiday season in the Bay Area.

Andy asked for a new Halloween costume, and Kristy had to say, "No."

"We don't have a lot of money right now. Maybe you could make your own costume? Or wear last year's?"

"*Nobody* wears home-made costumes anymore, *M-o-m-m-m*! And everyone at school will remember my costume from last year, I'm pretty sure."

"I'm sorry, I just can't do it right now," she cried. It was always so hard when she had to tell him he couldn't have the same things that many of the other kids in his class had.

"Hey, I know," she said. "How about you go as a pirate, like I suggested yesterday? A pirate would be easy to do, and you wouldn't guess it was a home-made costume. All you'd need is a hat, some make-up, and some old clothes. And you can re-use that sword you made for the school play."

"I dunno. A pirate isn't very cool. I wanted to be Captain America."

"*I* can make a pirate look cool. And you can wear make-up that makes you look fierce and bloodthirsty. With a bloody scar on your cheek. I can make one out of a gummy worm."

"Okay," Andy replied, after a long, sullen pause. "Okay."

The problem was, where was she going to get a pirate hat in time for Halloween? The holiday was only two days away. Most pirate hats came in full costume sets, which she didn't want to pay for. Maybe she'd try thrift stores or Craigslist.

The familiar knock on the door interrupted Kristy's internal meanderings. It was Red Onion night again. Kristy opened the door to Wictor, holding out a Red Onion package.

"Happy Halloween, Miss!" he said.

"Happy Halloween, Wictor."

"You got nice pumpkins?"

"Yes, we've got nice pumpkins. We just haven't carved them yet."

His eyes shone, as if he was excited about something.

"Tonight, there's something special inside box. For

Halloween."

"Oh yes." Last year, she recalled, the Red Onion Halloween box had included a window cling in the shape of a witch and an extra jumbo-sized cookie that resembled a black cat. "I remember."

Wictor beamed. "You're gonna like this year's extra, I bet."

She opened the box eagerly after Wictor left. "I hope it's the jumbo cookie again!" she cried out loud.

There was a flat opaque plastic bag on top of the usual Red Onion dinner ingredients. Her fingers felt through the bag, childishly trying to guess the contents. Some kind of heavy cloth. She tried to imagine what was inside. Maybe a little Halloween wall hanging, made of felt, with some cute saying on it. She ripped open the tape at the top of the bag and removed the contents.

Heavy black felt, folded; maybe she was right about the wall hanging. But no, it was the wrong shape. She unfolded it—and let out a little gasp. It was a tri-cornered hat in black felt, child-sized. A little steaming and maybe some gold braid from the notions counter at Michael's and it would make a dandy pirate's hat.

How did they know? thought Kristy wildly. Or more accurately, how did *he* know? She had a strong gut feeling that it was Wictor who was responsible for the hat, even though it was sealed in standard Red Onion promotional packaging.

She felt an icepick trace down her spine and Jell-O take over her knees; then she dropped the hat on the floor instinctively. It was too, too *creepy*. Something was very wrong.

Andy came out of the bedroom she'd made for him

out of the den; it had no closet, but she'd added two big dressers to the room, and everything worked out fine. "Hey, was that Wictor I heard? Yum-yum. Hey, what's that on the floor? It looks like a hat!" He picked it up and tried it on. It fit perfectly.

"Andy, listen to me—" Kristy began, uneasily.

"You're right after all, Mom," he burst out. "A cool hat like this will make a great Halloween costume!"

Kristy was thinking hard and fast. *It was just a weird coincidence. The hat came from the Red Onion marketing department, not from Wictor! And Andy liked it! No more arguments with him about the freakin' Halloween costume.*

Aloud she said, "It's a great hat. Now, let's go find some old clothes we can turn into a pirate vest and pants to match!"

She resolved to act cheerful around Andy all through dinner later that evening, but still felt uneasy inside. She realized, with a slight shock, that she no longer wanted to see or talk to Wictor anymore, free food be damned.

The next time he knocked, she dimmed the living room lights and pretended that she wasn't home. He rapped the door several times in succession—knock, *knock-knock*, knock and then knock, *knock-knock*, knock again, but finally gave up. She peered through a gap in the front drapes and watched him leave the Red Onion package on the doorstep. After waiting a few minutes, he walked away, his shoulders sagging.

Wictor seemed to disappear after he passed the hedge at the end of the walkway. He was very thin, and his baggy clothes only emphasized it. She felt sad and guilty for hiding from him.

* * *

December rustled in on dried leaves of winter despair. Kristy's callbacks for prospective jobs dwindled to nothing. She tried to keep busy with online classes and running in the park.

The only bright spot was that her deadbeat ex had finally come through with the back child support, and now she had to figure out how to divide it. She added and subtracted compulsively on her phone's calculator as she totaled up her monthly expenses.

First the fixed expenses: Rent. Check. Car payment: Check. Medical insurance: Check. Credit card payment: the minimum. Then the variables: Utilities. Cut as much as possible. Entertainment. Nothing that isn't free. DVDs borrowed from the public library. Food…

She hesitated to write anything down for "food". Those Red Onion boxes three times a week had done much to cut her meals budget to the bare minimum. She often got two dinners and two lunches out of every package.

But she never wanted to count on the packages, so she was at a loss on what to write. Finally, she just tapped out, "???"

While Kristy worked her checklist, Andy was in the living room, crowding ornaments onto their Christmas tree. It was just a little tabletop tree set on the coffee table; they'd bought it that afternoon—on discount—because it leaned a little.

"We never buy anything unless it's on sale!" he'd moaned, when they were at the tree lot. But he'd gotten in the spirit of things when Kristy challenged him to see if he could fit all of their ornaments on the tiny tree.

Anything to keep his mind off of the big Christmas gift he wasn't gonna get. Instead, waiting for Andy under the tabletop tree were a couple of board games, a new pencil case, and some pajamas.

Then she heard the familiar knock.

Knock. *Knock-knock.* Knock.

It was Red Onion night again. Kristy felt a little queasy, as she always did now, when she heard Wictor's knock. She didn't pretend she wasn't home anymore, the way she had just after he brought the pirate's hat. But she did try to minimize her contact with him. The situation just didn't feel right.

She opened the door.

"Christmas box for fair lady," he said, beaming.

For the first time, she saw—really *saw*—how skinny and fragile he looked. She realized all of a sudden that he always wore the same clothes: blue pants and white baseball shirt, over a blue, long-sleeved tee. Plus, the distinctive Red Onion cap and name tag the delivery guys always wore.

Poor guy—he probably just made minimum wage. Kristy wondered where he lived? He wouldn't be making enough to live even in Antioch on minimum wage, as downscale as Antioch was compared to most of Contra Costa County.

"Anything extra in the box for Christmas?" she asked, feeling tender toward him. She could afford to be a little generous with her time. Christmas was only three days away, and he looked like he needed some Yuletide kindness very badly.

Wictor beamed more. "Very *special* Christmas gift for

you."

She realized painfully that it was too cold and crisp of an evening for him to be dressed that way. A rare cold spell had descended on all of the East Bay. There was even a frost the night before. Mrs. Chung from the apartment next door had taken her potted tangerine tree inside to avoid frost damage.

However, cold snap or no, Wictor didn't seem to be effected. He wasn't even shivering.

Maybe he lived with his parents. If so, she hoped they would look after him better in the future. He was too skinny, and he needed some new clothes. And a haircut. His hair was shaggy and unkempt.

"Where do you live, Wictor? Do you live with your family?"

"No family. Just me."

"You have no family here, in this country?"

"No family *anywhere*."

"Oh…I'm very sorry. Hey, do you have some time to come inside for a little while? It's cold and you have no coat. I have mulled cider warming on the stove."

Wictor's face collapsed into sheer, unadulterated happiness. She could almost feel the hopeful warmth from his face, like embers from a fire.

"Sure."

She opened the door wider and Wictor took one step forward, then stopped. His right foot hovered, trembling, over the threshold, then he set it back down on the cement doorstep.

His face crumpled. "I can't," he said. "I…I got other packages."

"Are you sure?"

"Yes." He looked crushed but stuck stubbornly to his position. "Other packages."

"Okay. Well, thank you. Let me get you your holiday tip."

"*No tip!* You look in new box. Special Christmas promotion."

"Are you sure? Okay. I promise. Have a nice evening and Merry Christmas, Wictor."

She closed the door and sat down with the box on the sofa. In front of her, on the coffee table, the tiny tabletop tree was now leaning more than ever, overburdened with ornaments meant for a much larger tree.

Andy jumped up from the floor and plunked down next to his mother.

"Was that Wictor? What's in the box for dinner?"

"Let's see."

The dinner this time was composed of fixings and ingredients for roast turkey breast, stuffing, gravy, fresh cranberry sauce, and red potatoes.

As she pulled each item out of the box, she didn't see any promotional items wrapped in the familiar Red Onion packaging. She was disappointed, but then *at last*, she found it: a small box, nestled under the gourmet stuffing mix, wrapped in gold Christmas foil, and tied with a red ribbon.

It was strange that the little gold box was so small, Kristy thought. No cookies this time.

When she opened it, she saw why it was small, and pulled out a glittering item.

"*This* is *not* a promotion from the Red Onion marketing department!" she gasped. Beside her, Andy gasped also.

It was a sparkling ring in a heavy, platinum setting, with a large center diamond surrounded by smaller baguette stones. The setting was old-fashioned and ornate, and the stones didn't look like cubic zirconia.

"Wow! That looks like it cost a ton of money," exclaimed Andy.

"It does indeed. I can't accept this. Wictor meant well, but if this is genuine, he needs to keep it for himself. It looks like an heirloom. But how do I give it back without hurting his feelings?"

"Maybe you should call the Red Onion people?"

"You're right. I tried emailing them before and nothing happened. Tomorrow morning I'll call and get it all straightened out."

She put the little box in the top drawer of her bedroom dresser for safekeeping.

* * *

Kristy dropped Andy off at school and then drove back home. It took her almost an hour to find a customer service number for Red Onion; they did everything by chat and email. But she finally found it and called.

The woman on the other end of the phone had a heavy foreign accent and Kristy struggled to make herself understood.

"Your delivery boy—*man*—left an expensive gift in my Red Onion box and I can't keep it. Maybe you could explain it to him. I don't want to hurt his feelings."

"You have complaint about him?"

Kristy plowed on. "*No!* Not a complaint. Wictor. His

name is Wictor. He does the route in Antioch, California, near my house." She gave the customer service woman her address and phone number.

The sound of furious keyboarding assaulted Kristy's ears. Finally:

"Wictor. You mean *Viktor?* A-D-R-I-J-A N-A?"

"Yes, I believe that's him."

"He's not our delivery man now. Not active."

"That's *impossible*! I saw him only yesterday. He dropped off a package with turkey and cranberries."

More loud keyboarding.

"Your account was cancelled in September, Missus."

"But I've been getting Red Onion boxes three days a week since then from Wictor. I tried to tell you guys!"

"You make fun? His records show he's dead since September. Company tried to locate his family, no one found. His delivery van was hit by a truck. Is that all now, Missus?"

"*Dead!* But that's impossible! There must be some mistake!"

Click. The customer service agent hung up. She clearly thought Kristy was either crazy or a troll.

It couldn't be. It was crazy. But then, Kristy started to think, almost against her own will, about the things Wictor had done in the past few months, seeing them in a different light—

She pushed back her thoughts and switched to her phone's browser mode. There was one more thing she needed to do. She searched for the name Viktor Adrijana. She reasoned that not many people would have a name like that in Antioch.

Only a few hits came up. One was a small item in the

local news portal, *The East Bay Times*.

    ANTIOCH — A car accident near Lone Tree Way took the life of Viktor Adrijana, age 20, 2530 Pine Street. Adrijana was a delivery driver for an online food service provider. His employer is trying to locate his survivors. Those with any information about his family can contact our ombudsman department and it will forward the information on to his employer.

It was dated September twenty-seventh. The same week she'd been laid off. Just before she'd cancelled her Red Onion account.

Kristy felt her heart racing and her body seemed stiff and uncoordinated. It was impossible, there must have been a mistake. Damn! And yet—and *yet*—

It all fit. The fact that Wictor always wore the same clothes every time she saw him. His inability to walk across her threshold. The way he'd known about Andy's pirate costume.

And then Wictor had given her the diamond ring— he didn't need it, of course. It was something he wanted her to have. He had no family—he said so himself.

She looked at the clock on her phone. It would be several hours before she would have to pick up Andy at his school. There was a jeweler downtown that bought antique jewelry and did appraisals. She'd driven past it many times. Meyer's Prime Jewelry and Watches. She felt horribly guilty about it, but she wanted to know if the ring was genuine. She suspected it was something precious that had been in Wictor's family for generations.

"But I don't have anything to feel guilty about!" she protested to herself. "He *wanted* me to have it."

She had to cross Lone Tree Way to get to the jewelry store, and something stabbed at her heart as she thought of the accident. She remembered sadly what Wictor had said about his job; how much he was afraid of crazy, impatient drivers.

* * *

"Very fine quality," said the man at the desk at Meyer's, putting down his jeweler's loupe. "Yes, it's genuine. The jeweler's marks are not from this country. Eastern European, maybe? The setting is kind of Oriental. And it's old, maybe a hundred years old or more."

"Is it...is it worth a lot?"

"At a good auction, it would probably bring around twenty thousand dollars. I can buy it from you right now for sixteen." He gave a small cough. "I do have to make a profit."

Kristy didn't know how to answer. "It...it was a gift...from a friend," she said haltingly.

"Seventeen-five, and that's firm. Think about it. It's a standing offer—you can always come back."

"Okay."

Kristy drove back to her apartment in a daze. She crossed Lone Tree and thought again about Wictor and the accident. When she pulled under the carport in front of her apartment, she almost expected to see him standing at the top of the stairs leading to her door, smiling, thin and waiflike in his baseball shirt and Red Onion hat.

But no one was there.

She let herself in and placed the small gold box in the center of the dining table. Then she sat down in front of her laptop and began checking voicemail and emails. There were still a couple of hours left before the end of

Andy's school day.

Busy work would take her mind off of Wictor. She tried to focus on other things, but the thought of him was always there, lurking like a shadow in a cemetery. Almost worse than that was that she didn't have anybody she could talk to about Wictor or the ring; most people would call her crazy.

I've got to figure out what to do with this all by myself, she realized. *And I'm just an ordinary single mom who's barely more than a kid herself.* She'd always felt like the wolf was slavering on the other side of her front door, ever since Andy's dad had left her and Andy to fend for themselves.

Scrolling through her inbox, her mood lifted when she saw an email from Lorraine with the subject line *All Settled In.*

"Hi Kristy—I hope things are going okay. Just bought a house here, for exactly 1/3 (one-third!) of what I got for my old condo in Daly City. It's got a big back yard and plenty of gardening space. You and Andy can come visit anytime. The old owners left behind this big play structure in the yard with a cool treehouse at the top (hint hint)!"

The email included a photo of Lorraine standing in front of a small Craftsman-style house, elegantly restored, on an aggressively green lot. Kristy sighed wistfully, thinking of what it would be like to have a garden and a big treehouse for Andy to play in.

She turned back to her inbox.

There was another new email, from a woman at a company called BriteCore. She'd interviewed with them over Skype several times weeks ago, then forgotten all about them when they'd gone radio silent.

"Hi Kristy—Sorry it took so long to get back to you!

BriteCore is pleased to offer you the position of chief copy editor in our marketing department. As you know, this is a remote position that can be done from home or anywhere with an Internet connection..."

She reread it twice before the full impact set in. *A remote position! I can do it from anywhere! I don't have to live in Antioch anymore...I can live in Oregon! And all I need is a stake to get started with...*

A stake. Like seventeen thousand dollars. Suddenly, she knew why Wictor had left her the ring. Yes, seventeen thousand would make a nice stake with which to start a new life in a new city, a new state.

Knock. *Knock-knock.* Knock.

Wictor.

Kristy trembled as she pushed herself toward her front door. She was terrified, but she owed Wictor that much. Even though she now knew what he was. Even though it wasn't evening, and it wasn't even Red Onion day.

She opened the door, expecting to see Wictor's familiar face, beaming below the bill of his Red Onion hat, his arms holding out the familiar package.

There was nothing. She scanned the walkway below the stairs, and the hedges near the carport; no one was there.

Then her eye caught something sitting at the bottom of her feet, placed with care on her doorstep.

It was a Red Onion hat. She picked it up, instinctively knowing that she would never see Wictor again.

"Thank you, Wictor," she whispered, clutching the hat. "Best Christmas present I ever got."

The Boo Hag

"The best ghosts of America live in New England, but the most seductive ones live in the South, chiefly Louisiana."

McDermott had often heard Grayling open his lecture on Southern Gothic literature with those words. Something to do with the French, the old man would joke—the perfidious French, combined with the deep, wide, brown Mississippi river, whose sluggish muck obscured centuries of dark doings. McDermott thought it all a bit stereotypical and threadbare of Grayling to characterize the literature in such a way, but he never dared question it in the professor's hearing.

As clichéd as they were, Grayling's lectures prompted McDermott to pack up his draft dissertation, reference volumes, and notes, and book himself into a bed-and-breakfast establishment in New Orleans for a month, so that he could contemplate the old man's **pulchritudinous** Southern ghosts first-hand.

His narrow little four-story lodging house was more than two hundred years old; it had free Wi-Fi and was painted the most delightful shade of coral pink, with sugar white trim. It was on the quieter side of Frenchman's Street, six or seven blocks from the Quarter, insulated somewhat from the sound of the live jazz clubs by a stand of closely planted lavender crepe myrtle trees and an impressively spreading magnolia.

Surely, McDermott thought, *a street named after a Frenchman would be as good a place as any to start out looking for the city's seductive ghosts.* Having spent his first night in New Orleans drinking and snoozing in relative quiet, he walked toward Jackson Square the next day at ten o'clock in the morning. The humidity, rising off the huge, ever-dominating river, was already beginning its first stifling embrace of the random acts of humanity gathered in the Square. There were palm readers, charm sellers, and card readers set up around the base of General Jackson's rearing equestrian statue, most sitting behind little folding tables, partnered with molded plastic lawn chairs.

"Read your palm for twenty dollah, suh," called out a woman lazily, from behind one of the folding tables. She was younger than most of the others, with skin the color of cocoa powder mixed with vanilla ice cream, wide of eye and thin as a railroad spike. Really more of a girl than a woman.

"You don't look much like a gypsy," smiled McDermott, taking one of the white plastic lawn chairs. He was feeling generous with time and money; it was a June morning in the Deep South that had yet to turn unbearably muggy and sweaty, and he thought himself lucky, for the moment.

The girl didn't smile back. "Lines on your skin can be the same an' such the world round." She took his twenty and stuffed it into a Styrofoam cup full of other bills.

Her hands were soft and cool as she inspected his right palm. "Damn," she exclaimed softly. "You ain't got hardly no *lifeline*. So shallow it fades out here 'n there. Ain't easy to tell how long it is an' such."

McDermott shifted in the plastic molded chair. The seat of his khaki slacks was already starting to stick to the plastic with a bit of damp from the rising heat.

"Is that bad?"

"Ain't no tellin.' Could be bad, could be good. That's a lifeline for a man with a lotta buried notions and such. You don't do a whole lotta livin' on the top where people can see, know what I mean? And you gotta long, deep *headline*, running across, 'cuz you do 'most everything in yo' head, know what I mean?"

McDermott nodded. Her words were painfully true, more than he wanted to admit. Even though he was full of the inborn skepticism of a man made for scholarly pursuits.

"You a teacher?"

"College professor. Or will be soon."

"Damn." She turned back to his palm.

"This line's the *heartline*—it's all broken, not straight. That means you fall easily for any gal that's gotta sob story and a smile."

McDermott chuckled. "I haven't had a date in three years, though."

"Maybe not that kinda girl. Maybe a child? A little girl?"

It was past ten-thirty now, but he suddenly started to feel cold. The sweat of his khakis on the plastic seat even felt like a chill, a melted ice cube.

He drew back his hand as if burned.

"What little one?" he croaked. The girl regarded him critically, eyes growing wider, the whites expanding like the white of a frying egg. She seemed to be on the verge of saying something, but then thought better of it. Her face became a smooth brown mask, smiling and bland for the tourist dollars.

"You just gotta big heart for children. It's good to have a heart like that. That's what the ladies want for a man."

McDermott stood up awkwardly, knocking the flimsy chair on the pavement accidentally.

"I think my time is up. Thank you, Miss," he said somewhat stiffly.

He pulled out a couple of singles for a tip and stuffed them into the Styrofoam cup along with the twenty.

"Enjoy y'all's visit," she said. He turned away and took a few steps, only to feel a cool hand grabbing his arm from behind.

"I gotta tip for y'all. If you ever feel like something's ain't quite right where you at, put out a straw broom, or a checkered dishrag, or anything with a lotta little things to count. Lines, holes, li'l flowers, dots."

"Why?"

"Just remember, that 'n such. Hey missus, read your palm for twenty dollah?"

She'd already found another customer, and he decided to go back to Frenchman's Street, have a drink, and take advantage of the free Wi-Fi with his laptop.

He still had to get through that annotated book of short stories by Eudora Welty. Free Wi-Fi, air conditioning, and a little mini-bar filled with airplane cocktail bottles—suddenly, it all felt like a desperately needed lifeline. *No pun intended,* he mused.

* * *

"She couldn't have known about Sylvie," McDermott muttered to himself, looking up from the Welty book. "It was all just a vague guess. I said I didn't date much anymore, and she moved on to kids. A perceptive woman, full of shrewdness born of much observation of human nature, but nothing more."

Having solved that issue, he fished another tiny Mai-Tai flask out of the mini-bar and drank it straight from the bottle. It was evening now; the jazz clubs were starting up and the cheerfulness of the music was catching, even in its faint form.

He had come to New Orleans to prove to Grayling the similarities between New England Gothic literature and the Southern Gothic variety—that was roughly his dissertation subject. He had hoped to find something transcendent in New Orleans, beyond crumbling mansions, moss-draped trees and hoodoo priestesses selling charms.

But the trip to Jackson Square had been a validation for Grayling's point of view about Southern Gothic literature, he realized upon further reflection. There were people in New Orleans who seriously believed in the protective metaphysical properties of polka-dots, as if it were the most natural thing in the world. He had difficulty relating the idea to Hawthorne's *House of the Seven Gables*.

That reminded him; the polka-dots. Must be some sort of local legend. He emailed Grayling about it after first consulting a reference book on Southern folklore and coming up empty. Maybe he was looking in the wrong place—old Grayling would surely know. He tumbled into bed after drawing back the quilted coverlet—for the first time he was conscious of the pattern. Tiny sprigs of lilac in diagonal rows on a white background, hundreds of them. The other side of the coverlet was solid—a plain lavender quilting.

"I guess I am safe from ghosties and ghoulies as long

as I'm sleeping under this coverlet," he laughed softly, and then he was ashamed of himself, for letting that girl's nonsense remarks get to him.

Some hours later, having finished the Welty book and taken copious notes in a Word file on his laptop, he started on a biography of Erskine Caldwell, while snuggling under the lilac-sprigged coverlet. And then he fell deeply asleep, dreaming a dream that he would probably not remember in the morning.

He awoke before five, gasping for breath, believing—nonsensically, he later thought—that he couldn't breathe because there was something heavy sitting on his chest. And he'd kicked off the coverlet in the night, probably because the air conditioning had gone off at some point, for its motor lay silent now. The coverlet sprawled on the carpeted floor next to the bed, with the solid, lavender side up, most of the printed side pressed to the floor, with its lilac sprigs obscured.

Why am I so tired? I feel like an old man who's just climbed a dozen flights of stairs, he wondered in a grumpy mood. He put it down to the melatonin he took to help him sleep. The stuff made him groggy in the morning and stimulated some outrageous dreams that seemed hyper-real while he was having them.

He grabbed the coverlet and pulled it back up onto the bed, and dozed under it, exhausted, until it was time for breakfast. He then dragged himself to the little guest dining room on the first floor and poured coffee, hoping to revitalize. The coffee *did* make him feel somewhat human again, if not exactly ready to run a marathon, or even to stroll back to Jackson Square.

The landlady, Miz Faillie, was already in the dining

room, putting out clean napkins and filling sugar bowls. Her face was pink-on-pink, framed by graying ringlets; her bust was stuffed full and firm like a bolster on a chintz-covered couch.

She trilled at him in her tinkly Southern voice. "Gods and nightgowns! Is that you, Mr.—uh—Mr. McDermott? I hardly recognized you all. Not sleepin' 'speshually well, are you?"

"I slept well, mostly. I seem to be out of breath, but maybe it's the humidity that's affecting me. We don't have this steam bath climate in Boston, of course."

"Ah, of course."

"Miz Faillie? I went down to Jackson Square yesterday and had my palm read by one of the ladies there."

Miz Faillie made another tinkly little laugh. "Never would've 'spected it of someone like you."

"I just felt like doing something touristy. Believe me, I'm not likely to repeat it." McDermott related his experience from the previous morning, leaving out the comments about the children, but covering everything else.

"Is there some old folk custom about counting little things to keep bad spirits away? Polka dots and chintz nosegays?"

Miz Faillie wrinkled her pewter brows in thought. "Well, there's the Boo Hag, but that's in the Carolinas. And countin' li'l things, so Ah've heard, is for the *spirits*, not for people. Keeps 'em busy and then they can't attack a body. But that's in the Carolinas, not in Louisiana. We're likely to have different spirits in *Louisiana*."

"Maybe my fortune teller was from the Carolinas, originally?"

"Yay-ess, that could be," she replied in a doubtful

tone. "But we don't get Boo Hags in Louisiana, so I don't trifle about it." She was serenely confident, as if she believed in spirits fully, but only those that were native to the Pelican State.

"Oh, I understand," murmured McDermott in a diplomatic tone. "Thanks for your helpfulness."

"What are you fixin' to do today, young man?"

"I plan to hire a car and drive up to Natchitoches Parish to see a museum there. But it's too far to make the trip all in one day, so I'll be staying the night over and driving back in the morning."

"Museum? What museum in Nak-tish?"

"It's a museum about a late 19th Century author named Kate Chopin. She lived there."

"Oh yes, we get a lot of folks during the annual New Orleans literary festival and that Shope-Ann woman is mentioned sometimes. Not really sure what it is that she wrote, but if you get a chance, be sure to visit the Alligator Park at the oxbow lake. Those are some amazin' snappers."

McDermott believed that Miz Faillie's taste in writing extended more to scripted chatter from the Home Shopping Channel and afternoon soap operas; he had heard them a couple of times through the door of her office/apartment on the first floor. He had also briefly peeked into the office when the door was left ajar and was amused—and somewhat alarmed—to see a row of stuffed cats lined up on the floor in front of a big mahogany desk, each with a small bowl of milk set before it. Upon poking his head in further, he realized they were not toys—they were *taxidermy*. He wondered if he could find a way to work that into his dissertation.

She smiled and returned to her dining room duties,

while McDermott helped himself to scrambled eggs and bacon from the chafing dish on the sideboard. He loaded up his plate, thinking he needed the protein, and drank two more cups of coffee. Feeling refreshed, he went back to his room and checked his email for Grayling's reply.

"It's an old folk belief from the Gullah people on the islands off the coast of South Carolina. Other ethnic groups picked it up and embroidered it with their own takes. Probably originated from West Africa. Called a Boo Hag," Grayling's email began. *"It's a half-spirit of a departed person who isn't at peace. The soul-half goes to the afterlife, but the spirit-half separates and stays in this world to torment the living."*

"Yes, my temporary landlady told me what she knew about it," McDermott typed in reply. *"But what exactly does it do to 'torment' the living, may I ask?"*

He also outlined his trip to Natchitoches and hit "send" back to Grayling. McDermott then packed the laptop in its carrying case and filled his carry-on with a change of clothes, and took a taxi to the car rental place to start his journey to Natchitoches.

* * *

"Burned!" McDermott muttered to himself. "The damned thing's burned. And that crazy old bat Faillie didn't even tell me!"

Thirty minutes earlier, he'd arrived in town and asked the way to Kate Chopin's Bayou Folk Museum, only to be told that the building and everything inside had burned down completely a dozen years before. Now he was sitting in a bar across the street from the B&B he'd booked himself into, at a bit before two in the afternoon.

Five hours' drive from New Orleans for nothing! Why hadn't he looked it up previously on the Internet? He had just assumed that it would be right there, where Grayling had once told him it would be.

He signaled for another bourbon and water from the bartender to drown out his feelings of foolishness and embarrassment. The table he sat at looked out onto the street. McDermott watched the locals drift by as if they had all the time in the world—so different from the way people moved in Boston.

Then he saw her: the child. Small, red-haired, wearing a violet corduroy or velvet jumper over a thin white tee shirt. She seemed to be alone, standing in the middle of the sidewalk on the other side of the street, in front of his B&B. Who on earth would leave a child that small alone on a busy street? She couldn't be more than three years, the same age as Sylvie...and she reminded him so very, very much of how Sylvie had looked on that last day, except that Sylvie had shiny black hair, not red. Not especially like this most unusual red—red as a firetruck, almost. He had seen adult women with obviously dyed hair wearing that shade, but never a child. It was so odd. So very like Sylvie, except for the hair. Sylvie in the purple jumper, made of some plushy material, on that terrible day in the park.

The red-haired girl was standing still as a mausoleum on the sidewalk, as if held in place by unseen roots. But then she was gone suddenly—*as if something had pulled her straight up* into a large magnolia tree, and she disappeared into the thick, leathery leaves. No one on the street seemed to have noticed anything astray. McDermott clenched his eyes shut for several seconds, then opened them again. The street looked as it did before he'd noticed the strange child.

He reasoned it was an illusion, born of equal parts of John Barleycorn and Grayling's florid, descriptive prose from the email. "*A half-spirit of the departed…*" he recalled from his mentor's words.

Moira had warned him about Grayling once.

"That man lives in your head in a very unhealthy way," she'd exclaimed. "Why d'ya let him?"

He winced at the memory. Poor dear Moira: she might have been his wife if fate hadn't intervened with its very nasty and dirty thumb on the scale of his life. Moira would have made the perfect academic wife and little Sylvie could have charmed the pants off anyone in the department, even Grayling.

It was hard to explain the great man to anyone who didn't know Grayling well. The vast stores of a peculiarly pugnacious type of knowledge, the constant challenging and hectoring on points of intellect, no matter how obscure or small; the Pulitzer Prize, the reviewer slot at the *New York Times' Review of Books*, and the fortnightly column at *The New Yorker*. Grayling was intimidating as hell, and yet, somehow, the great man had chosen McDermott, a humble working-class orphan, as his protégé.

The pressure of living up to Grayling's expectations had gotten to him three years ago, when he and Moira and dear little Sylvie lived together, and they were happy after a fashion, except for the ever-present anxiety caused by Grayling's exacting standards.

But then there was that final Saturday morning in the Commons, when Moira left him with Sylvie, while she went to hunt for hotdogs and lemonade. He had been reading O'Connor's *Wise Blood* and making copious notes, as he always did when reading for purpose, glancing up every now and then at three-year-old Sylvie, playing in the sand box, solemnly and with a great sense of purpose, sifting sand back and forth between two plastic pails. He had noticed idly that the sandbox was close to a bike trail and cyclists would occasionally pedal by, dressed in frozen sherbet hues of yellow, lime, or raspberry Lycra. He had never thought it through enough, however, to sense anything wrong.

Everything was over in a matter of less than a minute; little Sylvie toddling onto the bike path, the cyclist whizzing along in a shiny yellow and lime-colored blur, unable to stop, and Sylvie's tiny purple-clad body flying through the air, instantly dead from landing on her head—*she had been far from the track the last time he had looked!*—and Moira dropping the hot dog tray and running toward the nightmarish scene.

He clenched his eyes together, tightly, as if to blot out the painful rumination. It was time to pay his tab and leave.

He thought he'd walk around the Old Town of Natchitoches with its elegant French colonial architecture, before checking in to the B&B. There was an indie bookstore with a Chopin display in the front window; the barkeep had also told him about a famous dry goods store, still in business, that was so old Kate Chopin had actually shopped there in her day.

At the bookstore, McDermott bought a guide about places in Natchitoches Parish associated with Chopin, and then he found the ramshackle and decidedly old-fashioned dry goods store. He puttered through rows of cast iron skillets and Dutch ovens, tablecloths and towels, and baskets of French-milled soap.

He supposed he should buy something for Grayling's daughter, Doreen, who kept house for the widowed professor. He felt sorry for her, as she also acted as a kind of secretary to the great man—a thankless task if there ever was one. Grayling would think it brown-nosing to favor Doreen with a gift, but McDermott felt he owed her for certain favors. Maybe something pretty would be appreciated.

His eye caught a linen tablecloth set with eight napkins. There was a toile pattern on the tablecloth and napkins, in light magenta on a cream background, of scenes from the 19th Century —women in bonnets, horses and carriages, mansions with Greek columns—and the vignettes danced in little clumps all over the fabric. The set didn't look like something Doreen could just order up from Amazon—it was a bit more special than that.

"Is this made locally?" he asked the clerk at the cash register.

"Why yes, after a fashion. That's an old, old linen pattern that's made at a textile mill down near Shreveport, and some local ladies sew them up!"

"How interesting." He had the set gift-wrapped after the clerk rang it up.

It was well past three when he reached the B&B, freely sweating from the heat and humidity. This B&B wasn't as charming as the coral stucco one on Frenchman's Street in New Orleans, but it was serviceable. He checked in at the manager's office, still clutching his packages, the book and the gift-wrapped toile tablecloth with napkins.

He tried not to stare. McDermott had expected another fluffy, pink-faced woman of a certain age, like Miz

Faillie back in New Orleans. But no, the manager was a man and a dwarf, middle-aged and resentful looking, with shocking red hair.

McDermott at once began to wonder if the girl he saw earlier was a relative of the dwarf, considering the similarities with the hair. Obviously, the way she disappeared was an illusion, born of rye and massive internal guilt, but the girl herself…the girl could possibly have been real after all—and maybe not actually a child.

He realized with flushed cheeks that he'd stared at the manager more than he intended.

"I run the place with my sister, Lizzie. She's *little* too," said the manager, who introduced himself as Darcy Quinn. "Mother was fond of *Pride and Prejudice*. That's how I got my first name. You know Jane Austen?"

"Yes. I think I saw your sister earlier as a matter of fact. Was she wearing a plushy purple dress today?"

"I dunno. I never take much notice of women's dresses, myself. I'll let ya know when I see her."

"All right." McDermott made his way to his room on the second floor. There was a solid peach-colored coverlet—no lilac sprigs in sight—pale ecru walls, and plain white curtains over blinds. Free Wi-Fi here too, though.

He set up his laptop on the small table near the front window and logged on to read his email. He scrolled through all messages until he came across Grayling's latest reply. THE BOO HAG: WHAT IT DOES read the subject line.

"According to many legends, the Boo Hag attacks when the subject is asleep. It sits on the subject's chest and sticks its mouth on the subject's mouth and sucks out the breath until the subject

suffocates. The Boo Hag can be distracted from its task but can't be fought any other way." Grayling included a link to an American Folklore site section dealing with the traditions of the Boo Hag. McDermott skimmed it and noted with a curious sense of relief that some of the traditions around the specter seemed naive and almost absurd.

"Put out a dish towel with a pattern for it to count... Put out a big hairbrush with lots of bristles." In some tellings, the Boo Hag was also supposed to be fire engine red without skin, only blood and muscle, because it sometimes "borrowed" its victim's skin. It was also often   depicted as having wild red hair and pointed teeth.

McDermott smiled to himself wryly at the outlandish descriptions of the Boo Hag. "And anyway," he said aloud, "I've got it on good authority from Miz Faillie that Boo Hags don't exist in Louisiana, only in the Carolinas."

He emailed Grayling back that it was a good trip except for the museum not existing anymore, but the photography book about Chopin's old haunts seemed a good substitute. And then he settled down to write more notes.

That was the last thing he remembered before the...*thing*...attacked him. He'd somehow lain his head down sideways on the table and was snoring with his right cheek pressed against the tabletop. He couldn't breathe. The thing had grabbed him from behind and twisted his head up from the table with horny claws and was pressing a fetid maw against his mouth and nose.

He struggled to gain consciousness while grabbing instinctively at the creature. It seemed to not have a corporeal form; his hands felt mush, even as the thing began to suck the breath from his mouth and nose. He flailed and thrashed, trying to get a hold on his tormentor.

A rush of half-realized things ran through his mind, a jumble of images and impressions of Sylvie, Moira in the park, Grayling, even poor, spinsterish Doreen. The frantic intrusions of irrelevant memories in the midst of danger—so foolish and so human.

It's going to kill me. I'm going to die tonight, in this strange room and town, so far from home. He struggled with desperate resolve, but the thing gripped him with iron, scaly talons of black and scarlet. There was no way to escape its grip. In between the awful sucking sounds the thing made a clicking-clacking noise, and McDermott was reminded of those twin Lucite balls on strings that children smack together as a game.

"*The most seductive ghosts live in the South,*" he imagined Grayling intoning in his pretentious Harvard accent, while McDermott suffocated, his lungs straining for air. What would the red-haired dwarf and his sister think of him when they found him? What would Grayling think? Or Doreen?

He had a sharp inspiration at the thought of Doreen, and he saw it as his only chance, crazy as it was. He worked his left arm out from where it was pinned under his chest by the thing, and he grabbed wildly around on the table until he found it: the package with the toile tablecloth and napkins from the famous dry goods store. He clawed the gift wrap off desperately, grateful that the girl at the store had done a slapdash job with the Scotch tape. And then he worked part of the box lid off and grabbed a napkin, unfurled it and tossed it away into the air. The cloth made no sound when it hit the floor. Perhaps the thing didn't see it? But then there was a loosening of the talon-hard grip and a pull-back from the suck-suck-sucking…and McDermott grabbed another napkin and tossed it in the air behind him. Which made the thing loosen its grip in total, and squat down to examine the two patches of linen with the little clumps of scenery and charming figures repeated over and over again.

McDermott was free. He could finally see the scarlet-skinned and wildly red-haired creature in the dim, small light of the table lamp, crouched over the two napkins, stabbing the patterns with one striped talon, used almost like a pointer finger. The long, red hair was streaming over its back and its tattered and moldy purple rag of a corduroy tunic.

The thing seemed oblivious to McDermott now. But he felt barely alive and ready to pass out, gasping for breaths that couldn't come fast enough. With his final strength, he threw the tablecloth and the rest of the napkins on the floor, and then he swirled into the darkness, falling from the chair onto the carpet, only a few feet from the thing.

He awoke to someone shaking him by the shoulder. He started violently: were the talons back? But it was only the "little person," Mr. Quinn. "You were hollerin' to beat the band there just now, feller—I used the passkey to get in and see if you were all right. You a big drinker there?"

McDermott pulled himself up. It was still dark, and the dim table lamp shone a weakly golden light on the little man's face.

"Sometimes," McDermott admitted. "But I fell asleep without drinking anything, at least not since two o'clock in the afternoon."

"Musta been havin' a whale of a nightmare. Ya shore did wreck up this room!"

McDermott shuddered. "I'm not well, maybe I overtired myself yesterday. I need to rest up for a while." He felt—in a sheepish way—that he would sleep soundly as long as the tablecloth and napkins were visible on the floor or the bed.

"All right. But if you're here past noon when day comes, I gotta charge y'all for an extra day."

"It's okay. Can you give me a hand up?"

He slept far into the day, regaining a little of his strength by dinnertime. He'd spread out the toile tablecloth carefully on top of his peach bedspread and slept under it, just in case. Was it all just a dream, as the dwarf had said? He often had even more realistic nightmares under the influence of melatonin. His head felt befuddled, and he couldn't decide; but there was one thing for sure, whatever was happening, it had something to do with Sylvie.

When he arrived in New Orleans the next day after the return five-hour drive, he boxed up the tablecloth and napkins, intending to leave them as a gift for Miz Faillie when he checked out. There was no way to remove the painful associations the linen set held for him now, and if he gave it to Doreen as originally planned, she would be sure to drag it out the next time he had dinner at Grayling's. He'd get Doreen some French perfume in the Quarter instead. Feeling grimly mischievous, he attached a note to the boxed set that read, *"Dear Miz Faillie, I've learned that some Carolina ghosts can indeed show up in the noble state of Louisiana. Take care."* He almost smiled when he pictured her at her big mahogany desk, reading the note, just after filling up the milk bowls for her taxidermy cats.

McDermott stayed in New Orleans for two more weeks, blessedly uneventful. By the time he was checking his luggage at Louis Armstrong International for the flight back to Boston, he almost felt new again. His trip had turned out successful after all, and he had a lot of new ideas and notes, which he couldn't wait to work into his dissertation. He even jauntily hummed *What a Wonderful World* as he filled out his forms. No more thoughts of, or "sightings" of the supposed Boo Hag, including during a two-day trip to Welty's house in Jackson, Mississippi. The only thing that marred the latter part of his trip was a small spat with Sairy, the chambermaid at Miz Faillie's, when she removed the lilac-sprigged coverlet for cleaning and replaced it with a plain white one. He'd insisted she put it back immediately, but when she said it was in the wash, he made her find another coverlet with a busy floral pattern on it. He was a bit embarrassed, thinking of his behavior with Sairy, but Miz Faillie didn't say anything when he checked out, and he considered the matter closed. He made sure to leave an extra-large tip for the maid on the dresser top.

McDermott was sitting in the terminal at Louis Armstrong, waiting to board, when something made him look up from his travel paperback (a Ludlum title—pure escapism after all the heavy reading on Southern Gothic authors) and turn his eye toward a group of chattering children. Girl Scouts, perhaps? They were all girls and all wearing uniforms of some sort, except for a much younger child a few of the girls were crowded around, laughing with and cooing over, the way older girls do with a little one. A much smaller girl, about three or four, with bright red hair.

With a sense of dread, McDermott was sure the child

was wearing a plushy purple jumper, even though he couldn't see it from his vantage point. He imagined with a sick thud in his chest that she had red hair instead of black because she was only a half-spirit—half-Sylvie, half-red-haired-monster.

The little girl was making the other girls laugh by imitating with her hands the motion of an eggbeater. Round and round. No, not an eggbeater, he realized with growing horror—a *bicycle*. A horrible, fast-moving bicycle, round and round. McDermott stood up and took a couple of steps toward the girls—and then he stopped.

"Don't go there!" something warned him in very definite tones. He sat down again and opened his Ludlum, although he couldn't read the print at all, due to his agitated state. After a few moments, he looked up and saw that the girls were quiet. The smaller child with the red hair was gone.

On the plane, the stewardess asked if he needed a blanket for the flight. "No, I've got my own," he said, pulling a new throw out of his carry-on satchel. It was black, covered in tiny white polka-dots. McDermott had purchased it in New Orleans the day before while buying Doreen's perfume. Before him— he suspected—lay years, perhaps decades, of traveling and living with things stamped with polka dots and flower sprigs and little squiggles. It would be his small penance for Sylvie. Maybe, it would also someday be his redemption—after there was enough looking behind him and counting polka-dots— that Sylvie might rest.

He balanced his head on the pillow the stewardess gave him, snuggled under the throw, and slept like a tombstone most of the way home to Boston.

Regeneration Wood

"The house is brand new; there is no possibility that it could be haunted," Jen told Madame Blavashevsky. "Me, Daniel, and our little Jack are the first-ever occupants. So, you see, our house can't have any history to it. It's even shot through and through with that 'new' smell—fresh paint, caulking paste, wood sealant, carpet fibers! And it's surrounded by other equally new houses, rows and rows of them, in that recent development called Pine Breeze."

When the "disturbances" began, she'd searched for every bit of information about the land that Pine Breeze was built upon, uncovering nothing. No ancient Indian burial grounds (take that—Stephen King!). No workmen killed on site in a construction accident. No old cemetery headstones moved with the bodies left behind (take that—Steven Spielberg!). No swampy sinkholes allegedly habituated by slimy alien creatures or ghostly transparent spirits. But the disturbances were undeniable. Strange sounds emanating from the floorboards, missing small items, fuzzy images reflected in mirrors.

Which is why she decided to consult Marya "Call Me Madame" Blavashevsky, a spiritualist who wore fake gypsy scarves with copious jet beads, and, incongruously, a pair of aviator-style eyeglasses that became passé in the late 90s.

"My dear girl," counseled Madame, "a poltergeist or malevolent spirit can attach itself to a person, not a house, and follow them from place to place."

"Lovely," said Jen. "And yet, neither I nor Daniel

have ever had any spectral experiences in our whole lives, until now. Never. It would be a very new poltergeist indeed! Like from two weeks ago. And Jack is only 18 months and the most cheerful and contented toddler you've ever seen, so I don't think it's stuck on him. Since we moved in, he does keep talking about something called 'Bobo,' which we think is one of his stuffed animals, but that's it."

Madame shrugged. "One never knows when or where one picks them up. I'm having a two-for-one special on seances right now, if you're interested."

"I'll take a pass, for now." Jen had seen enough horror movies to be wary of seances held in potentially haunted houses.

The rest of the day was uneventful after Jen left Madame's house. She put little Jack down to sleep after dinner, and then she and Daniel huddled together on the couch in their brand new family room, watching a family movie on Netflix.

"Anything but horror," she'd stipulated, as they scrolled through the listings.

The family movie was dull but relaxing. Jen could feel her eyelids droop and a little doze come on at intervals. Daniel nudged her awake several times.

"Honey, you're missing all the important parts!"

"Sorry, dear. Had a rough day of work, and then I went to that appointment about the sewer pipes." Thinking Daniel would laugh about it, she'd lied that Madame was a specialist who could advise them if the strange sounds they'd been hearing were due to noisy sewer pipes.

"And what did the sewer specialist say, by the way? You didn't tell me?"

"Nothing useful. And now look, that couple in the movie are having another baby. Wouldn't it be nice to have a little brother or sister for Jack?" Jen had never wanted Jack to be an only child, but circumstances were tricky. Daniel sighed. "We've been over and over it. It's dangerous for you to have another one. The doctor said so."

"We could adopt," she said stubbornly. "Or take in a foster child."

"You've got your hands full with Jack and your job," Daniel said crossly. "Imagine wanting more craziness in this household. And we can barely afford to keep ourselves afloat, what with the mortgage on the house."

Jen didn't answer. She bolted upward in a rigid, sudden move. It was dark in the family room; they usually kept only a single lamp on while watching television. But in the dim light, the shadowy form lying on the loveseat directly opposite the couch looked like the body of a small child, stretched out with its arms seemingly crossed over the chest, and the head held upright on one arm of the seat.

"Daniel. There's…it looks like there's a kid lying on the loveseat. There!" she stammered, pointing at the seat, stifling the urge to scream.

"I-I think I see it. Maybe I'm imagining it, but something *smells* dead," whispered Daniel, blocking his nose with his palm. He stood up then and grabbed the fireplace poker from its holder.

"What? You're going to go look at it?"

"Yes. I have to. Stay where you are."

Daniel took a few steps toward the loveseat, poker raised, then stopped. The dark form was moving. Jen swallowed a small cry as she stared, terrified, at what was happening.

The small figure slowly sat up, swung its feet to the ground, stood and ran away in a little pattering motion. Jen heard the pattering noise move across the dining room and then into the hall, where it became indistinct and disappeared.

Daniel turned toward her, wearing his familiar "what the fuck?" face, times two. "A little kid," he said to Jen in a cracked voice, "laid out as if in a coffin or on a slab. Clear as day."

"Did—did—you hear the footsteps going into the dining room? And then toward the hallway?"

Daniel swallowed hard and nodded. "Yes."

"What are we going to do? We can't move out! We've just moved in!"

"There must be some logical explanation, Jen. There *must* be…"

All of a sudden, he was interrupted by a piercing howl from down the hall, and they both realized that Jack was awake and frightened of something.

Jen bolted to the child's bedroom, with Daniel following closely. She flipped on the light and grabbed the screaming toddler out of his crib. His little face was red, and he was breathing quickly between ear-splitting howls. Jen walked him out of the room, bouncing him gently on her hip, soothing him with soft words of comfort. Terse and white-faced, Daniel said he would stay behind and search Jack's room for any sign of a disturbance.

Jen took the squalling toddler into her and Daniel's room and rocked him until he quieted and went to sleep. She was lying on her side next to him, stroking his wispy blonde hair, when Daniel came into the room, looking grim. He was holding a length of plastic or vinyl tubing, which looked like a narrower version of a garden hose.

"I found this coiled up on the floor near Jack's crib," he said grimly, thrusting it toward Jen. "I searched high and low in his room—this is the only unusual item I came across. Do you recognize it?"

The tubing was old and had strange discolorations coating the inside of it.

"Ooohhh, get that thing away from me. I've never seen it before in my life! It's nasty looking, isn't it?" She shuddered. "Can't imagine what it's used for, or how it got into Jack's room. Do you think it was left by…the ghost?"

"Ghost, ghost!" he cried in frustration. "Are we really at the point where we think we have a ghost? I can't accept that—it's ridiculous!"

"Shhh! You'll wake the baby! After tonight, can we say we *don't* have a ghost? The noises under the floors. The missing objects. And now, an actual dead child on our loveseat! You saw it—you heard it. One thing's for certain—the ghost or ghosts are not just appearing to us— they're after Jack, too!" Jen's voice rose and tears squeezed out of the corners of her eyes.

There was this apparition, the other things, and then the mirrors! Her mirrors occasionally showed fuzzy images of indistinct objects, which crept up on the gazer when least expected. She often thought the images looked like some kind of laboratory. At other times, they resembled a type of machinery, with a lot of old-fashioned brass and chrome. There were also noises that seemed to be coming from the floor: a kind of grinding at times, then an annoying, high-pitched whirring sound, and intermittently, a crying, homeless-kitten noise that tore at Jen's heart.

"Okay, okay, calm down. He can sleep with us

tonight in our bed and tomorrow, I'll move his crib into our room until we figure out what's going on."

Jen felt a little mollified. "Okay. Go turn off the television—and take that tube *thing* out of my sight too. I don't feel like finishing that movie tonight—or ever."

* * *

Jen was relieved that Jack seemed no worse for wear in the morning. He was his old cheerful self as she bundled him up and dropped him off at his daycare. On the way home, she stopped for a soy latte at Starbucks, and lingered at a table in the corner, delaying the inevitable chore of returning home. She worked part-time managing a website that sold customized T-shirts online. She knew she had a lot to do before she picked up Jack at 2 p.m., but still, she dawdled, ordering another latte and a muffin she didn't need to eat.

I just can't go and face the loveseat, the mirrors and everything else, she thought, tearing the paper wrap off the muffin and biting a chunk from it.

"Lost in thought?" interrupted a woman leaning over Jen's table, speaking in a rushed sequence of vowels and consonants. "Fancy meeting you here. I mean, it's a bit out of the way from the neighborhood, isn't it? There's a closer Starbucks on Jermaine Street, three blocks from the Clara Barton Elementary School."

Jen shook off her thoughts and focused on a well-packed woman in her late 30s, with a mass of copper corkscrew curls, periwinkle eyes, and blotches of ginger freckles on her face and the backs of her hands. She was holding a cardboard cup of hot tea and a couple of madeleines.

"Uh, hullo? Have we met?"

"Diane St. Benedict. I live three doors down from you in Pine Breeze. We met at the neighborhood mixer last week. I work part-time for the homeowners' association. Otherwise, I'm mom to two girls—a fifth-grader who goes to Clara Barton and a senior at Pinevale High. My senior will be going off to college in the fall." Diane's aggressively cheerful face took on a sudden look of sadness as she mentioned her college-bound child, and then it was gone.

"Oh. Of course. I'm afraid I'm not good company today."

"Mind if I sit?" Diane took a chair without bothering to hear a reply. "You look very upset about something. I'm sorry, can I help? Is it the terrible thing that happened with Mr. Wilkinson? Are you having second thoughts about Pine Breeze?"

"What? Wilkinson? I don't know any Wilkinsons."

"You haven't heard? Seriously?"

"Nothing rings a bell."

"He lived on Magnolia Street in Pine Breeze. A newbie, only arrived a week before you guys did. Single guy in his late fifties. Committed suicide this morning."

"How awful!"

Diane took a sip of her tea and stuffed a madeleine in her mouth. She used a few moments to chew and then said, "Isn't it? He obviously had mental health issues. Between the two of us, he complained several times about his house to the association. Said there were strange sounds coming from the floorboards and thought something was in them. He seemed rather frightened."

"Oh, no!" Jen knocked over her latte cup and then

tried to mop it up with an inadequate napkin. "Oh, sorry—I'm so clumsy," she said, as the frothy liquid spread all over the table.

Diane jumped up and grabbed a bunch of napkins from the counter, and returned with them to help clean up the spill. "My goodness, what a mess. Did I bring up some bad memories, hon? I'm sorry if I did. I didn't realize the news of Mr. Wilkinson's hanging himself would be so upsetting. I should really learn to watch my big motormouth."

"It's okay," mumbled Jen, standing up and gathering her purse and keys. "I'm sorry, but I really have to go. I work remotely and I've got a lot of orders to process. Bye-bye, Diane."

"Can we do lunch sometime?" Diane called after her.

* * *

Something in the floorboards! Jen was almost relieved as she pulled into her garage. "We're not the only ones who've noticed it!" she told herself. But what was the problem with the floorboards? They were only slats of wood.

She walked into the house from the garage. As she did, she noticed that Daniel had left the length of tubing he found in Jack's room on the credenza near the door. Gingerly she picked it up and took it with her into the living room.

It bears closer inspection, she thought, feeling a bit nauseous. She sat on the living room sofa with the tubing, half expecting to see a body materialize on the easy chair opposite her seat. Or on the coffee table. But there was nothing. The living room, at least, seemed safe. And for once she was glad she'd given in to Daniel and allowed carpet in the living room instead of hardwood floors…which were everywhere else in the house.

She examined the tubing, and found a tiny, stamped logo at one end, with the lettering almost worn off. Jen retrieved a magnifying glass from her sewing kit and applied it to the lettering. "Scargill Bereavement Supplies, Ltd. Columbus, Oh. Est. 1904."

What on earth were "bereavement supplies"? Jen rubbed her temples in confusion. *Consult Dr. Google*, fluttered a voice in her head.

She pulled her smartphone out of her purse and googled Scargill Bereavement Supplies. To her surprise, a website of that name came up in the search. She clicked on the link and started to read.

Mortuary supplies! Scargill supplied equipment for funeral homes and morgues. Their motto was, "Sympathy is our business—your loss is our pain."

"Catchy," Jen mused aloud. "Really rolls off the tongue. And the award for Worst Advertising Slogan in the World goes to…Scargill Bereavement Supplies."

Jen felt slightly sick as she scrolled through Scargill's product line. Then she saw it—a simple length of tubing the same size as the one in her lap.

"Tough and reliable hose for use with an arterial tube. Easy clean and long-lasting .1/2-inch diameter."

For use with an arterial tube…

She searched for "arterial tube" on the site, although she already had a more-than-faint inkling of what it was. Up came a diagram showing the metal arterial tube attached on one end to a long vinyl hose, which led to a sink with a large drain.

We recommend the ½ inch hose for fastest draining of bodily fluids.

Jen cried out and pushed the hose off her lap. *The brown discolorations*, she thought, feeling as if she wanted to vomit, *the brown discolorations!*

After a few minutes of shock, she came back to herself and started thinking. The ghost had something to do with a morgue or a funeral home. It all fit. The body laid out on the loveseat, the "laboratory" images in the mirrors, the grinding sounds coming from the floor—and now this. An actual material object with a sinister connection. Jen shivered.

But what was the connection to Pine Breeze? There was never a mortuary or morgue situated on any part of Pine Breeze. She'd checked and all of the development was built on virgin land, carved out of the hills. There were still deer, coyotes, and mountain lions living on the ridge above the streets, houses, and green belts of Pine Breeze.

Bzzzzzzzzz.

It was her phone, flashing the name of Diane St. Benedict as the caller. Jen found to her surprise that she wanted to talk to Diane, whom she'd found pushy and annoying earlier at the coffee shop. It occurred to her that Diane, as an employee of the homeowner's association, probably knew more things about Pine Breeze than Jen could look up on her own. Plus, she was clearly a busybody, and doubtless, made it her business to know everyone else's.

"Hello? Jennifer? I hope I'm not keeping you from processing your orders! Hope you don't mind, but I got your number from the association. I just wanted to call and make sure you were okay. You seemed awfully upset at Starbucks this morning, about poor Mr. Wilkinson."

"Diane, thank you for calling. Yes, it was a bit of a shock to hear about the man who hung himself, right in his house on Magnolia Street. I push my little one in his stroller up and down Magnolia Street all the time. But I'm fine now."

"Are you sure? Nothing I can do for you?"

Jen took a deep breath. She wasn't sure how much information she wanted to trust Diane with.

"Well, now that you mention it, I have to confess. We've been having trouble with our floors, too. Strange noises seem to be coming from them. It's probably just the settling of the house, but sometimes it gets awfully spooky."

"Really? I hope it's not turning you off of Pine Breeze—it's a great place for kids."

"No, no, it's not that. I'm wondering if you knew anything special about the hardwood floors they put in?"

"Special? I don't know. Unless it's the greenbuilding stuff, but that's everything, not just the floors."

"Greenbuilding?"

"Didn't you read the brochure? Everything about Pine Breeze is as environmentally friendly as possible. Natural insulation instead of synthetic, double-paned windows, skylights for extra natural light, optional solar roof, and reclaimed wooden floors."

Jen's heart fluttered.

"Reclaimed wood? What do you mean?"

"You know—from a company that buys old wood from buildings that are going down, restores it, and sells it as flooring to new construction projects. All of the houses in Pine Breeze have reclaimed hardwood floors—at least, for the people who picked hardwood instead of wall-to-wall carpet. Which is most of us."

A couple of odd thumping noises came from the dining room that connected to the living room, and Jen shuddered. She pounced on Diane's comments. "Do you know the name of the company that supplies the reclaimed wood?"

"I can tell you in just a second… Let's see, it's in my contact list on my phone… Here it is! Regeneration Wood. I'll text you the contact info if you want."

"Yes, please."

"Done. So, what are you gonna talk about with Regeneration Wood? Just curious."

"I'm interested in knowing where the reclaimed wood in my floors came from. Maybe there's some kind of mold or beetles in it that's causing these weird noises, and they've dealt with this before."

* * *

The salesman's office at Regeneration Wood was decorated with slabs and chunks of different wood samples. They were mounted on wall plaques or impaled on iron stands. The salesman twisted a chunk of some tigery-looking square of wood around in his hands while absent-mindedly listening to Jennifer.

"I'm interested in the sources of your reclaimed wood," she began. "Specifically, the wood that was used for the houses in Pine Breeze."

"May I ask why you need this information?"

"It's a school project," she lied. "For my nephew.

He's doing something on greenbuilding for his environmental studies class."

"Ah, I see. Well, the Pine Breeze wood was locally sourced. Some of it came from old barns from the farming days of Pinevale. Some of it came from Old Town Pinevale, when the city tore down that block of crumbling Victorian buildings for the new convention center about five years ago."

"Oh, I remember that. There was some protest about an old hotel."

"The Grand Continental. Quite the showplace in its day. Had a checkered past. When the grand hotel era passed, the bottom two floors became a mortuary, and the top two floors were used for warehouse space. Then it fell empty for quite a while, before it was demolished."

Jen drew a sharp breath. "The reclaimed wood from the mortuary? It was used for Pine Breeze houses?"

"All of the wood from what was once the Grand Continental. It's very high-quality, old-growth oak with an antique wormy patina. The unique blend of colors is due to a reactive stain we apply that brings out the natural oxidation in the wood. It's then kiln-dried, tongue-and-groove machined, and clear-coated."

"Is there any way of knowing which houses got the wood from the floors used as a mortuary?"

"No, it was all part of a single lot. Say, is something the matter?"

"Oh, no. Not exactly. I mean, I think I've got what I need for my niece's report."

"Nephew. You said it was for your nephew's report."

Jen flustered. "Did I? How silly of me. My niece is a

tomboy who cuts her hair like a boy. Anyway, thank you so much for your time. I know my way out."

* * *

"They think they're home," explained Madame, as Jen fidgeted with her purse strap, while seated on Madame's patchy velour couch. "The ghosts. They only see the wood in the floors, not anything else. But it's enough for them."

"But it's *not* their home—it's *ours!* Mine, Jack's and Daniel's. *Our home!*"

Madame Blavashevsky pushed her unfashionable glasses down her nose and fixed Jen with a clear-eyed stare. "They don't know that, my dear."

"What if we pulled up all the floors and replaced them with new hardwood? Would that make them leave?"

"It could. Or it could make them angry. You wouldn't like them when they're angry."

"I don't like them *now.*"

"How many of them have you seen? Do any seem hostile or threatening?"

"We've only *seen* one—the child lying in the family room—which we think also left that horrible thing in Jack's bedroom. We think Jack may have seen it."

"Child ghosts are often problematic for people who have children of their own. It's seeking your child out, because it wants to be with someone its own age or close to it for a playmate. It doesn't know any better."

Jean leaned forward, practically touching Madame's knee with her own. "Isn't there some kind of a, you know…an exorcism thing…that we can do?"

"A clearing ceremony? The problem is that there are

potentially so many... Almost any lost soul who went through that mortuary could attach itself to your house. Few mediums can handle more than one."

Jen sank back into the velour couch. "If it's only the child though, and the other ghosts don't do anything much but make noise? You could get rid of it, couldn't you?"

"I could try. But we need more information. I'd start with the child—try to communicate with it, ask it why it's hanging around."

Jen shivered. "I guess I can try." It was almost two o'clock by the cuckoo timepiece on Madame's wall. "I have to go pick up Jack now, and then maybe talk to a kid ghost."

"Be careful. It must be a very powerful spirit, if it can make physical objects appear."

"Thanks for the warning."

* * *

"Bobo. Bobo."

Jack was sitting on the living room carpet, pointing at something in the dining room. It was an hour since Jen had picked him up from his daycare. He'd been happily playing with his plastic blocks until now.

"Not now, sweetie. I've got to reply to this customer email," Jen said from the living room couch, her head buried in her laptop.

"Bobo! Bobo!" The toddler was getting louder and more insistent.

Jen closed her laptop with a sigh. "Okay, what is it?"

She followed his pointing finger into the dining room. "Oh, I might as well check it out, you little troublemaker! Who or what on earth's Bobo?" She walked breezily into the dining room and stopped short, then screamed.

Sitting at the big table was a small child with a blonde cowlick, barely tall enough to peek over the tabletop. He looked about three years old, the same size as the child she'd seen on the loveseat. He had a mournful look on his face and large, heavy dark circles around his eyes. His skin was very pale and speckled in places with faint greenish-brown blotches.

Jen gathered up her courage. Remembering Madame's words about trying to talk to the child, she asked in a shaky voice, "Who are you? Do you want us to do something for you?"

The little boy said nothing. He continued to stare at Jen with his dark-ringed eyes. Gingerly, she moved closer, until she could smell the faint odor of death emanating from the boy. She found she got used to the smell after a while, and then didn't notice it as much.

"Bobo! Bobo!" cried a delighted voice from behind her. She turned to see Jack toddling into the dining room, pointing at the pale boy at the table.

The boy smiled and Jen could see discolored teeth that revolted her. Still, it seemed like a genuine smile.

Why, they know *each other,* Jen thought. *The little ghost is Bobo! But why was Jack scared of him last night?*

Jack didn't seem scared of the child now. He toddled over to the table eagerly, as if greeting a playmate at the Pine Breeze sandbox. Jen gasped and pulled him back.

The pale boy frowned and looked disappointed. He lifted something shiny and metallic up from his lap and placed it on the table. Then he disappeared, fading into the air like dissipating steam. Jack began to cry. "Bobo gone-gone!" he howled. Jen realized that his screams from the other night may have been when Bobo left him suddenly, as he just did now.

"I have to find out more about Bobo," she told herself, picking up Jack and comforting him. She moved cautiously toward the table and picked up the long, pointed metal object. She knew instantly what it was.

An arterial tube, used for draining blood and other fluid out of a dead body.

* * *

Jen put Jack down for his afternoon nap and settled in the living room to search online for information about the history of the Grand Continental Hotel. She found a message forum from a community group's failed attempt to save the hotel from destruction. Most of the messages were from five years before and many of the links were broken.

She read through the messages and saw several references to the mortuary, which had operated from the 50s to the early 80s. Then the mortuary closed down due to some sort of terrible "scandal."

She looked for more references to the scandal and came across one post from a member with the screen name "GrandHotelForever" that contained a link. To her surprise, the link still worked. It led to a local Historical Society blog post about the history of the hotel.

The mortuary was called Clayton Bros. and it had been the only funeral home in Pinevale for three decades. There was a sidebar article called "The Horror of Bobby

Sholty."

Bobby. Bobo?

"Clayton Bros. received the body of little Bobby Sholty, age 3, on April 17, 1983. The child had been pronounced dead the same day from a high fever that had sent him into a coma. Unfortunately, little Bobby revived when he was on the mortuary slab just as the funeral technician was preparing his body for embalming and began to cry for his mother. It was too late, as the child had already been drained of a good deal of blood via mortuary equipment. The technician called for an ambulance, but little Bobby died a second time before the vehicle arrived. Clayton Bros. was sued by the boy's parents and the business never recovered from the scandal. It shut down for good in January 1984, and the bottom two floors of the former Grand Continental Hotel remained empty until community leaders voted to remove the entire building in June 2014."

Jen closed her laptop, stunned. Oh, poor Bobby Sholty! What a terrible fate for the little tyke. She could feel tears forming in her eyes. And she realized now why Bobo kept leaving old embalming tools for them to find.

Then she smelled it—the faint, rotted smell of death. She turned around and peered over the top of the couch to see Bobo, pale and small, standing in the arched doorway that separated the dining room from the living room.

He took a tiny step toward her. Jen felt fear rising up to her teeth but tried to suppress it.

"I know what happened to you now, Bobo. You don't have to keep leaving those awful things for me."

He nodded very slightly and took another step closer. The smell of death got a bit stronger.

"What happened to you was a terrible, terrible thing. It should never happen to anyone, let alone an innocent child."

He nodded again and took two more steps, holding out his arms. Jen realized, horrified, that he probably wanted to hug her.

He stopped suddenly at the edge of the living room, where the carpet met the hardwood of the dining room, and looked at her with horribly sad eyes. He lifted a foot as if to step ahead again, but put it down reluctantly.

He can't step where there's carpet! Jen realized silently, in a sudden flash. *He can only appear in the rooms with wood floors.*

Aloud she said, "You'd like to stay with us, wouldn't you? To play with Jack and make up for all the years you missed of your childhood?"

Bobo nodded slightly again, and put his outstretched arms down to his side.

Jen started thinking quickly. Was it really so terrible, having the ghost of a child in the house?

They could move Jack's crib into the spare bedroom, which had carpet—that way, Jack would only be with Bobo when Jen could keep an eye on them together. Her and Daniel's room was carpeted—no problem. The two bathrooms and the kitchen were tiled. Bobo could have the other rooms most of the time—maybe they could learn to share the family room.

"You'd have to stop taking things and stop making those noises with the floors. And you must never, ever hurt any of us, especially Jack. Do you understand?"

Bobo nodded again. He didn't seem to be able to speak to anyone but Jack.

"Then you can stay. You're welcome to stay."

It would be almost like having another child in the house, Jen realized. Wasn't that what she wanted? What's more, a child who would never grow up and leave. Jen thought of Diane Benedict's sadness when she mentioned her elder daughter leaving home next year for college. Bobo would never leave home. He would be her child forever.

She looked at Bobo, who'd disappeared again, melting back into whatever world he lived in when he wasn't showing up in the rooms with wooden floors.

She heard Daniel's key in the front door and realized it was past five. She needed to throw something together for dinner. She also realized that Jack was stirring in his temporary crib spot in their bedroom; he needed a bath after dinner and a story. Maybe they would sit in his old room and invite Bobo to hear the story, too.

She would have to finesse things with Daniel about the changes they would have to make to live peaceably with Bobo. Not lay it on him all at once. She heard something pattering in the dining room, and then the noise disappeared down the hall, and she thought, *I'll have to get used to that. Maybe add air freshener to deal with the occasional odor, too.*

"Hi, honey," Daniel called from the front entrance way. "I'm home."

"In the living room," she called back, opening her laptop and pretending to work.

He found her on the couch and leaned down for a peck on the cheek.

"How was my ghost hunter's day today?" he asked, only half-joking. "Any new spectral sightings or other eruptions of strangeness happen while I've been gone?"

Jen smiled up at him weakly. "Nothing too bad," she said. "I've been thinking up a way for us to add to our family without costing too much money. I'll tell you after dinner."

The Warriors of the Sand

"If there was ever a *true* ghost town, it's Shelby," Marina read out from her smartphone, "up in Mono County near the Nevada border."

Kyle kept his eyes resolutely on the road, both hands on the steering wheel. "Hmmm," he grunted in reply.

Undaunted, she continued reading from a website article about historical Shelby: "A hundred and fifty years in the past, Shelby had a thriving goldmine and a population of about ten thousand souls. However, after the mine played out, Shelby's fortunes ebbed, and then the last few diehard residents abruptly left during the Great Depression in the early 30s."

The couple drove east from San Francisco toward Mono County: he, a prosperous corporate attorney and she, a freelance commercial photographer. It was a long and unfamiliar drive for both of them, toward a landscape they didn't even know existed until a week ago, when Marina had heard about it from a friend in her advanced landscape photography course.

"If I sell any of the Shelby photos, the whole trip is tax-deductible," she reminded him, as they headed toward the semi-isolated badlands of the sparsely populated county.

"Damn." Marina's data connection abruptly died as they started to hit remote countryside. "That's the end for now of my travelogue on Shelby."

"I guess it's nice to know I gave up my weekend for

a tax deduction. Why are we going to *this* place again?"

"Because Shelby is *different* from the other old mining ghost towns in California. Mainly, because of how it was *left* by the people who lived there. With canned foods still sitting on the kitchen shelves, the tractors in the fields, the cars parked in the street.

"There were even neatly made beds in the hotel's bedrooms, and full whiskey bottles stacked in the saloons. Nobody knows *why* the people of Shelby left so much behind. But it was completely vacant by 1931."

"This is interesting *why*?"

Marina sighed. "You're so hopeless. Don't you have any curiosity? Why am I with such an unromantic boyfriend?"

"Because of my inescapable charm, clean hygiene, and impeccable dental work," he said, turning briefly to favor her with a toothy grin.

"That must be it." Marina rolled her eyes in mock-contempt. "My friend says the State Parks Service took over and decided to preserve Shelby just as it was left, a piece of living history. The only people who ever really go there are movie location scouts and artists or photographers, like me. Maybe the occasional history buff."

They arrived at their motel in Mono City, some twenty miles downwind from Shelby, on Friday night; it was mid-spring, and the weather was chill and blustery. In the morning, after a full night's sleep, Marina collected a Shelby guide pamphlet from a small stack at the front desk. She also borrowed an old book about the town from a desk in the lobby. She scanned the book over breakfast at their motel's adjoining Silver Dollar Pancake House, reading out little tidbits of information to Kyle over poached eggs, as he pretended to listen.

"Listen to this—it wasn't on the website!" she cried. "There were several notorious lynchings in the history of Shelby, and the judge who presided over the 'frontier justice' was actually named Lynch. Philip Lynch. Isn't that a weird coincidence?"

"Yes, I suppose so," replied Kyle in a detached voice; he was busy reading the *New York Times* on his smartphone. "Good thing they've got free Wi-Fi here, to my everlasting shock and awe."

"You're just not into this, are you? I always attend your tacky legal events without *kvetching*—now it's *your* turn to support *my* career."

"Yes, dear." Kyle didn't look up from his digital version of *The Times*. Normally, he only logged onto the Internet to read *The Times*, the *Bleacher Report*, and *The Wall Street Journal*.

"You'll like it better when we actually get there. I'm sure it'll be really interesting and cool, almost like being in an old spaghetti Western." She hummed the theme from *The Good, the Bad and the Ugly*, which Kyle pointedly ignored.

She returned the old history book to the motel's desk clerk after breakfast. The young man looked up briefly from a portable TV, where he'd been watching a gameshow. "You can't take nothin' out of Shelby," he admonished her, placing the book aside. He spoke with an odd inflection over the words *you can't take nothin,'* and Marina took note of it defensively.

She protested, "Of *course*. I would *never* disturb anything at a State Park! It's against the law to take things from the parks."

"Well, in that case, have a good trip with your lawyer boyfriend," came the laconic reply, over the sound of a female contestant screeching hysterically about the price of Tide.

They pulled away from the motel parking lot a few minutes later, and Kyle reminded Marina that Shelby really was a ghost town in the middle of nowhere. "It won't have Wi-Fi or even voice service," he pointed out. "No checking the Internet every five minutes on your phone."

"You don't have to remind me of it, I know," she retorted, as their car continued to creep up the serpent-shaped, two-lane road to Shelby. "I *do* spend too much time on the Internet, and I *am* trying to break the habit."

She looked out of the passenger's side window and watched the road turn lonelier, and the landscape on either side become more forbidding, more wild.

"I've only been on a few minutes today so far, to see what the rating was for my 'Kitler' photo of Mr. Smuggles."

"What the hell is a *Kitler*? I'm almost afraid to ask."

"A Kitler is a cat who looks like Hitler," Marina explained. "There's a whole website devoted to them. You post a picture of your Kitler, and then other people vote on its resemblance to Hitler. There are thousands of cats posted there."

"For fuck's sake, that is just ridiculous. What a way to waste time."

"The last time I looked, just one person had voted on Mr. Smuggles, and he only got a 4.5 out of 10. I guess he doesn't really look all that much like Hitler."

"For fuck's sake," repeated Kyle.

"You already said that."

"I meant, for fuck's sake, we're here. Unless I miss my guess, there lies Shelby over yonder in them thar hills."

He gestured toward a hulking arrangement of weathered wooden buildings, painted a faded rusty brown, looming out of the monotonous scrub landscape. "They almost look like Norman turrets brooding over a desert battlefield from the Crusades. *Ahoy* Saladin—"

"It's the stamp plant, silly!" Marina exclaimed. "That's where the mine workers brought in the rocks and boulders for crushing. Then they would extract the gold and silver ore from the crushed rock."

Kyle followed the map in Marina's guide pamphlet to a small kiosk and parking lot marked with the Parks Service's logo. "No rangers are around," he said. "That seems odd."

Marina left a five-dollar bill in a donation box at the kiosk.

"What a lonely job for a ranger," said Kyle. "Imagine being stuck out here by yourself, day in and day out, in a broke-ass ghost town that looks like this."

"Some people might see a rare beauty in the bleakness and solitude," retorted Marina. "Let's go walk around a bit and look for a place to set up the tripod and other equipment for a shoot."

They headed in the general direction of the looming stamp mill, crossing an overgrown field in which sat a weather-beaten cabin. A vintage truck was rotting away in the field, with gray-green prairie grass bursting out of its cab and engine.

"Who would leave behind a truck like that?" wondered Marina aloud. "It would have been valuable in the Depression years. Especially with money so hard to come by in those days."

"Couldn't say," replied Kyle. "Maybe it broke down, and the owners didn't have any money to have it fixed."

They followed the map, cutting through waist-high fields of grass, encountering yet more abandoned old cars, plus rusted-over farm and mining equipment, until they found the main street.

"This is creepy. We're the only ones here," said Marina. The main street was not paved; it was a long stretch of windswept sand, with dilapidated buildings on either side. Some of the buildings were listing to one side badly; all were weather-beaten, with paint and varnish peeling off like flayed animal skin, and decaying in inglorious silence.

"Looks like Gary Cooper might be coming down the street soon at high noon," said Kyle.

"It really does look like that, doesn't it? Like a Wild West movie set. And yet people actually lived here for almost eighty years. There was a church, a school, a hotel, even an Odd Fellows Hall."

"Let's check out some of the buildings."

They walked into the Shelby General Store, taking in shelves that were still lined with canned goods and dusty old glass bottles. They saw a wooden planked counter with a cash register in rusty metal scrollwork sitting on top, several upright flour and barley barrels, and an old-fashioned coffee grinder ready for customers who didn't exist.

"I don't get it," said Marina. "Why would they leave the food behind? The guide pamphlet said the heavier stuff was left because it was too hard to move down the hill, but what about the food? Who would leave cans of food and coffee behind? Or bottles of medicine? People would have been destitute during the Depression—surely *someone* would have taken the food and medicine."

Kyle shrugged. "I dunno, really. Hey, there's a saloon! Let's go."

"Look at the sign; its name is The Golden Fleece. Must have been very grand in its heyday!"

Inside, a hulking and elaborate pool table dominated the main room; it had a felt top of a still-vibrant light blue shade, and mahogany legs carved with sculptures of rearing lions. Nearby was a wall-rack of pool cues. A long time ago, someone had left two of the cues on the felt covering, as if the players had just set them down to order something from the room's long bar, which was made of dark, dust-covered wood.

The two visitors exclaimed at the mirrored shelves behind the bar—ones that contained an impressive array of spirits, in addition to bottles of syrups and tonics, beer, and champagne. At the bar's far end, a phantom barman had placed a glass decanter and a grouping of shot glasses, each stacked bottom-side up. The barman had turned a solitary shot glass upward, as if waiting to be filled.

"These are very cool," said Kyle, picking up the upturned shot glass. "Wouldn't they look great above the bar at home?"

"*Kyle!* Don't touch anything!"

"Can't I take just one home with me, as a souvenir?"

"No! Of course not!"

"Why not?"

"It's *stealing!*"

"It isn't—no one owns this stuff. They left it all here."

"It belongs to the Parks Service now," reminded Marina, firmly. "What would happen if everybody took a souvenir? Soon nothing would be left."

"I didn't see anything in the guide brochure about not taking things. Nor at the parking station," protested Kyle.

"*Hmmm*…you're *right*. Usually, they put up a sign warning you not to take anything away, even if it's a pinecone or a wildflower. But, anyway, it's wrong, so put that shot glass back. Let's go over to the old hotel—it looks interesting."

Kyle grumbled and made an exaggerated show of putting the shot glass back on the bar. He followed Marina reluctantly outside and down the street to the Shelby Grand Hotel, a three-story brick structure that stood next to the Oddfellows Hall. Unlike the Oddfellows Hall, Kyle pointed out, the hotel wasn't listing crazily to one side. From the street, the building appeared sober and true—even still somewhat habitable, after a little cleaning up.

"What was that?" cried Kyle, all of a sudden.

"What was *what?*"

"I dunno," he said. "I thought I saw something hanging from a window at the jail across the street. Like a body. With bony bare feet, jutting out of a saggy pair of pant legs."

"There's nothing there," said Marina, firmly. "You probably saw a whirlwind spiral of sand. I've seen several since we've been here. Maybe you've got a guilty conscience."

"Guilty about what?"

"Everybody has *something* to be guilty about. Let's go into the hotel."

"Hey, look," said Kyle, after pushing open the front double doors of the Shelby Grand. "The front desk still has room keys in its cubbyholes. And there's a bell and an antique typewriter on the counter."

Marina looked around with amazement on her face. She pointed to a little corner off the desk, which housed an ancient telephone switchboard. Some of the lines were still plugged into their moldering, respective slots.

"I wonder what it was like a hundred years ago. People milling about in the lobby, the switchboard operator connecting calls, the bellhops in shiny buttons rushing to get the guests' luggage," she said dreamily. "So romantic! It must have been something to see."

"Yeah, so *romantic*," said Kyle. "There would be no air conditioning and no deodorant. Everyone would smell like B.O. The street would be full of horseshit. *You'*d be wearing a long dress with ten petticoats underneath, even in a hundred-and-five-degree heat."

"Well, I'd be *used* to it because that's all I would have known. Look over there!"

She gestured toward a long console table in a prominent corner of the lobby, with a glass case on top running the length of it.

"That must be where they keep *The Warriors of the Sand!*" exclaimed Marina. "I read about it in the book at the motel."

They went to look at the case. Marina wiped the dust off the glass top with a corner of her jean jacket. Inside, the case contained a plaster cast—so long it was made of three separate plaster sections—of a stunningly beautiful sand drawing.

"It's a *masterpiece!*" she exclaimed. The plaster had

captured a scene of Indian warriors riding out for battle in full regalia, with their painted mustangs, feathered lances, Henry repeating rifles, and quivers of arrows.

"It's remarkably lifelike," she said. "All done with just a sharpened stick and wet sand. There's something almost *religious* about it. If you look at it long enough—it's almost as if—I swear—you could see them moving. With the ponies all nervous and tossing their manes, and the war regalia flapping in the wind."

"So, what was the story on this thing?" asked Kyle.

"Apparently there was a young man named Scribbler Jack, a half-white, half-Indian who would make extra money by drawing scenes in wet sand in the street for pedestrians and bar patrons," Marina answered. "The hotel manager's wife was entranced by this particular scene, and she ordered that plaster be poured to preserve it before the wind blew it away."

"I wonder what happened to Scribbler Jack? Seems a shame if this is all that's left of his remarkable talent."

Kyle absentmindedly stuck his hands in the pockets of his anorak. "Hey, what the—it's gone!"

"Gone? What's gone?"

Kyle felt abashed. "I took one of the shot glasses after all, from the saloon. I grabbed it when you weren't looking and stuffed it in the pocket of my anorak. But now it's not there!"

"You *stole* it? How *could* you?"

"I'm sorry. I didn't mean any harm. I just really wanted a souvenir. But now it's gone, and I don't know how that happened."

"It must have dropped out on the ground while you were walking around. We can find it if we retrace our steps.

Then, when we find it, *we are going to put it back exactly where it was before.*"

"Okay, okay, Miss Prissy-Face."

They retraced their steps, all the way back to the Golden Fleece. There was no sign of the shot glass on the ground they covered.

Inside the saloon, they looked all over the floor, near the pool table, under the barstools and then—on the old bar itself.

At the far end of the bar, the grouping of overturned glasses and the whiskey decanter was still there. Including the solitary, upturned shot glass, waiting an eternity for a ghostly refill, just as it had looked when they first entered the saloon.

"Can't be," said Kyle. "I *took* the one that was right-side up."

"There must have been *two* upturned shot glasses," answered Marina. "We just didn't notice it at the time."

"No, there was only *one*."

"You must have dropped the other one," she said stubbornly, sweeping the floor again with her eyes.

"I'm taking it again," said Kyle.

"*Kyle!*"

"It's just an experiment. I'll put it back afterward, I swear." He grabbed the upturned shot glass and stuffed it back into his anorak pocket. "Shouldn't you be setting up your equipment and getting some shots? You're going to miss the best light."

"All right, let's go get the stuff out of the car," she said. Kyle noticed she didn't seem particularly interested in photographing Shelby anymore.

"What I really want to do is just go back to the

Shelby Hotel and look closer at *The Warriors of the Sand*. I'm sure I hadn't yet *begun* to see all of the exquisite details."

"You looked a long time already."

"I guess I'll have to take at least a few quick shots out here," she grumbled. "But the real story's in the hotel with the sand cast. I wonder if I've got the right equipment to shoot it properly."

She and Kyle cut through the fields again, past the rusting cars and farm equipment, back to their lonely car. It was still the only vehicle parked in the lot. Kyle opened the trunk and took all the photography equipment out. He shouldered the tripod while Marina grabbed her favorite camera, and they set off once again to the town, wading through the abandoned pastureland.

"Maybe we should start at the church," she said. "I could see if a greeting card company would want to buy a shot of it for Christmas cards."

The church formed a simple wooden structure with a peaked roof and a steeple; it was weather-beaten, with most of the white paint peeled off, and slightly listing to the right. It supported a plain iron cross on top of the steeple. Against the backdrop of the bleak, yellow-green-gray hills and surrounded by abandoned fields, the church would translate well to photography, Marina informed Kyle.

"Here," she added, indicating a spot in front of the church. Kyle set everything up as instructed. Then he straightened and stretched, putting his hands absently again into his anorak pockets, while Marina adjusted her camera on the tripod.

"It's *gone*!" he cried. "Marina, the shot glass is gone again!"

"Are you sure?" she said, plainly irritated. "You must have dropped it in the field while you were lugging the tripod around."

"Maybe so," said Kyle. "Call me crazy, but first I'm gonna go back to the saloon and see if it's back in place at the end of the bar."

Marina shouted, *"Oh for fuck's sake!"* but Kyle had already started loping back down the sandy main street toward the Golden Fleece saloon and couldn't hear her words. Reluctantly, she ran after him into the saloon, leaving her tripod, camera, and other equipment behind.

"There it is!" said Kyle. "It's back in its place at the end of the bar!"

This time Marina didn't dispute the number of shot glasses at the bar. "You're right. There were five downturned ones and one upturned one. And that's how many of them are there *now!"*

"What's going on? What *is* this place?"

"You know something …I've been thinking—that clerk at the motel told me *'You can't take anything out of Shelby.'* I thought he was warning me about taking souvenirs… But what if he meant it *literally?* That you can't, *physically,* take anything away from here?"

"But that's crazy, 'Rina—just crazy." Kyle shook his head. "Maybe I should try to take something else, one of those old bottles…for instance—"

He slid behind the bar and grabbed a tonic bottle off one of the shelves.

"Mornin', folks," came a steely, hard man's voice from behind them.

Kyle and Marina turned to see a figure silhouetted in the doorway of the saloon. When the figure moved closer, they saw a man in an old-fashioned uniform: a dark-blue, brass-buttoned jacket, light blue pants, and muddied, tall boots with spurs. His wide-brimmed hat bore the crossed-rifle, brass insignia of the U.S. Cavalry on the hatband. He lifted it toward Marina politely, and she could see he had blue eyes and a bright red beard, mustache, and eyebrows.

"Um, good morning," replied Kyle, somewhat spooked. "My girlfriend here is a professional photographer. And I suppose you're the ranger from the Parks Service who looks after this place?"

"I'm the *caretaker* here, yes," said the man in uniform.

"Oh, I see. Do they make you wear that as part of the living history exhibit?" asked Marina.

"It's required for my position, yes," answered Red-Beard, with a nod. "I see you've got a bottle there in your hand, sir. You weren't planning to run off with it, were you?"

Kyle's face flushed red, almost as red as the ranger's beard. "Umm, no—not really. I was just looking at it." Hastily, he placed it back on the bar.

The ranger nodded. "You can't really take anything out of here anyway," he said. "Most people around these parts know that."

"What do you mean?"

"Everything here's stuck here, just like them warriors in the glass case at the hotel."

Kyle and Marina looked at each other in disbelief, and Kyle snorted a strangled little laugh of nervousness.

"I don't follow you," said Marina. "What's the connection with that?"

The ranger crooked his stern mouth into the trace of a faint half-smile.

"Let's set down a piece, I don't have anything else to do today, unless some other folks come by, and it don't look like that'll happen."

Red-Beard nodded toward a dusty saloon table with some rickety chairs around it. "Them chairs are okay to set on. In case you were wonderin'."

"This I gotta hear," said Kyle, taking a seat at the indicated table, and Marina followed suit.

"It started with Scribbler Jack, the half-breed drawin'-boy. As was the usual case in those days, neither the white side nor the Indian side wanted much to do with him. His mother's people, the Paiute, decided he was bad medicine because he could draw figgers that looked real, like the white man's art."

The ranger sighed and sounded almost sad.

"The Paiute didn't like them figgers at all. There was a rumor goin' around the Indian camps that the white man's pitcher box could steal a man's spirit, and I guess some of 'em thought Scribbler Jack's figgers were more of the same. They weren't alone neither—when the pitcher boxes first came to town, even some white Christian folks were scared of them. 'Unholy graven images' said some. As for Scribbler Jack, he kinda made a bargain with his tribe; he promised he'd only draw his figgers in the wet sand. When the sand dried and the wind came up, the figgers would be gone. They weren't permanent-like, so any spirits they stole would be released with the wind."

"He made a pretty good livin' round here, drawing his figgers in the sand with a sharp stick, settin' out a tin cup for folks to show their appreciation. He liked to set up in front of the hotel because a lot of fancy folks ate there."

"But he wouldn't draw on anything but sand?" asked

Marina, fascinated.

"Aye—Scribbler Jack would never draw his figgers on paper, or anything else permanent, even though some of the fancy folk offered him money for it. He only worked in the wet sand."

"But—but—he let the warriors be preserved..." she protested.

"There was no *lettin'* about it, Missy," said the ranger, shaking his head. "Jack worked till sundown on a hot Sunday afternoon to draw them warriors, pouring the water on the sand a little bit at a time. Folks crowded around him to watch, eggin' him on. They were all excited, pointin' and shoutin'—'*Oh, those warriors, look how real they are, those horses, those hooves!*' It was a real sight to see.

"Unfortunately for Scribbler Jack, it was *too* good a sight to see. The hotel manager's wife said it would be a crime to let them warriors go back to the wind, when the sand dried out. 'It's a masterpiece!' she cried. 'We can't let it go.'"

The ranger paused for a moment, and an expression of discomfort flitted over his face. He rubbed his upper right arm, somewhat absently, with his left hand. "Excuse me for a piece, I get *pains* sometime in my arm," he apologized. "I dunno why, but I get them now and then... I must be pretty old by now—I've been here a long, long time."

Kyle cleared his throat. He made a face to Marina that said *not right in the head,* and she nodded back, with a faint, knowing smirk.

The ranger continued his story after a few moments, the pains apparently gone.

"She screamed for someone to get the plasterer and

he came a-runnin', even if it was a Sunday. Scribbler Jack kept objectin', mind you, but nobody wanted to listen to a half-breed. When it was all done, he snuck into the hotel several times, tryin' to destroy them plaster casts, but he was always caught. Then they got that glass case and locked it, and that made him even madder. He tried one last time, goin' there with a big rock at night to smash the case, but the manager caught him and shot him. Shot him right there in the lobby of the Shelby Hotel. Claimed it was self-defense, and Judge Lynch was happy to oblige and let him go. Ol' Jack was taken to a bunk at the old jail and that's where he died the next morning. Poor fella had to look at ol' Barefoot Burke hangin' from a window upstairs while he passed."

Kyle pulled back from the table in fear. "Barefoot Burke? Hanging from the window?"

Red-Beard nodded. "One of Judge Lynch's specials. Got his neck stretched that morning. He never wore shoes. Lookin' at that thing probably hurried poor Jack to his final reward. Why'd you ask?"

"I *saw* a man hanging from the top window, while we were walking to the hotel. He had long, bare feet."

The ranger rubbed his sore arm again. "It coulda been a dust spiral," he finally allowed. "Plays tricks on the mind. Barefoot Burke has been gone a very long time, I reckon."

"That's what *I* said. But what about Jack?" Marina interrupted. "And the warriors and the plaster casts—?"

"Well, that's what I've been *tryin'* to tell you. Before he died, ol' Jack told the Doc, *'This town'll be locked in as long as them warriors are locked in that glass case.'*"

"*Locked in?* What did he mean by that?" asked

Marina.

"It happened kinda slow-like, after that. But people started noticin', as the years wore on. A load of ore would disappear on its way to Mono City. When the ranchers tried to drive their beef out, the cattle would spook and stampede. It kept gettin' worse, and people started leavin', first just a trickle, then a flood. Some of their things would disappear when they tried to leave, and eventually, it got so bad, people were just leavin' everything behind, except the clothes on their back. But nobody wanted to talk about what was happenin', because they didn't want to admit there were things that couldn't be explained by their Bibles.

"And that's why you *can't* take anything out of Shelby. You can try to take that there tonic bottle—" he nodded at the bar where Kyle had left it—"but that ain't gonna do no good."

Kyle and Marina sat in silence, trying to make sense of the ranger's tale.

"Thank you for the story," said Marina, finally. "That was worth the trip up here, just for that."

"'Tain't nothin', ma'am." He rummaged inside his jacket and consulted an antique pocket watch. "It's past noontime. Time to get back to my rounds. Afternoon, ma'am," he said, standing and tipping his hat again to Marina.

The ranger nodded at Kyle and then walked out of the saloon.

"Well," said Kyle finally. "That was quite a story. I guess it's time for us to be going, also. Your tripod is waiting for you back at the church, m'lady."

"Yes, I guess we'd better go."

They walked out onto Main Street and saw that the

sun was high in the sky; the ranger's timepiece had been accurate, for its age.

"That's funny," said Kyle. "I don't see old Red-Beard anywhere on the street. He only left about two minutes ago."

"Maybe he took a shortcut." Marina spoke in a distracted tone. "He probably knows this place like the back of his hand. You know what, Kyle?"

"What?"

"It isn't *right*, what happened to Scribbler Jack."

"Yeah, I know. A terrible injustice—letting the manager off for killing him."

"That's not what I meant. Yes, that part was terrible, but it's the fact that they wouldn't respect his wishes about *The Warriors of the Sand*. It wasn't right to lock them up like that."

"*Lock them up?* You can't tell me you believe that nonsense? It was clearly made up just to discourage people from taking things. That ranger has probably told it to hundreds of visitors."

"Well, if you don't believe it, you can always go back inside the saloon and try to take that tonic bottle out to the car. And what about Barefoot Burke?"

A dark, fidgety emotion passed over Kyle's face. "Uh, no thanks, I've had enough of that saloon and its contents. Enough of this whole place, as a matter of fact. And I probably read about Barefoot Burke somewhere and just didn't remember it. You don't seem too enthusiastic about taking photos anymore, anyway. How about we just go back to the motel in Mono City, have a bite to eat, and get some rest? We can come back tomorrow."

Marina sighed. "Okay. I just can't get my mind off

poor Scribbler Jack, though. It's like they *violated* him. The whole town just looks different now. Maybe tomorrow it'll be different."

They retrieved the tripod and other equipment from outside the church and then trudged back to the little Parks Service kiosk where the rental car was parked.

"We're the only car here," said Kyle. "How'd that ranger get here?"

"He probably lives somewhere close by, just off the highway. He probably walks to work when the weather's good."

"Yeah, probably," said Kyle.

* * *

All the rest of the day, Marina gave off an air of being distracted and ill at ease. Kyle attempted to cheer her up, but she could only manage a few weak smiles—even when he called up the Kitler website and reported that the rating for Mr. Smuggles had improved to 5.3.

"Well, that's nice for the cat," she said in a bland voice.

Kyle was mystified. "Since when is Mr. Smuggles 'the cat?' You dote on that creature!"

"Piffles," she harrumphed back.

She went to bed early, pleading exhaustion, and he went up a bit later, after a drink at the motel's little bar. They watched an old episode of *Star Trek: The Next Generation* on the motel's all-too-basic cable service, and then turned out the lights at nine-thirty.

Marina was troubled all through the night. Kyle had never known her to talk in her sleep, ever, and they had been living together for more than two years. But that night she did talk in her sleep, muttering words that clearly concerned Shelby and Scribbler Jack, although he couldn't quite make out their meaning.

Paiute War and *bluecoats* and *horse soldiers*. And even some garbled words of an unidentifiable foreign language. Marina didn't fall into a real sleep until a good deal after midnight, but when she did, she slept deeply until morning. She woke to find Kyle hovering over her with donuts and hot coffee on a tray from the motel lobby.

"Good morning, sweetie," he said. "Want some hot coffee?"

She sat up in bed. "Smells really good, even for motel coffee. Thanks!"

"You had a terrible night last night," said Kyle, sitting down on the side of the bed.

"Really? I don't remember anything at all."

"You kept saying nonsense about the Indians, and then there was one part when you apparently started talking in Klingon."

"Did I?" Marina laughed. "Well, I'll tell you, I *was* a little *spooked* by that ghost story the ranger told us yesterday."

"Oh, I knew you were. Look, sweetie, I've been to a few of these old Gold Rush towns, and the locals do whatever they can to bring in the tourists. They tell ghost stories; they dress up like Annie Oakley and Buffalo Bill; they claim that Joaquin Murrieta or some other desperado used their town as a hideout. That ranger just did his job *too well,* and besides, he probably didn't realize he was dealing with a delicate artistic temperament like yours."

"But what about the shot glass you tried to take out

of the saloon? You have to admit, that was *very* strange."

"I've been thinking about that. I think it fell out of my anorak pocket both times, just like you said it did. It fell on the ground, and the ranger was walking around on his rounds, and he found it twice and put it back. That's the only rational explanation."

"I guess that could be," admitted Marina. "He sure showed up at the right time, didn't he? Like he'd been watching us for a while and knew what we were up to."

"That's my girl." Kyle leaned over and gave her a quick kiss. "Do you still want to go out there and get your photographs?"

"Oh, yes!" said Marina, suddenly alert, back to her old, enthusiastic self. "It looks like it's going to be a wonderful day, too, much nicer than yesterday. The light will be gorgeous."

They drove back to Shelby, and this time, Marina packed both of her cameras in the trunk, plus the tripod: the big camera for taking landscapes on the tripod, and a smaller one for shooting interiors.

They parked in the Park Service's lot, in the same spot as they'd done the day before. Once again, theirs was the only car in the lot.

"I hope we don't see Ranger Rick today," said Marina. "There was something about that cavalry uniform, and the way he wore it, that creeped me out. It didn't look like it came from an online re-enactment catalog. Like it was homemade, or something."

"I hope we don't see him either. He clearly thinks we're troublemakers."

They unloaded the car and strode through the abandoned fields toward Shelby. "Look at all the wildflowers! Aren't they beautiful? I didn't even notice them yesterday. And the sun's so bright, even the stamp mill looks kind of cheerful."

Once again, they found the church, and Kyle set up the tripod and Marina adjusted her big camera on it. She took several pictures of the church. "These are gonna be good," she said happily. "I got some of the wildflowers in the foreground."

"Okay, that's about it for the church. Kyle, why don't you take the tripod and the big camera over to the school? I want to get that too. And while you're setting up, I'm going over to the hotel with the other camera to get some pics of the interior. I love that old typewriter on the front desk counter—how much do you think that thing weighs? It looks like a rock."

Kyle looked a little uneasy at talk of the hotel. But Marina seemed so cheerful and enthusiastic, that he relaxed. "Sure, I'll meet you over at the school once you are finished at the hotel."

They gave each other a short kiss, and then parted after reaching Main Street. Marina headed one way toward the hotel, and Kyle went the other way to the school.

The school building was a handsome structure, Kyle told himself, as he unfolded the tripod and set it up in a likely spot and affixed the large camera to it. It was one of the better-preserved buildings, a two-story wooden clapboard structure with a copula on the roof that contained what looked like the original cast-iron school bell. He walked all the way around it and then peeked inside. He saw a few rows of wooden desks in the main classroom—the old-fashioned kind with inkwells in the corners—and an antique map pulled down over the chalkboard, showing the borders of the nation circa 1880. The walls were lined with shelves filled with crumbling books, and there was a prim rolltop desk in one corner.

Kyle heard something moving behind him and turned quickly. It was only a small cloud of dust and sand kicked up by the wind. "Dust spiral," he recalled Marina lecturing, before. "They do get around."

Then he noticed that at his feet was a drawing in the sand. He bent and looked closer. It depicted a pair of eagle feathers, crossed at the quills, exquisitely drawn. "Someone's been here!" he told himself. "Hell of an artist. Maybe they were here yesterday after we left. But how'd this drawing survive the wind?"

Later, he sat on the steps of the school building to wait for Marina to come back, thinking troubled thoughts about the curious feather drawing. He waited a long time, and then eventually consulted his watch, amazed to see that he'd been waiting for an hour and a half.

"I should go over to the hotel and see what Rina's up to," he said aloud. "She doesn't have that much time to shoot before we have to drive back to the motel, pack up, and then hit the road for the city."

He jogged over to the old hotel, feeling a kind of dread with every stride. He stopped shortly in front of the Golden Fleece, thinking he'd heard someone moving about inside, and wondered if the red-bearded park ranger was lurking about, watching them. But then he moved on; the first priority was to see if Marina was all right, or if she needed help. When he reached his destination, there was a strange field of pewter sky and charcoal clouds around the hotel, and the building itself looked dark and forbidding.

"Where did all that sun go?" he wondered. "How did

we ever think that hotel was charming and quaint?"

He jerked open the grand old double doors and slipped inside the lobby. In the gloom, his eyes located Marina after a moment or two; she was standing in the corner, near the glass case that held *The Warriors of the Sand*, and there was something about her stance that wasn't quite right. He approached quickly and saw that she was standing on the carpet in a ring of white powder, surrounded by broken pieces of some white thing. Her small camera was on the floor next to her, still in its case.

Then he noticed that there was a good deal of broken glass on the floor around Marina too, mixed in with the white dusty powder.

"I had to let them *out*," she said, in the same dreamy, preoccupied manner she had shown the previous evening. "It wasn't right."

Then he saw what had happened. She'd taken the heavy old antique typewriter from the front desk and used it to smash open the glass case. With the case destroyed, she'd removed the three adjoining plaster casts of *The Warriors of the Sand*, and smashed them also, leaving broken plaster pieces and dust all over the threadbare carpet. The typewriter, now mangled and twisted, lay nearby.

"*Rina, for God's sake, what have you done?*" Kyle cried. "You've *vandalized* it!"

"It belonged to Scribbler Jack," she said. "It didn't belong to the hotel, don't you see? I *had* to do it."

"We need to leave, now!" Kyle cried, grabbing Marina's arm. "I think I saw the ranger over at the saloon. He could come in here any minute, and then you'd really be in trouble. This could mean a huge fine or even jail time! You've destroyed valuable state property."

Marina smiled an odd, crooked half-smile, as if unaware of what she'd really done.

"You act like you've lost your mind!" he cried. "Yesterday, you almost took my head off for wanting to steal a lousy little shot glass!"

He picked up the small camera and pulled her along by the arm with his free hand, out onto the verandah of the old hotel, keeping his eye cocked for any sign of the red-bearded park ranger. He squinted down the sandy length of Main Street—

"What the—?"

A huge cloud of dust rolled straight toward them: thick, advancing yellow-gray dust and swirling sand. And the sun was bright again, incredibly bright, almost blinding.

As the cloud came closer, Kyle could hear a kind of dull pounding, which made a faint collective roar, and then he heard high-pitched whooping of shouts in some peculiar tongue, and he saw, for the first time, the flashes of the sharp hooves and the fiery snorting nostrils, the buckskin-clad legs kicking painted mustang flanks, the sun glinting off the fittings of scores of raised Henry rifles, and the polished stone heads of arrows fitted to a hundred raised bows—

"I had to let them out, don't you see?" said Marina in a strange, mechanical, pleading voice, from beside him. *"It's what he wanted."*

"But they're coming right toward us!" screamed Kyle, and then his voice was strangled in the dust and sand.

Across the street, the solitary, red-bearded man in cavalry blue moved out onto the creaking boardwalk in front of the saloon, and silently watched the mustang ponies gallop past in an enormous cloud of dust and sand.

An ancient memory stirred in his consciousness.

"There's nothing I can do now—it's a full-on Indian warrior raid and you poor folks ain't gonna get out of it," he said to the cloud of dust, sand, whooping figures, and horses. "Such a pretty girl and nice young fella." He shook his head with a regretful motion and started to rub his painful right upper arm. "I remember now—it's from that arrow I took back in the Paiute War of Eighteen Sixty-Ought."

The Blue-Green Map of the World

From the time I came to live at Casa Del Mar, I was fascinated with the blue-green room at the end of the corridor on the third floor. As a young bride, I used it a few times as a tearoom until Howard, my husband, had it triple-locked. It was Missy's special place—Missy, the first wife. It was odd the way he treated her memory. After all, she had died respectably in a car crash; she hadn't run away with the second gardener. But Howard could barely stand to speak her name.

Then Howard died last year, and my stepson, Howard Jr., decamped for the States to look after what remained of the family's once-vast industrial empire. I was left alone in the many-roomed Casa on Santa Serafina— my island home for twenty years. One afternoon in September, I had a sudden epiphany. Howard had been gone for almost a year, and there was nothing keeping me from enjoying Missy's room again. I was free to go where I pleased, without fear of his scolding.

I snatched the house's master keys from the desk of Mrs. Matamoros, the housekeeper. They jangled disconcertingly as I trod off to the third floor.

The third floor was the gloomiest part of the house. I passed shadows within shadows, stone gargoyles perched in awkward corners, and double rows of portraits of Howard's ancestors, the Roddicks. I sensed their dour eyes on my back and wondered if Missy had once felt the same.

I tried every key until I found the three correct ones.

I pushed the door open and was assaulted with a powerful smell of mustiness and old age. But soon I was used to it, and I circled the room curiously. It was as I remembered it. Wooden floors, a big window that looked down into the north garden. Missy was an artist, and her art supplies and canvases were still scattered around carelessly. There was the charming aquamarine velvet sofa and tea table, still set up in the center of the room.

The best feature, however, was a map of the world that Missy had painted on the walls in the last year of her life, and it was strange and beautiful. The map was all done in myriad hues of blue, green, and blue-green—the latter being her favorite; she was crazy about any shade of teal, aqua, turquoise. I'd removed the decor in her turquoise bedroom and aqua bathroom and replaced it with my own colors, but the special room, with the map of the world— that I'd wanted left alone.

The walls had retained their vibrant splendor. The continents were still there, populated by fanciful animals, plants, fruits and flowers. I was particularly fond of a family of turquoise bears she'd painted on Russia and the cobalt kangaroos she'd made to decorate Australia. If I stared at the map long enough, all of the flora and fauna seemed to be swaying to a gentle, unheard rhythm that was fascinating to see.

The exceptions to the blue-green color scheme were a network of orange-red circles in random places, which I guessed symbolized areas of the world that were important to Missy. Besides Missy's native London, the only one I saw as relevant was a splotch of red off the Pacific Coast of South America: Santa Serafina.

Missy's giant easel and paint supplies were pushed

uncremoniously into a corner, next to a galvanized sink and a small electric kiln; she'd done ceramics as well as painting. There was a stack of canvases balanced on the easel. I flipped through them, until I found one that I hadn't noticed before. It depicted the head and shoulders of a young woman with the face completed, although not the hair or neck. Missy had given the subject an unusual expression that made her look cruel, almost demonic, despite features of great beauty. A legend was painted at the bottom of the canvas, reading "Milena" in block letters.

Who was Milena? I'd never heard the name in all my years at Casa Del Mar. But whoever it was, Missy didn't like her. I noticed the faintest outlines of tiny, twisting, evil creatures—spiders, lizards, snakes, and scorpions—lurking under Milena's beautiful translucent skin. Who would paint something like that? I'd heard that Missy had turned "strange" just before she died, and the portrait seemed to confirm it.

"You desire to open up this room again, Señora?" said a familiar voice behind me, a plain hint of disapproval in it. The tone was odd, even for Mrs. Matamoros, who habitually spoke English with a stilted, archaic flavor. Almost like a challenge rather than a question.

I turned to face her, standing in the doorway. "Yes, I want to make it a sewing room. The light's much better up here than it is in my current sewing room."

Mrs. Matamoros's face registered a subtle alarm. "It gets dusty up here. Señora will catch a cough."

"It's only dusty because it hasn't been cleaned in twenty years! There won't be dust after cleaning."

She set her lips in a thin line and looked slightly to the side, away from the portrait. "No one will clean here."

"But why?"

She shrugged. "Village superstitions."

"What superstitions? And who is Milena? I found a portrait of her on the easel."

I wasn't aware that Missy had been a source of superstitions in the village. But it was hard to keep housekeeping staff over the years—that was undeniable. The villagers still called us Los Gringos, even though Howard's family had lived on Santa Serafina for four generations.

"Perhaps Señora should inquire for herself in the village."

I noticed how she'd sidestepped the question about Milena. "Was there a housemaid of that name, from the village?"

"There have been many housemaids here over the past thirty years, Señora. One can't remember them all."

I saw that I wasn't going to receive any further information about Milena, so I sent Mrs. Matamoros back to her kitchen.

In the end, I cleaned the room myself. Fortunately, though, I was able to get Mrs. Matamoros to help lug my sewing machine and table up to Missy's room, with all of my spools, fabric bolts, and patterns. She stopped just short of the doorway, so I had to push everything into the room on my own, but I managed.

I put my table and machine in front of the big window with the fantastic light. I could see the garden, full of banana and mango groves. Chickens ran free among the trees and their faint squawking drifted all the way up to the third floor when the window was open. No wonder Missy had loved this room. So sunny and cheerful—it was like an architectural protest against the gloom and darkness of the rest of the Casa.

Soon I was spending my free time in the room, happily finishing a quilt I'd started years ago and then abandoned. When I tired of the quilt, I sat on the sofa, drank tea, and watched the blue-green map of the world.

Yet it was a week later when I first began to feel something peculiar. It was hard to quantify. A kind of heaviness in the air, as if something unseen was moving through it. And then came the day—a perfectly ordinary, sun-drenched tropical day—when I saw the woman standing in the garden below, looking up at the window. She was wearing a short black dress. Her face was indistinct, but she had the stance of a young woman. She looked straight at me as I peered through the window.

Then she held out her arms straight out in front of her, in a kind of supplicating gesture. I cried out in shock.

She had no hands. I rubbed my eyes and looked again. No hands at all that I could see. The arms ended in pitiful stumps. I pulled away from the window, revolted, and when I made myself look again, she was gone.

I ran down to the garden and looked all around for a half-hour, but I could find no trace of the handless visitor. I asked one of the gardeners if they had seen a strange woman and he shook his head, astonished at my description of her. "Nada, Señora," he said, backing slightly away from me with a peculiar look on his face. I gave up and went back into the house.

"I just imagined it," I scolded myself. "Caused by a fragment of undigested beef, as Jacob Marley would say." But why on earth would such a gruesomely specific image be produced by my imagination? I did not watch horror movies or read macabre literature.

Nevertheless, I avoided my sewing room for several days, until my curiosity got the better of me. The feeling of heaviness was still palpable in the air, but otherwise the room was as I'd left it. I ran to the window and looked down into the north garden. To my relief, there was no strange visitor, only the gardener I'd spoken to before. He waved when he saw me at the window.

I sat down at my sewing table and tried to put *it* out of my mind. Eventually, I found myself working happily again. How I loved to sew! I was not a painter like Missy, but I felt that my quilts were a form of art. I often gave them to the villagers of Santa Sarafina: baby-sized ones for infants, double-bed-sized ones for newlyweds.

After a couple of hours, I sensed that the heavy feeling in the air was getting stronger. I felt a certain mass of it directly behind me and turned around. There was a young woman sitting on the sofa. Wearing the short black dress. This time I could see her face clearly. It was Milena. The girl in the portrait.

"Oh!" I cried. She didn't seem to hear me. Instead, she held out her arms again toward me—the arms that ended in thin air where the hands were supposed to be. It seemed like she wanted something from me, and I shrank back at the thought of what it was.

Speechless, I trembled and stared at her, trying to discern if she were real or an apparition. I realized with a pounding heart that she must be an apparition after all, for she looked no older than her portrait, from more than twenty years ago.

Milena, Milena…who are you? Or, rather, what are you? I thought. I wanted to leave desperately, but I shuddered at the thought of getting up and walking past her to get to the door.

Amazed at my own audacity, I spoke to her. Or it. Or whatever the proper appellation was.

"Are you...Milena?" I croaked, barely able to speak.

There was no answer.

"The...girl...in the portrait?"

Again, no answer. Just staring, with her arms outstretched in front of her and the two revolting stumps pointing through the air. Then she dropped her arms and hid the stumps in her lap.

Instead of her arms, she extended her legs, and for the first time, I saw, open-mouthed, that she now had no feet as well as no hands. They were just round, pale, bloodless stumps.

I cried out again, too frightened to move.

It was a stalemate after that, with me and Milena just sitting and gazing at each other, until the door flew open and Mrs. Matamoros's tall, dark shape was framed in the doorway.

"Luncheon is served in the small parlor, Señora," she said stiffly. "Do you prefer to eat it there or shall I have Esperanza bring it up here for you?"

"You don't see it?" I asked, flabbergasted. "The young woman sitting on the sofa?"

"There is no one on the sofa, Señora."

I was perplexed. The sofa faced away from the door, but she would have been able to see the back of...Milena's...head.

"I am staring right at her. She is wearing a short black dress and has a tortoise shell barrette holding her hair back on one side."

Mrs. Matamoros began backing away slowly. "There is no one, Señora. A...trick...of...the shadows. That is all. Luncheon is served in the small parlor." She turned around and lunged away. I could hear her sharp, quick heels battering the wooden floor as she fled.

"But Mrs. Matamoros!" I called after her in a futile protest.

I turned my eyes back to the sofa.

It was empty.

* * *

I needed to find out about Milena. I wrote off taciturn, stubborn Mrs. M., but I thought the estate manager, Tomaso, a better bet. He was around when Missy was alive, as a young campesino working the fields on the estate.

"Tomaso," I began, settling into a chair in front of his desk. In Spanish, I asked, "I wonder if you remember a girl called Milena, who may have worked at Casa Del Mar when the first Señora lived here?"

"Milena? I can't say that I have any memory of a girl of that name." He played with a ballpoint pen on his desk.

"It would be in the estate records, would it not?"

"It would have been more than two decades ago, Señora."

"There would be account books showing wages, etc."

He gave an elaborate Latinate shrug. "Why do you ask?"

"I found a portrait of a girl with that name. In the old studio that the first Señora maintained."

He almost spit his coffee in surprise. "The old

Señora's studio?"

"Yes," I said. "Is there something wrong with it? Come now, Tomaso. Tell me the truth."

He leaned back in his chair with a sigh. "I knew her. She was very beautiful. All the young campesinos like me...we fought each other if there was ever a chance to go up to the big Casa on an errand—just to have a glimpse of her. But...she went away suddenly. Some thought she stole away to the mainland to meet a lover. No one knows what really happened to her. That's all there is to tell."

"Is it, Tomaso? Why do villagers have superstitions about the old Señora and the Casa?"

He looked down and avoided my gaze. "They think the first Señora did away with her."

"What!" I switched to English. The story was getting too complicated for my high school Spanish to handle. "Why would Missy—I mean the old Señora—why would she do a thing like that?"

Tomaso continued looking down. "It was a long time ago, Señora," he finally said.

I saw it in a sudden flash. The reluctance of Mrs. Matamoros to talk about Milena to me. Howard's closing up Missy's studio.

"Howard? and Milena? They were...*together*?"

"It was long before you came here, Señora. The other Señora—she was so angry. So jealous. And the rumors flew. They said she was loco, or a witch who cast an evil spell on Milena. She kidnapped Milena and threw her in a secret dungeon. Some said, if she painted a portrait of someone, that person would die. There were dozens of different scenarios, each more outlandish than the last."

It was my turn to sink back in my chair. "Thank you

Tomaso, you've been kind. One more question?"

"Señora?"

"Do you think that Milena could still be alive and living somewhere, hiding in the Casa?"

Tomaso laughed. "No! Milena was not the one to bury herself away. She was the type of woman who loved being envied and desired."

"Who are her people? Do they still live in the village?"

"She was an orphan from the church school."

"Ah. Then Padre Madrigal might know something?"

Again, the elaborate shrug. "Priests always do seem to know things other people do not, is that not true, Señora?"

* * *

Casa Del Mar was fairly self-sufficient. Produce, fish and livestock were in bountiful supply. We even grew our own coffee beans. When Howard was alive, we would go into town every Friday night to eat at one of the three restaurants. I always drove down the hill to the tiny post office to pick up any special order from the mainland or the States. Periodically, I would visit the meager shops on the Main Street. Other than that, I had little reason to visit the village.

Neither Howard nor I were Catholic, but we donated money to the Iglesias San Pedro y San Pablo and its adjacent school anyway. It was good business practice, Howard said, because you never knew when the locals would turn against you.

That was typical of Howard, who still saw himself as

a gringo Yankee despite his family's long tenure on the island. The founder of Casa Del Mar, Howard's robber baron great-grandfather, believed that the States were a place of "barbarity and ill-refinement," and had established a feudal estate of eccentric splendor here, in order to raise his spawn as proper ladies and gentlemen. One hundred and thirty-five years later, the spawn had dwindled to just Howard, Jr., and by extension, myself.

Now I was taking tea with Padre Madrigal, and I realized I had never sat in the rectory parlor before. Howard always messengered the donation checks, and I usually only saw the padre at village festivals. I was slightly embarrassed about it.

"I was away at seminary when the girl disappeared," said the priest, a thin, intense man in his early forties. "But of course, I've heard all the stories. A sad case. I prefer to believe she took the weekly ferry to the mainland and started a new life, which I pray is a happy one."

"You don't think she came to a violent end?"

"I don't have any evidence either way, Señora."

"Well, I do." I suddenly found myself telling everything to Padre Madrigal, including my last terrible sighting of Milena with her missing peripherals. "Do you believe the dead can haunt us?" I asked as I finished my story.

"That is an extraordinary tale, Señora." He smiled kindly. "To answer your question, the dead are always with us, in our thoughts, our prayers, our memories."

"That may be true of lost loved ones, but I don't have any memories of her! I've never heard of Milena until I saw her portrait."

Padre Madrigal lifted his cup of tea, took a long

thoughtful sip, and said in a regretful tone, "Señora, I don't want to offend, but is it possible you saw a servant girl in the room? A new one from the village, whom you didn't know? And you transposed the portrait's face onto hers?"

"What about the missing hands and feet?"

"I can't speak to that. Perhaps you heard an old legend and dreamed you saw it. The afternoons on Santa Serafina are very warm and many get drowsy at the noon hour."

I was almost convinced of the padre's theory. But even so, I wanted guidance on what to do if I actually had seen a ghost.

"If there *was* something...supernatural...in that room, how would I go about getting rid of it? The Church believes in exorcisms, doesn't it?"

"Only rarely. I wouldn't even know how to go about it."

"But you have a theory? If it were true?"

"We Catholics do believe that the dead rise corporeally on the last day. If the remains are missing something, when they rise, they will not be complete in their bodies. If what you saw was real, perhaps the girl is dead and was buried...incomplete. But it's most likely you saw something perfectly reasonable and interpreted it wrongly. A widow alone in the big Casa on the hill, still recovering from grief...the mind will play its tricks."

"I'm not alone up there," I protested. "I have the house and garden staff. But if I take your meaning—you think Milena was killed and buried...*incomplete*...and wants me to find her missing parts? Is that what you think?"

"It's not what I think at all," he said sternly. "I am just speaking hypothetically, about the way the Church views burial and resurrection. There is no proof that Milena came to a violent end."

"What about Missy? The old Señora? Did you know her well?"

"Not before I went to the seminary. But later, when I took over here, I knew her briefly. She would bring donations to the school. She was pleasant, but she always acted as if…how do you Anglos say it? She 'kept to herself'."

"But why do the villagers think she was bad, then?"

"They didn't, until the last year or so before she died. She shut herself up in her art studio and would let no one come in, not even to clean. Working on a big project, she said. And she was cruel to the servants, where before she had been kind. Rumors started that she was practicing the black arts. And then the girl Milena disappeared. That's enough, in a superstitious village on a small, isolated island."

"The blue-green map of the world," I said.

"Pardon?"

"That's what the big project was. A giant map of the world painted over all the walls, in different shades of blue and green. Except for a network of red-orange circles in various random places, which I don't understand the purpose of."

"That sounds interesting."

"It's a beautiful piece of work. But I suppose it's not to everyone's taste." I put my empty teacup down and stood up. "Gracias for the tea and the information, Padre. I must go back to the Casa now as it is almost dinner time and Mrs. M will be very disappointed if I eat in town."

Padre Madrigal stood up and bowed slightly. "I'm

not sure what help I gave you, but I hope you will see no more gruesome apparitions at the Casa. I would not go into the blue-green room for now."

* * *

My head was full of thoughts about Missy as I returned to the Casa. I knew little about her, aside from Mrs. Matamoros telling me endlessly how she liked her housekeeping done. Plus, childhood stories from Howard Jr. I remembered that he had photo albums of her up in his suite on the second floor.

I felt a thrill of naughtiness as I trespassed into my stepson's rooms. He'd been eight when I'd married his father, a stick of a boy with huge woeful eyes, looking at me with undisguised suspicion. I was only twenty-two, myself, but somehow I won him over. He always held back a little though, as if he thought too much closeness with me was disloyal to his mother.

There was a photo of Missy on the dressing bureau, wearing a blue-green dress. She was pretty in a washed-out way, but very ordinary-looking otherwise. I couldn't see her as someone consumed with evil passions and a lust for revenge. More likely, as someone who enjoyed afternoon bridge games, followed by fruity cocktails.

I searched through the dressing bureau and found nothing. However, a drawer in a bulbous mahogany desk yielded several photo albums. I flipped through them, fascinated. There were numerous family photos of a young Howard with Missy and Howard, Jr. I noticed that Howard, Sr., started to look less happy as the photos progressed in time, and eventually disappeared from them entirely.

So, their marriage wasn't happy, even before Milena, I thought. Somehow that made me feel good. Howard and I had been quite happy together, although I must admit, I did not ever have a passionate attachment to my husband. Ours was more of a companionable marriage, based on compatibility and mutual need.

Something fell out of the last album, startling me. A thick, creamy envelope, addressed to Howard Jr., that had never been opened. The envelope was printed with Missy's name in the return address space. I recognized it as her monogrammed stationery, pieces of which sometimes still turned up around the house.

I wondered why Howard Jr. had never opened the letter? Possibly, Missy tucked it in a pocket of the album without telling him, and he'd just never found it.

I opened it, of course; I had a prickly-necked sixth sense that it contained information about Milena. Since Howard, Jr. didn't know of its existence, I did not see a need to hide its opening.

Inside was a handwritten note that read:

How, My Dearest:

By the time you read this, I may be gone—away for a long time, maybe forever. I thought the Problem was finished, after completing the Map. But I was wrong, Rest assured that I will always love you.

Mommy.

The date was the day Missy died. I wondered: Did she run her car off that cliff intentionally? That's what it sounded like. It also seemed obvious that Milena was the Problem she wanted "removed." But what did the map of the world have to do with anything?

I felt a sudden chill and the odd sense of heaviness I'd sensed in the map room. My back was to the door. I spun around to face it and saw an unspeakable presence floating a few inches above the floor.

It was Milena. Or rather, *part* of Milena. Her torso, wearing the same black dress, with arms and legs. But no hands or feet.

And…no *head*.

Her neck was a stump jutting out of the collar of her black dress. The neck twisted to and fro as if it were looking for something. But there was no head with eyes to see it.

I heard a scream and realized it was mine. I instinctively ran into the dressing chamber that was attached to Howard Jr.'s bedroom. I closed and locked the door. Shortly afterward, I could hear something thumping on the door. Shuddering, I pictured Milena's arm stumps battering against the dressing room door. I struggled to remain conscious, fearing some horrible consequence.

Then one of her thin arm-stumps began forcing its way under the dressing room door, inch by inch. Force, inch, force. I cowered against the back wall of the small room, wanting to scream again, but unable to do so.

"I'll find them, Milena," I whispered hoarsely at the thrusting stump in Spanish. "I'll put you back together, I promise."

The stump halted. Then it began inching back, slowly.

I waited a good long time after that, and then I fearfully peeked out of the door into the main bedroom. Only Mrs. Matamoros was there, giving me a stern and accusatory look.

"I was looking for something that Howard Jr., borrowed from me," I said weakly, almost crying with relief that it was just Mrs. M.

* * *

That night, I dreamed of the latest hideous apparition of Milena, even though I kept my bedside lamp on all through the darkest hours. My sleep was restless, but I dropped off soundly toward dawn. When I awoke, the sun was shining bright, and I had an inspiration.

"The red-orange circles! Perhaps they are a code of some sort. That's why her note mentions the map."

I pulled myself out of bed and went down to breakfast. Mrs. Matamoros had laid out scrambled eggs and fresh mangoes in the breakfast room. I dawdled over breakfast, torn between my desire to test my theory about the red-orange circles and my fear of seeing Milena again. I shuddered to think of what body part she'd have lost the next time she appeared—her torso sawn in half, maybe? My god, I was becoming a Gruesome Greta in my old age. That poor girl.

I made myself go up to the map room after lunch. Armed with a cross I'd stolen from Mrs. M's private prayer closet, I opened the door with trepidation, expecting to see Milena's wretched spirit awaiting me on the other side. There was nothing, but the musty smell was back after a few days' emptiness.

I pulled my chair up to the wall painted with the red circle that was closest to my table,   and pondered the map before me. It was the Australasia section, and the circle was over Melbourne in Southern Australia.

Melbourne? Why pick Melbourne? I wrote Melbourne on a notepad, stood up, and moved on to the other circles. There was the one for London, Missy's birthplace. I wrote down London on my notepad. Then there was one in North America—Indianapolis in the State of Indiana. That seemed a bit odd for the cosmopolitan Missy. I wrote down "Indianapolis." Then another for Nairobi...

Then I saw the pattern! The first letter of each place spelled out "Milena." The E was Ecuador, and the final A was Afghanistan.

M-I-L-E-N-A. Plus the circle that stood for Santa Serafina. *Milena in Serafina? It sort of rhymed,* I thought idiotically.

I sensed that odd heavy feeling in the air again, and braced myself, looking around for Milena, who always seemed to show up whenever I got that feeling. But there was nothing. I returned to my pondering. I was now standing in front of Afghanistan. It was covered with sky-blue sheep and turquoise goats. I chanced to look down and I noticed something unusual. Some of the floorboards beneath me looked odd. I knelt down to examine them more closely.

They were nailed down with larger, newer-looking nails, unlike the surrounding floorboards, which had smaller, older nails. And the edges of some of the suspect boards protruded a bit.

I went down to the garden and asked a gardener to find me a hammer and a chisel. Tools secured, I went up to the map room and began to remove the floorboards beneath Afghanistan. There was a pocket under the boards, and what it contained was horrific.

Two skeletal hands, with mummified strips of skin and tendons clinging to them. I thought sickly that she probably mummified them in low heat in her kiln. I turned away, stifling the urge to vomit. Regaining control, I placed the loose floorboards back and stood up.

It took all my presence of mind to continue my investigation. I examined the other red circles and I saw that the floorboards under each one looked slightly "off," also. At that point, I decided I needed help. Mrs. Matamoros knew something; I was sure. I had to make her tell me everything.

I didn't have to go far to find her. She was just outside the door of the sewing room, her face registering deep surprise when she saw me exit the room.

"You've found her." The baldness of her statement shocked me.

"Yes."

Mrs. Matamoros reached out to steady herself on a tall cabinet standing in the hallway. She made the sign of the cross with her other hand and muttered: "*Madre de Dios, Madre de Dios.*"

"She was chopped up and hidden under the floorboards around the room. Did you know about this?"

"*Mio Dios!* No! I swear by the Holy Mother, that I did not know this."

"But you knew Milena was dead?"

"Yes. But I didn't know what happened to her…*after.*"

"You knew that Missy killed her."

Mrs. Matamoros laughed almost hysterically. "The first Señora? No, that is not what happened."

"I don't understand. Mrs. Matamoros, please, no

more games. I saw Milena's decomposed hands under the floor."

"She did not kill Milena. She only *disposed* of her."

"But then...how did Milena die?"

Mrs. Matamoros looked away, into a dark recess of the hall. "Do you really want to know? Do you really *need* to know?"

I felt some horrible realization growing inside of me. I could scarcely process it—it was so astounding.

"Yes, I do." I finally said, in a shaky voice.

"I think you know now. It was the Señor."

"Howard? *My* Howard?"

She nodded. "I am devastated that I must tell you this."

"What happened?"

"An argument. A lover's argument. You know they were...*together*...Milena and the Señor?"

I nodded, feeling numb.

"Milena wanted to be the new Señora. To rule as chatelaine at the Casa. And for the old Señora to be sent away. She hated her with such a cruel hate! The Señor was almost willing to give in, but she became wild, and he pushed her. She fell and hit her head on a stone gargoyle. Those gargoyles that the old Roddicks loved so much. It happened in the library on the first floor. He did not mean it, and he did not want to be punished for it."

"But...what did Missy have to do with it?"

"She told him she would dispose of the... *cadaver*... and they were never to speak of it again. I did not know what she did with it until now."

It was my turn to grab for something to steady myself with. I clutched at a tall planter near me, containing a potted palm.

My Howard, a killer! Even if it was an accident, he had covered it up. And I had been married to him for twenty years.

"We must call the *policia*. And Padre Madrigal, to officiate at the burial."

Mrs. Matamoros shook her head, alarmed. "No, Señora, we cannot."

"Why? Everyone involved is dead. Surely someone would want to know what happened to Milena."

"There is no one. And you and I will pay a heavy price if it becomes known what happened."

"How?"

"The villagers. They will never let you forget it. It won't matter that you had nothing to do with it. The Casa will be tainted in their eyes forever. And your life will become unpleasant. *My life* will become unpleasant. No one will work here, no one will speak to us. I have no place else to go. That is why I kept silent. I believed it was my right."

"Your *right*? What do you mean?"

"Can't you guess? She was my daughter," Mrs. M's voice broke and I saw she was fighting back a tear.

"There was a man, an older man—I was just seventeen. My mother arranged for the nuns to take her and raise her. She did not know who I was, but I watched over her, visited her, and when she became of age, I procured a position for her here. And she betrayed me by dishonoring herself with the Señor. Of course, I could not judge—I was no stranger to dishonor either. But it was wanton and cruel to the first Señora. She broke their family, and I was ashamed. I was the only person with a claim on her, and if I did not want the secret told, it was my right."

"But why has she come back...after all this time? I've *seen* her. And you saw her too, that day she was sitting on the sofa. You lied to me about it."

"I did see her. The old Señor saw her also—that was why he closed up the room. When you came, he opened it, saw nothing, and thought you'd be amused by it. But she appeared again, and he closed it for twenty years. You brought her back, by opening it."

I considered this charge silently. "I didn't know why it was locked. I loved the map on the wall so much."

Another horrifying thought occurred to me then. "And Missy? Her death...it wasn't *anything* that Howard did?"

"No, Señora. She died truly as the result of an accident. She saw Milena and tried to run away from Casa Del Mar forever. Driving very fast down the hill, and...she went over."

"We must put Milena back together and bury her. It's what she wants. And we must do it soon. I fear her soul is very angry and very restless after being locked up for so long."

* * *

I retrieved all of Milena's body parts. An ugly, difficult task. The worst was when I found the head under the red circle that symbolized Santa Serafina. That seemed significant somehow, although I never figured out why. Then I had the room triple-locked again, and the door sealed with large nails as an extra precaution.

I also had a new garden created on the fringes of the

old gardens, a lush place for a handsome statue of the Holy Mother. I thought it would please Mrs. M.

We buried Milena in that garden. I invited Padre Madrigal to come and bless the statue, and that was the closest thing to a funeral that Milena ever had.

It seemed to suffice. I saw her once more, standing in the new garden next to her mother. Mrs. Matamoros was saying her rosary and was so immersed in her prayers that she didn't see or sense the otherworldly presence—nor did she notice me, pausing just outside the garden on my morning walk. But I saw her—I saw *them* together.

Milena was whole again.

About The Author

A native Californian, Jane Nightshade is a former public relations manager turned horror writer. Her fiction has appeared in numerous anthologies and magazines, and has been dramatized by NoSleep Podcast and Octoberpod. She is the author of *The Drowning Game, A Novella of the Supernatural,* available in digital form on Amazon. Her non-fiction writing has been published by several major horror sites. Online, Jane mostly hangs out on Twitter at @JaneNightshade.

© Brian Watson BKWatson PHotographie

www.ingramcontent.com/pod-product-compliance
Lightning Source LLC
Chambersburg PA
CBHW031115030726
47496CB00002BA/550